STIRBUGS & SCREWS

A Novel by
Arnold James Isbister

e-mail: aji@shaw.ca

ACKNOWLEDGEMENTS

I wish to acknowledge my wife Karen Isbister along with my daughter Michelle McGilp, and my many friends and family throughout my life who inspired fictional characters in this novel. A special thanks to Murray, JT and many other colleagues who covered my back. And to those minstrels of music; Kris Kristofferson, the Rolling Stones, CCR and John Fogerty, Eddie Cochran and Ricky Nelson I give thanks for those moments in my life they froze into memory with their music.

Finally, the places I have called home; Shelby, Sandy Lake, Canwood and Saskatoon… thank you.

Abnormal in this world is relative but none is more bizarre than the mind that has broken the bounds of self and body, wandering a world of fantasy unable to find the door it came through. Escape to another world - where we might glimpse the mysteries we sought answers to. Death, the other unknown, is but another world where we find the answers and maybe the freedom.

Embraced, unloved, she croons
A lullaby, sounds of the night.
Wings of fright echo in flight,
He draws closer, wishes the light.

To her nature she gives blessing,
Sedate the will, coddle the drone.
Beastly demons prevail the throne
Thanking her for all she has given.

His pained memory unwanted,
Time weighs the moment fought.
Blighted by vengeance sought
Perverts reason without thought.

The Psych Center
-by Sam

Prologue

They roped him, entangled his body in knots of wet sinew, hide and rope. The young men strained their muscles, tightening the bounds to a painful quilt over his bare body. He sat at the entrance to the teepee, cross-legged, stoic, silent with a look of defiance. Inspected visually and physically by two Elders, the other four young men lifted him into the center of the tepee. I could see him in the shadow as the men drew the flaps and closed the entrance. Along the base of the traditional tepee were symbols in colour; jagged lines, straight borders, circles and above in the center of the teepee pictographs of Thunderbirds.

Everyone, and there were many, stared in stillness at the tepee as I looked around, observing the atmosphere. I had heard of this secret rite in hushed talks around the campfire but never saw the actual ceremony. There was the Sun Dance now outlawed by the Church and Government but this event was dark and hidden even among the Reserve residents. It was ageless and had persisted through countless generations.

The young men began a drum song, the beat rose in tempo and volume becoming so strong I physically felt it in my chest as it rose to a crescendo. The reverberations shook my body. Then – all became silent. My heart kept the drumbeat in my ears as the silence deafened. Suddenly there was a rush of wind; everyone drew in a breath. The wind died to a calm and from inside, the sound of a rattle, clear yet subtle rose above the tepee. A soft murmur ran through the crowd. The rattle became louder then again, suddenly, deathly silent in an instant as

6

anticipation rose. I began to feel the trepidation amongst the people, my eyes betrayed my fear when I looked up to my Father and pulled on his hand for security. He looked down putting his finger to his mouth. We both turned towards the tepee. Another burst of wind, another gasp from the spectators as a small cloud of dust gathered around the base. I thought my eyes were playing tricks on me but I'm sure the tent moved; I wasn't the only one. I looked again, looked hard and the teepee began to tremble slightly, the crowd stepped back a foot or two. Abruptly the tremble increased to a violent shake, the tepee emitted a groaning sound as a weight bent the poles. The people startled with a collective jump, some turning their backs and scuttling a few short steps away from the teepee. An unfamiliar sound came from inside and I began to whimper, swallowing the cry that was in my throat. My Dad shook my hand as a warning to be silent, motionless. The sounds became a voice, an eerie voice with no substance, a tin echo in a dream. In the tent, a conversation began with a myriad of voices, then like before, all became silent. The shaking subsided with a trail of smoke wafting upward through the top. A minute later in the hush, a man stepped forward, parting the crowd as he walked with authority to the entrance. He stopped, turned around to the People then turned again and with the swipe of his hand he opened the tepee entrance. There trembling in a foetus position, was the man who had been bound in rope and rawhide, naked.... *with no rope or sinew around him*. He was free.

The Elders gave him water and smudged some sage smoke over his body. In a while he was up sitting cross-legged, the colour of his eyes seemed to have diminished. The old men gathered around him talking in whispers.

7

The odd time, one would stand upright and look over the crowd. They now all stood up facing the audience and asked the spectators to put any questions to the man. None of the people held their silence; each asking for advice, news of recently departed, whereabouts of lost objects, who their love would be, on success, on their future and so on, until the sun went down. He answered correctly, truthfully all that was asked of him, providing such guidance and information that only they would know. The audience dwindled slowly and as the Elders helped him to his feet his eyes fell on my Dad. An uneasy quiet hung in the air while he walked over. He leaned to my Dad, whispered something in a hushed tone then stared at me with black eyes. I was very young at the time but I never forgot that scene and the spell it had cast. It was called the *Shaking-Tent Ceremony* used rarely to evoke the Spirits to appear.

I asked my Dad later what it was that the *Bound-Man* had whispered. In Cree he explained quoting one word, "*Wah-nus-kay-win*" and that I would come to know what it meant later in Life. I knew then it referred to something 'gone' and a state of being.

Chapter 1

I dreamt I was in Paradise. God was there but too busy to see me; to his right was a triangle of men, one had braids who kept vocalising a message to me but no words were heard. After awakening a lucid sense remained as I recalled the dream with its vibrant colors as a feeling, not visual. My bedroom felt barren, a melancholy overcame me as the dream washed away. Time for work....

My first impression was how gloomy it felt, despite the never-ending windows with cascading sunrays flooding the floors. A hard whiteness of sterility, sanctity prevailed the atmosphere and the silence floated on the wings of a Raven. There was always that other world in here. Windows' blaring heat fought the air-conditioning, blinding sunlight scuttled to the shadows as we continued along the whole atrium. No matter where you were, you had an unobstructed view of who was in the "centre park". Greenery abounded in trees, shrubs and rows of painted flowers filled the atrium with benches and walkways strategically placed.

Down the hallway I heard screams...then silence.

The endless corridor I was in circled the atrium or 'park' with individual units of 12 to 32 cells branching off like spokes from the hub. This was the Federal Psych Center that housed '*stirbugs and screws*' - **stirbugs** being those inmates that have lost their sanity from prolonged incarceration or just plain crazy and **screws** being us, the guards.

This was my first day at work although I had been inside for indoctrination and training, this felt different. The gloom felt was maybe a premonition of things to come, maybe resignation to a working life or was it from viewing the clientele shuffling mindlessly with looks of despair? *Bunch of Zombies* I thought reminiscing back to those 'B' movies in Shelby on a Saturday Matinee. A row of inmates, not quite in file, walked aimlessly as they followed a guard. Most were shuffling. Their 'gait' and a collage of other physical symptoms were a result of psychiatric meds needed to calm them or more appropriately, subdue them. These were killers, abductors, sexual predators too violent for the regular pens or who had "flipped out" while in other institutions. Ours was a multi-level, the highest security rating where even unmanageable inmates of the SHU (Special Handling Unit) were sent; we paid special attention to these clients and were escorted everywhere. The fix-all was medication, which had its merit but I hated seeing the outcome. How can you assess or analyse problems in personality disorders if the guy's a walking zombie, I often thought. On the other hand, these meds have saved many nurses and guards from assault, so who were we to think…we weren't supposed to.

I started my rounds, going from unit to unit just to see how things were done as part of my intern training. Each unit emphasized or specialized in certain assessment and treatment such as sexual offenders or the worst, the acute schizophrenic ward, where terms were indefinite and I never knew of anyone being released after being admitted to that particular ward. Imagine the Hell of Dante's Inferno, where unspeakable crimes and behaviour were the norm for the residents. You can't dream up the events that put them there or what they do to themselves. We had Olson, killer of kids in the 80's and Hoffman who shot and killed a family of 9. From here, they were shipped to Pentangushene in Quebec for permanent incarceration where they will die of old age – or be released. As I approached "SW", short for Southwest unit, the screams, howling and moans became louder, routine for the acute schizophrenic ward. I tensed up, not yet being acclimatized to the atmosphere. Pushing the button, waiting then entering the unit through a long hallway, I could hear coming from an adjoining hallway someone calling my name. Looking to my right was the "Hole" or "Seclusion" (an area for punishment or disassociation) where I could see in the dim light, a set of 4 doors, each with an 8x8 inch window. Inside one of these, I could see someone motioning. I took interest, approaching cautiously, wondering who in Hell would know me here in the Hole. He seemed to be quite tall as he stooped to the window. His hair was wild with eyes fully dilated as he fought to focus.

"Sam, Sam…hey Boss." His actions were animated, his eyes looking yellow and hollow below thick lines of blonde hair. He had finer features with a chiselled sinewy frame and not unattractive in a rough way. I thought amusingly of a hungry logger with his gaunt cheeks. He looked through me as I came closer, the focus gone in his eyes. "You gotta get me outa here Sam, I'm going fucking squirrelly." He had a guttural accent, almost Bronx I imagined.
"How do you know my name?" I had never seen this guy before.
"Oh, I know everybody here."

11

"Yeah, but you called me Sam and nobody knows me by that name, not here anyway."

"Yeah, well...."

"Do you know my real name?"

"Sure, it's Bran."

I froze, trying to think as a chill came over me. I thought back, flipping through a myriad of memories, but his face drew a blank. Could be that he knew me from a distance and we were just passing acquaintances. Only my closest childhood friends knew me as Sam, they had given the nickname to me as a joke and it stuck. I searched and searched for a connection in the past – nothing. His actions and that stare of familiarity unnerved me because he definitely knew me from somewhere. My composure shaken, I didn't say anything.

"Boss!" he shouted, this was a term for guard, one of the better ones. I looked up. "You're not listening to me."

"Yes I am." I thought carefully. "Where do you know me from?"

"Never mind that Boss, you gotta get me outta here."

"You know I can't do that. I haven't got the authority or the inclination. Why are you in here? What's your name?"

"Whoa, *inclination*? Some pretty big words for a screw; I assaulted some guard, he deserved it. My name? It's Charlie," he smiled at me. "I know you're just a screw with no balls, but I'm not talking about that." He bent closer to the dark observation window, smiling. "Listen Sam, all you have to do is just leave the keys," he whispered. "You know...forget them in the hole, accidentally drop them and walk on." He called me Sam again, like a dark secret shared only with your best friends.

I turned around abruptly, leaving, hearing his laughter follow me down the hallway as I went back to the security station. Walking past the other seclusion doors another inmate screamed at me as he banged his head on his window snarling obscenities. From Charlie's cell came a shout, "Shut up, Dimitri or I'll come over there!" Just like that everything became silent, even the other 2 seclusion inmates stopped their moaning and shuffled cell walk. I came onto the main pod for SW also under lock where the nurses and security stayed working out their shifts. They let me in and I sat there silent for quite a while when finally, the guard for this post asked what was wrong. I told him of this encounter and he laughed. "That's Charlie," he said then raising his voice, "and watch out for him. He killed his parents. He's crazy, but he's not dumb and he loves to play games with staff. He flips out every month, then goes to the hole for some quiet time. He flips out on purpose, just to get away from the "stir bugs" in the unit. In fact, staff here figures he isn't crazy, but he's done such a good job in his scam that he's convinced the psychologists, so he's in it for the long haul. Fooled his way to an indefinite term, he'll never get out."

"Where is he from?" I asked.

"Well, according to his history, he came from B.C. where he shot his mom and dad, think he was in Gr. 10 or 11 at the time. He skinned them too."

"Skinned them?"

"Yup. Skinned them like a pair of rabbits."

I pretended not to be shocked. Visualizing what the guard just said about skinning I asked, "He was never here?"

"Nope, not according to the records. He was born in BC they assume, went to school there and in high school over some religious argument he shot both his parents.

They put him in a delinquent remand facility till he turned 18 then he came to us. Nobody else can handle him so he's been with us for... a long time and will be here indefinitely, or till they figure out what to do with him. When they say indefinite that means forever." I introduced myself and he shook my hand, a strong shake that felt reassuring in this place. Murray subsequently filled me in on everybody, everything and would become a close friend of mine.

I felt somewhat relieved, but I didn't mention the "nickname thing". I didn't want anyone knowing this until I could figure it out myself. There was that familiarity too that can't be imitated. Another chill raised the hair on my neck as a millisecond snapshot from the past flashed through my mind. I remembered an old tale of my youth told before a campfire when the *2 Syds,* as we called them, spun a tale of the Devil. A true story they contended that scared the living daylights out of me back then.

The old folks used to say.... *You can capture the devil, but you can never keep him.*

I walked slowly to the filing cabinets fingering through the names. I asked the nurse on shift and she informed me that Charlie's real name was Louis. I found the file but it didn't tell me anymore than we already knew. The same nurse who I now noticed had long dark hair, introduced herself as Shannon Payette. The name was familiar, like Paulette - Paulette? I recalled a sunny afternoon in June of my graduating year, a faded image of one young girl in a blue bikini, splashing in the waters of our lake. She had a fantastic body with black hair dripping wet, beads of water on black, shining like

14

diamonds in the sunlight. She reminded me of Cleopatra with those dark swirls of black hair covering her white shoulders and I remembered her dark penetrating eyes. She died of breast cancer many years later and I never did get to see her after that short interlude we called high school. *If you want to see someone, go see him or her, don't procrastinate – life's too short*, I thought to myself. There were old friends in Canwood High and those of my elementary years in Shelby I had lost touch with over the years mainly because of a jaded outlook moulded from experience. When I made friends I seemed to lose them.

I looked over to the orange cell doors; from Charlie's cell room I hear voices. Why are there voices in his room? Then I realized he had a radio at the foot of his door on the cement floor. The unit nurses would let seclusion inmates borrow a radio providing they didn't abuse that right and it had to remain outside for safety's sake. Little privileges like this were also used as tools in getting them to cooperate or maybe divulge info about other inmates. Being locked in for 23 hours a day, these little things become essential to their sanity and sadly we used them for our benefit. I would learn this fast as SW Unit, also known as Churchill, would become my preferred station. From the surface, withholding or denying these 'favours' looks cruel, seems juvenile but often these were the only tools that worked in placating an inmate or defusing an escalating violent situation.

I had to visit other units for orientation and to introduce myself, so I left South West looking behind as I exited the unit, there's Charlie in his tiny window waving to me with a big smile. 'Welcome to Churchill' he seemed to be saying as I walked on and the sight of him waving struck me as funny. An image of the Queen popped into my

15

head with her waving to the multitudes from her balcony, her cell.

"You look like the Queen waving." I yelled back to him with a smirk on my face. I heard him slap his hands as he began to laugh, a cackle echoed off the grey masonry walls and died to a chuckle. At least someone appreciates my humour I concluded.

My eyes glanced to the floor as I proceeded to the main corridor door when I noticed a rivulet of red slowly oozing its way across the hallway. This was Dimitri's cell! I screamed to Murray, not taking my eyes off the slow meandering of blood, as it seemed to be alive in its movement. Engrossed, captured by the consequences I was imagining, I stood staring blankly. Murray pushed me aside, yelled for the nurses then radioed "Code 55!" Within seconds the hallway was full of guards and Nurses as they pulled Dimitri out. He had slashed his forearms and he was fighting but soon was calmed down with a syringe of some tranquilizer as they bandaged his arms and threw him back into seclusion only this time under 'suicide watch', and no perks such as a radio. A quick search turned up broken glass but from where they didn't know. I asked if I should stay but was advised to "carry on" to the next Unit while they did their reports and sanitized the area. I looked again at the scene unable to comprehend the time and action that transpired followed by the calm and quiet. In a few seconds all Hell broke loose with blood being smeared all over including uniforms. Now I stood there alone, the halls are dead quiet, noting left but the drying blood turning black then I hear a snicker. At the end, down the dark hallway is Charlie smiling, waving his fingers like you do to a child.

Chapter 2

It was summer, a hot summer I remember so well. We had been away from the reserve for 6 maybe 7 years. I was trying to *fit in* after moving back from Shelby, Montana during the school break of that momentous year. Not only were we now living in the country, but on an Indian Reserve. I was pretty green in both areas being fair skinned and city looking with my attire. My fair complexion came as a side-shoot from a Scottish line of Orkney explorers who came to the new world, then intermarried into the tribes of the West. My reserve brothers, because of this, didn't always accept me, although I was 'classed' as a full-status Indian. I had to work for that right to belong and also for a place to eat at the table through the time-honoured process of manual labour. Both were alien to me especially that I should work for my food. I didn't have a clue about 'manual labour,' now here I was in the middle of nowhere; haying, with a team of horses in 85 degrees Fahrenheit and a cloud of dirt clinging to my sweat in rural Saskatchewan. This was one of many types of 'manual labour' I would have the benefit of experiencing. I didn't even know that Saskatchewan was a province, our home province. I arrived and was informed violently with a fist-sandwich after I had cheekily mentioned my thought that the name espoused an image of 'Sasquatches', those ambiguous bush-dwellers otherwise known as 'Big-Foot'.

God, I hated this place, hated this life! I should be back in Shelby riding my bike, going to the Roxy Theatre, eating popcorn and seeing my friends! The anger fuelled my body with more heat, more sweat and the dirt plied on. I pulled on the reins halting the horses and hopped

17

off lying down on the cool grass. I looked to the sky spread-eagled. From up there I must look like an X I thought then added in a sigh, *definitely not an X that marks a treasure.*

A cool breeze coming across the field caressed my hair as I started to daydream. My mind drifted off as I wished to be back in Shelby, wished it with all my will. The heat lessened, the dirt was gone and I visualized biking down a dark grey asphalt road, the pungent smell of the 'black-top' hitting me as I could feel our home back on Cascade Avenue. The memory smelled alive, pleasant and I could sense myself there in real time, lucid. I closed my eyes, a smile growing on my face as I pictured myself on the way to pick up Pug for the Saturday Matinee.

"Pug" was my best friend, his name a derivative I had given him of Peter and Douglass, his first and second name. I came to know later that Pug was also a small dog with a funny face, which seemed perfect in hindsight. He had a puppy face. He called me by my name 'Bran' with no nickname or slant on the name. I mean what could you change to make it suitable for the age-old practice of nicknaming? How do you get anything from Bran that makes sense other than it's some sort of fibre good for digestion and being regular? There was Bran Flakes that everyone hated; guess I could have been called Bran Flakey. Maybe I was, behind my back, as we did for countless others.

Pug's gentle face came to me as the memories took hold, transporting me home to the streets of Shelby. This was what we looked forward to during the week; riding our bikes, going to movies and teasing the older girls we had crushes on. There was always some corny B-movie

18

special, like "It Came From the Ocean" or the "Swamp Thing" and every kid in Shelby would be there. After, we would hang around to see if 'our' girls were there. They were not really our girl friends but we were infatuated with them, fantasizing was the best we could do because I'm sure they hated us. We would send anonymous notes or phone them, then hang up from sheer terror as we heard their voices. I learned later that probably half of Shelby knew that it was us. If I had known that everybody knew, I probably would have quit school or something, maybe joined the French Foreign Legion. Sometimes, ignorance is bliss.

There was Linda, Mary Jane and *Heather MicGregrrr* whose name we would roll off our lips as we spouted off the syllables, in particular the final 'r' in a self-made accent born of movie Pirates and French noblemen we perceived as romantic. We must have sounded terrible. We learned from the movies and heroes we watched. We hadn't applied what we learned so far, but we would, we were in training. We knew women liked strong men and really liked kissing, even though they pushed us men away with the heels of their hands – just like in the old Westerns. And sometime, of course, you had to spank them too if they didn't do as you wished or they were becoming difficult. Even back then, I wasn't too sure about this one though because I had never seen it in real life. In my youthful wisdom, I found this unrealistic, not plausible. I often wondered who or what kind of guy made these films and what their home life was like...and the actors, did they really do this in real life?

Anyway, we thought we had it figured out after countless talks about Love and Sex, as every adolescent will do. Besides, we also would hear our older wiser brothers, uncles and their friend's talk, the "pros" that had access to such literary love classics as "I'm Hot and Horny" or "Steal My Cherry". You could tell that they were well read by their informative medical terms of the anatomy such as: the *organ, instrument, Big Stick* and my favourite, *manhood.* They knew the woman's body too which we, the uneducated, took to heart and broadened our vocabulary with their sensual, descriptive words such as *peaches, buns,* and *watermelons,* although this last particular term changed depending on the breast size, from small to large, but was always described by comparing them to fruit. Back then I often speculated about why fruit, not vegetables was used for the women's anatomy and not the men's. Why were carrots or onions never used for men's parts since these were both regarded as masculine? Instead we, the men, had a *rod* or *piston* as in mechanics. Vegetables! That was why, since we were the name-givers, vegetables were never used by men in describing women because we didn't like them. I analysed my discovery, imagining women's breasts being called cabbages or rutabagas... or radishes. I envisioned a scenario of two guys talking, "Wow – man, she's got a good set of rutabagas", or for the smaller sized... "She's got a set of radishes".

I laughed to myself at the thought, all alone in the hay meadow, the horses farting as they monotonously gnawed on some hay.

I remember the one time at the Roxy we tried to endear ourselves to the girls with what we thought of as a flattering compliment. The show now over, we followed them covertly to the Capitol Café. Working up some courage, we devised a plan sure to add admiring comment to their attributes. Taking off our long shirts, we stuffed these into our shorts for a raised behind, or "buns" as we were taught. Left with only t-shirts on the upper body we then stuffed these with water balloons. Mary Jane, Linda, Heather and another girl were at a window seat as we paraded by, Pug swinging his hips in a sexual manner and me bouncing along to accentuate their watermelons, one delicate hand aloft in grace. We thought this cute, flattering... but WOW, did they get mad at us. Using language I didn't think they knew, they chased us for four blocks. First time I realized I could run quite fast if the need arose. That one episode kind of rearranged my thinking of the gentler sex and those Western movies.

Two weeks later everything was fine. They saw us at the annual fair and smiled, in fact, Mary Jane even waved to me. Man, I was in love again.

I smiled, thinking about this as I resumed my chair on the mower and plugged along in a claustrophobic cloud of dirt with my horses. The horses meanwhile continued to fart, only now it was in my face as we crept along at a snail's pace, it would be another 3 hours before I could head home. Head home? *To what?* I thought, *no TV no radio – nothing!*

At night sleep came easy. Indeed I waited anxiously for the *Sandman* so that in my dreams I could visit Shelby again.

Chapter 3

I wrote to my friends in Shelby; even sent a couple letters to Mary Jane and Linda, the distance had made me braver. I received some replies, but after the summer months were gone, school started and the letters dwindled until there was nothing. With school came new friends, adventure and those old days I had currently looked at as blank pages before, now started to fill up. The odd time though, when alone, my memories would take me back for a visit. Little things like lighting the fire would spark an image like the time Pug and I tried to be cool by smoking and our hair in front got singed...our eyebrows too. We had used old dry cigarettes that flared up like torches. Our parents asked what happened and we innocently remarked on how we didn't know what they were talking about. We, in our adolescent wisdom opted for this generic everyday never-fail excuse, *"What? ...I don't know what you're talking about."* with hands raised and sad puppy eyes.

It was those little things that grabbed you and took you. A rainy day with puddles would bring recollections of the shiny wet pavement of the town streets after a rain. I remembered the days we biked together getting lost in the sound and smell of small town Shelby.

Now, I was lost in a cloud of filthy choking dust. There was so much of it I couldn't spit it out as a drool of mud dangled from my chin. This was my third day mowing barley and oats; tomorrow we were to begin thrashing and the week after that – school! School! I couldn't believe I would ever be excited about going to school. Up here, the only time you had friends and relatives together is when there was work to be done or a wedding to go to…or a funeral; everybody lived so far apart. The only other time, the best time, besides weddings (by invite) and funerals were dances at the huge local hall. At the time I thought the hall was huge but really it was no bigger than a small church, those quaint churches you find in villages. Dances were wild, the in-thing, an all-in-one event where the whole community showed up. There was also the bad side of it, the drinking, swearing and sometimes fighting not to mention the depraved wanton women lurking about for some innocent boy. I couldn't wait! Somehow I had to convince my God-fearing parents that I was old enough to go and was able and responsible to look after myself in this sinful den of frivolity. Contrary to what many outsiders thought (or saw) most of our People were adamant Christians. My Mom and Dad for instance never drank, smoked, cussed or told dirty jokes. God, I couldn't imagine my parents telling a joke about sex! They (as all did) never ever talked about Sex, hence our corrupted education on the topic. It became a kind of hands-on experience. The religious thing also had its hands on our culture in moulding old practises to new directions.

Names were one big difference; no longer were we naming our offspring after animals, events or incidents like being shot in the ribs one side and the shoulder on the other side thus named "shot-both-sides". I thought those names heroic, noble and awe inspiring. Now everybody was given biblical names such as Cain, Solomon, Jeremiah, Rachel, Ruth and so on and so on. My name was Bran? *Where in the Hell did that come from?* I fantasized going back to the past and meeting some great warrior and Chief with names like "One-Who Never-Dies" and "Mighty Bear" then offering my handle to

23

them, "Hello Great People, I am Bran ...named after a coarse breakfast meal consisting of ground kernels of grain." I would be laughed off the Great Plains! So identities changed as the Missionaries brought so-called civilized names, but the public still saw drunken Indians or savages. Even today nobody sees the 100 Christian God-fearing people; all they see is that one drunk Indian on the street corner.

I recall my own biased thoughts at the time. Having been brain washed by the movies I too was guilty of this thinking when first moving back to the reserve.

Around noon, after driving all night from Shelby, we arrived in Canwood, our hometown closest to the reserve. This was the day we finally arrived permanently at our new home – or old home. There on the corner was some drunk waiting for a ride back to the Reserve. To my horror Dad stops. The guy hops in, squeezing into the seat made for three, reeking of beer. He was loud, gruff and obnoxious – to me anyway. My Dad knew him, I assumed, by the way they talked, remarking on common topics and people they knew. He looks at me long and hard, making me uncomfortable as I squirmed in between my Mom and Dad. He scared me.

He puts his hand on my head and I move away. "Is this Bran?" he rasps in his alcoholic breath.
"Uh-huh," my Dad replies and turns to me, "This is Campbell, Bran. Say hello."
I whisper hello.

He smiles at me; suddenly he doesn't look so scary anymore. I glance at him under my eyebrows and see tears well up in his eyes. He looks out the truck side window, not really seeing anything as the streetlights disappear behind us. The conversation starts again as we turn off to the Sandy lake road.

When we get to the reserve, the roads end with dirt trails taking their place. Welcome to Nowhere Ville, I said to myself. Out there behind us was "modern civilization", here we go back to the horse-n-buggy days. These differences marked a huge change not only in my perceptions but also in me while I continued to discover the culture I had lost. All of this, the present and the past, had to be reassembled. The first order of business was to work and help with your family and community; everything else will fall into place. I reminded myself of this but it didn't curtail the cussing and whining I did when alone; there was no way my Dad would put up with such nonsense if he ever heard it so I kept it to myself. Following the summer haying was the harvesting, to which I looked forward to because of the mechanics, organizing and teamwork involved. This sounded interesting, with so many partaking and the camaraderie shared by jokes, pranks and storytelling. It was a prime learning experience for an up-and-coming teenager and at the end of it all was – the Dance.

We began early, real early as the horses need to be harnessed, all equipment prepared, oiled and cleaned. The tractor was aligned precisely with the thresher, the huge belt put on, tested and gas put in for the long day. Then we had breakfast, which was fantastic, with fresh bannock, bacon, eggs, potatoes, pancakes with syrup and coffee for all brewed in a 5 lb. lard pail. No percolators here, but the coffee seemed to taste better. There were twelve of us, and Mom had been up since 4 am getting everything ready for this ravenous bunch. Between forkfuls of pancakes, my eyes sized up the crowd. There was Campbell the hitchhiker, my uncles Cliff, Willard, Walter and a threesome named Moses, Solomon and Jeremiah. The others, about five more, I did not know yet. I was pretty excited, maybe a little apprehensive since this was my first attempt at real work. The previous mowing or binding (whatever that was), I didn't mind, but got tired of it quickly because it was being alone which I was having a hard time to reconcile. It was lonely being by yourself in a deserted field – a nagging reminder of my situation and future. Harvest, threshing didn't feel like work, it felt like a picnic.

The day wore on, everybody doing his "thing" as assigned and all working together like a well-oiled machine. The thresher banged away all day, coughing straw and chafe into the air. The area around it was thick, choked with dust as Walter, the engineer took care of it, primping, priming it with oil, grease and wax. The huge black belt extending from the tractor to the thresher moaned, sometimes squealing when it started to slip. This is when the wax or soap was put on the belt and you could hear the old tractor gulping for air as it 'grabbed' on providing more power. Team by team, we sided up to it, feeding it endless stokes of grain as it devoured them in a second. Wow, I thought, mesmerized by the scene, a person would be 'sausage' if he fell into that. After a couple trips, we all looked black with the dust and chafe sticking to the sweat on our skin.

By day's end I was tired, but felt good, so did everyone else as shown by their actions and talk. It got so we looked to the next day and the daily smorg of excellent food and that feeling of contributing. There was closeness, a family feel throughout the whole event, with the inevitable end to the harvest, but not to the friends made.

Now there was school to come, which I was looking forward to – with a little trepidation. There is always the unknown and this couldn't be more so. I had grown up here but that was before I started school. Since then, my life, my friends, my whole world had been in Shelby. To the kids on the reserve, I was that fat white kid from the States.

But, before school there will be the Dance.

CHAPTER 4

"PPA alarm in West One!"

Our radios blared. Everyone left whatever he had been doing and raced towards the area. West 1 was one of the two units making up the sexual offender wing separated from all other units. PPA alarm meant somebody was being attacked or assaulted. This was my first response after training had been completed. Unsure of the hierarchy procedure and not knowing what to expect, I followed the veterans; always a smart move. We were all in shape, moving like the wind down the glassed corridors. Coming to the wing, we could hear screaming already in the hallways with scurried movement blocking the main door to the unit. The Nurse remotely opened the door pointing to a cell, screaming "It's Will!" We barrelled through the door, knocking aside inmates standing around. They had grouped at the entry, not to block it but out of fear trying to get out. It was Will flipping out and he was the biggest, meanest Indian I had ever seen. Will was 6'7 in his stocking feet, about 270 lbs, dark with an intense glare, which was directed towards us. He blocked the door to his cell, he had someone in there. The pleading screams had subsided to grieving cries and moans, reminiscent of a funeral. We approached as trained, in circular fashion with the cell door and wall to Will's back. I saw a snake of black red liquid crawling, slithering out under his door and realized that it was blood. Someone else's blood because Will, breathing like a bull, eyes bulging and vacant, wasn't cut or bleeding. I knew this was about to get as hard-core as it gets, my initiation welcoming me to another world.

Suddenly Bill says to me "Bran! Say something to him in Indian."

"WHAT?" I hissed in a whisper.

"It might calm him down if he knows you speak his language."

"I don't speak Cree…or Blackfoot or Sioux or anything!" I angrily shot back. "Nothing?!" he asks. "No, nothing."

Then I remembered one word everyone uses when they meet.

"**Tansi**!" I yelled, which meant *Hello*.

He looked at me, eyes bulging. I thought *'oh God' here we go, I'm being singled out*. When inmates are cornered they will single out one person to vent their rage upon. Doesn't matter if he gets the shit kicked out of him, he will have the satisfaction of exacting pain on some poor soul. Looked like it was me this time. In his left hand he had a shank, a self made knife from whatever material he had access to. In this case it was the jagged cutting edge of an aluminium foil box that had been erroneously discarded by Nurses at a cookout or BBQ they had for the units. He had fastened it to an old toothbrush by burning the plastic and sinking the edge into the soft plastic. Quite a weapon of ingenuity and he was coming towards me. I readied myself thinking of a battle plan. I would dive for his legs if he rushed me; this way we would fall and the guards could grab him from behind.

We were never issued any weapons for defence since the clientele we had were crazy. The risk was too great of them seizing the weapons and resulting in a mass killing. So, it was bare hands in emergency situations until others from outside the central area could bring in batons, shields, gas and masks. A loaded weapon would never be brought into the general population areas. There were assigned vantage points for snipers if the incident dictated this course of action.

But he didn't rush me. Instead he hesitated and that was all we needed as everyone in the room jumped on him. With arms flailing, legs in the air, the sheer weight of 8 bodies brought him down. It took two men to bend his arm backward, another two to bring the other arm in place for the handcuffs. He looked up at me from the floor smiling, his teeth yellow and broken, blood coloring his lips. Soon others entered with a body chain that restricted all movement and a helmet with a face shield was put on him so he couldn't spit or bite us. Will was dragged to seclusion commonly known as the 'hole' or as our socially, politically adept bureaucrats referred to as 'disassociation'.

Now we had to attend to whoever the victim was in the cell. There was a soft plaintive moan emitting from a small room darkened purposely with a sheet slung across the window. There was also a smell that we gagged on getting closer to the door. On the bed we saw a body in blood, his arms and legs spread eagled with both limbs being tied together under the bed, on the bare chest was a red X marking a target. There was so much blood it was hard to determine the injury as we crowded the entry. The red now turning black was everywhere making a visual analysis impossible. The eyes looked sunken and dark. Suddenly the Doctor burst through us carrying a needle, his MD bag and some plastic tourniquets. We bent over his shoulders as he went in closer mumbling nonsensical medical terms to us. No one answered so he turned, looked at us and yelled, "Get a Nurse here! Now!" Someone in the back repeats the order to the unit bubble and a Nurse comes running in. "Call an ambulance, find his chart and inform the hospital of an immediate blood transfusion."

"Hey Doc," someone asks, "What's his condition?"

"Bad, critical. He won't survive if he doesn't get some blood in him soon."

"Jesus, what the fuck did Will do to him?"

Disregarding the question, Doc asks if anybody had a flashlight. Bill informs that he has a small one. The Doctor tells him calmly, "Look for eyeballs. We're missing some eyes." Craning our necks we bend even closer to investigate what the Doc had just said. Focusing on the victim's eyes, we could see holes where the eyeballs used to be. Big Bill immediately looks under and around the bed; others join in but no luck. The Doctor pulls off a blanket partially covering the victim who we now know is Rick, a 26-year-old pedophile convicted of assaulting 6 kids. "Never mind," Doctor Swade says, "I found them." There between Rick's legs where a scrotum used to be were 2 eyeballs staring back at us. "In fact you can look for 2 testicles now which are missing." Everyone moved from each other staring at the floor, at their feet, some even lifting their shoes up for closer inspection. Rick rasps out some words as the Doc lowers his head to his mouth. "Can't hear you Rick!" the Doc barks out, he was known to be quite abrupt, unforgiving with sexual offenders. Closer, he cranes his head, bending over till their faces are only an inch apart. Rick was still tied to the bed and immobile. Without warning like a snake striking he opens his mouth and latches his teeth onto the doctor's ear. Screaming, the Doc tries in vain to break away. We grab the inmate, push him back while Big Bill instinctively presses his eye sockets as trained but the victim has no

31

eyes so his fingers briefly disappear into the eye sockets and he quickly retrieves them looking shocked at what he had just done. I remember from my old farm days how we got bridles on reluctant horses so I pushed Bill away putting my fingers into Rick's mouth. With all my strength I pressed hard on his gums digging my thumbs into the flesh. He released his clamp but not before the doctor's ear had come off falling to the floor. Holding his vacant ear, screaming "You cock-sucking fucking diddler!" the doc stomps on the con's dangling leg. "Get me out here! I need a doctor! Fuck!" he hollers as he pushes through us. We all looked up at each other not saying a word. I had picked up the doctor's ear, which they would sew back on at the Hospital.

"What about his balls?" Bob asks. 'Bozo' we called him.
"What!?" the doc is incredulous looking at Bozo.
"His balls, we gotta find them."
"He ate them, all right? He ate them after Willie cut them off and made Rick swallow them! Jesus Christ get me to a doctor. Who gives a shit 'bout his balls!" Apparently Rick, the victim, had whispered this to him before enacting his own revenge on the doctor whose bedside demeanour he despised. "*Will made me eat my balls*," he had whispered, the last words he would say. The old cantankerous Doc was never one to pamper or 'pussy-foot' the inmates sometimes not treating them diligently if they swallowed a razor blade or glass. "*Oh it'll come out sooner or later.*' was one of his sayings. The Lifers here knew that. It was the punks and newcomers that would learn this the hard way in their ploy for drugs and soft time.... or sympathy that was as scarce as chicken-teeth here.

32

Later, as we investigated, the story unfolded that Rick had been bragging to other inmates about his exploits with young kids. To further his demise he had propositioned Will for some sex game. Although designated a sexual offender, Will always denied the charge; the truth would reveal him innocent of these assaults years from then but the label was already stamped upon him.

That was my first incident. After it was all over, everything calm, I began to shake. I felt my legs go weak like I had been walking a tightrope a mile long and a thousand feet high. The adrenalin rush was addictive; we were high... and caught in its grasp. In the following de-briefings, as we called our drink fests, we would replay the event over and over, calling this particular occurrence the "ear" or "Van Gogh" incident. It is funny or maybe sad how we remembered the Doc along with the other players and not so much the victim.

That was how it was though, no mercy; and you did the time if you did the crime. Don't expect anything but bad shit backing up from an overloaded sewer system... and that went for both the bugs and the screws.

Chapter 5

Later, as Campbell sobered up I came to like him. He was a quiet man when sober but drink had him caged in his memories. He had lost his son in a skating accident. While skating alone at night on the lake, he broke through a thin patch and slipped under the ice. They never found the body. In the spring Campbell started drinking in an effort to forget and just never stopped. Not having a body to bury grieved him and when he drank, he would begin to think that his boy was still alive …so he would drink and talk to his boy. I used to play with his son and I had only vague memories of this, but I remember he could play the violin, which his Dad loved listening to as I heard from the open-fire talks. My growing up, his recollections of us playing, probably added to his pain because he was always so quiet around me and I would catch him staring at me with haunted eyes. After the harvest season he would be gone, lost in his beer in some lonely bar or shack. My Dad said if there was a dance anyplace you could be certain he would be there; the violin brought back happy memories. Harvest was over and he was gone but there was the big fall dance coming up and I knew we would see him there.

I was going on twelve now and looking forward to my first dance but my parents had other ideas. My chances were pretty slim until the Council asked my Dad amongst others to be security. Because he didn't drink, they figured he was perfect for supervising and controlling the crowd, especially the young adults who were always looking to impress with their shenanigans. Besides my Dad was pretty tough and had a reputation that the young respected. So now my Dad and Mom were going to be there. Both, although very religious, loved dancing and the music, but in the crowd there was always some drunken idiot who would spoil the festivity, so usually my parents stayed home. But it looked like my wishes had been granted and I was going to be there.

About this time I started to look at girls a lot differently. Something had been happening in my body and mind that nobody had warned me of. This had been occurring since I was 10 and since nobody talked about sex or those 'organs' involved, I had no clue, as did most kids back then. Sex education came from older friends, brothers and uncles who took pleasure in corrupting your reasoning. You listened but you took what they said with suspicion. Getting "boners" or "setting up tepees" as my knowledgeable uncle would say, came at the most inappropriate times making life embarrassing. Traumatizing now at this age, it affected me in ways I would have laughed at two years ago. It would come in the middle of the night or early morning or just sitting there minding my own business. I had seen Pinocchio in my 'young years' and believed it. Did I have the Pinocchio curse on my 'instrument'? That thought scared me as I imagined my 'organ' growing 2 feet out! I wouldn't be able to go anywhere! Was this happening because I was telling lies? I didn't think so as I recalled some petty lies I had told without incident. Maybe it was because of dirty thoughts my Mom had warned about but nothing came to mind. Besides 'what the hell are dirty thoughts'? Looking at the older women in their tight sweaters bouncing to the beat of the music did seem to be a stimulus that aroused me. Why, I didn't know. Maybe that's why those older guys on radio and television news were so upset about this new music. With all this jumping around by young girls to the music they also got 'boners' and their instruments grew…. so maybe their Moms would find out and slap the backs of their head. That kind of made sense.

Some of my friends like Kelly, Shake, Johnny would talk about this so it wasn't a personal isolated problem or disease only I had encountered. This was so nice to know because I actually had concerns of what was going to happen next. Of course, later when we had the balls to do so, we asked the experts – our older brothers and uncles. Kelly and I, being more outspoken, took it upon ourselves to ask about this affliction. So one day we marched up to them with some swagger, puffed-up chests like we were the same as them. Not knowing the protocol of such situations, we blurted out.

"What makes our pricks get bigger?"

Before we could put it into proper context they erupted. They laughed till tears were coming down their cheeks then proceeded to inform everyone else within shouting distance, "Bran and Kel are getting hard-ons! They're putting up Tepees!"

"Noooo! It was Shake and Johnny who made us ask!" we shouted in desperation. It didn't work and we were relegated to ridicule for the next week. They even started to give us the nickname the "Boner-Boys". "Oh, here come the Boner-Boys." and they would bend over in epileptic fits of laughter, some falling to the ground. Whenever we saw the older boys, we disappeared or if escape was not possible as in a crowd, we waited, cringing. We would find the answers later through trial and error.

36

By this time I pretty well knew everyone my Dad knew from meetings, events and work gatherings such as cutting wood, branding and harvest. These were all done as events where much of the community came to help, knowing bountiful meals came with the work. My Mother was renowned for her baking and lavish meals. Besides, the usual gang, such as Solomon, Jeremiah, Moses, Brownie, Campbell and my uncles and cousins, there were the reserve drifters who would come if they were in the area at the time. Just to eat my Mom's cooking was all that some needed to be there.

One of these drifters was Young Syd, an irritable yet lovable free spirit who roamed the provinces in seasonal work. His Dad, Ole Syd, also named Sydney was a character out of Charles Dickens like a pirate and told stories like he was one. They were 2 peas in a pod, the younger being a fatter facsimile of the older; in our language there is no *Jr* or *Sr* to attend or affix to the proper name. Often around the campfire, after thrashing time or branding, both would start their stories with each filling what the other left out.

This made the stories more believable because one would verify the other and vice-versa, sometimes asking the other if this was, for instance, the "right time – or place".
I remember one such story where they collaborated on details and specifics that only they could know by being there in person. At least I thought so in my young mind. But this is one story that scared the hell out of me and would haunt me for years - especially if I had to walk alone at night.

One chilly autumn night before the dance, we were seated around a fire. The day's harvest was done; our bellies were full after a bountiful meal and we languished there in a splendid stupor. It was quiet, serene, with all eyes staring blankly at the flames dancing to their own music. Ole Syd also in his own daze lifts his head to the moon. In Cree he whispers, "*A-we-mis-pook. - There will be snow soon.*" saying this to himself as everyone turns to him. Nobody says anything while they follow his gaze to the haloed moon then back to the fire. We know he is about to tell a story so we wait in anticipation, everyone silent, the embers crackling.

He begins in old Cree, "*O-tana-n'kosis-a-yow* - my young son that is here," points with his lips, "used to be in a very bad way." He waited while everyone turned to Sydney junior, so named after him but we called him young Syd. "He had no respect, no love, no feelings for anybody. He was drinking, chasing married women, gambling, fighting, not caring who he hurt as long as he got what he wanted. He would play poker for 3 nights straight without sleeping then go on a drinking binge if he won some money." Young Syd nodded his agreement, staring into the fire. "One time as he was losing all his wages at a poker game, a stranger in a long black coat came in. There were about 20 of us at Frank's house, six were seated at the table. This fella asked if he could play and they said yes. No one bothers to ask who he is and if anybody knew him. As a joke they asked where his money was. He looked up from under his hat, his eyes lost in the shadow except for the reflection of the kerosene lamp and stove fire. With the orange reflecting in his eyes, he reaches into his black long coat. He brings out bills and bills of money and slams it down on the table. "Is this what you want?" he asks in a hard voice, smiling while his yellow teeth showed. Nobody answers but all smile back as they think of the money they can win. Syd here was seated beside him."

"On the right side of him." Young Syd adds to inform the circle.

"They play for 3 days and 2 nights, no sleep. Syd here is winning big, lots of money piled up!" he exclaims. "As the next hand is dealt, one card flies off the table and under. He looks for it but can't find it so he closes his hand over the cards to his chest so none could see his cards and kneels." Ole Syd acts out the part with his hand to chest. "He still can't see any card so he lifts up the blanket draping over the table." Ole Syd slowly gestures this action.

"He looks around underneath the table squinting to see, then turns his head toward the stranger. His eyes look down to the boots and he sees none. Instead, before him is a pair of hooves, cloven hooves – like a cow! Syd goes to get up and bangs his head on the table. He pushes backward and falls on his ass on the wooden floor. The stranger looks down on him, smiling, *"What's wrong son? See the Devil?"*

"I took off then. Ran to the door and took off." Young Syd says, clapping his hands then points as he stands. He now takes charge and tells his story but he's nervous, jittery. "While I was staring at his feet, I couldn't believe what I was seeing. I slowly touched his cloves, because I could not believe my eyes, then I felt the hair like a horse and the cold bone of a hoof. This is what made me jump and get out of there." Syd shakes his head in disbelief. Everyone mumbles in words I couldn't hear as they looked around to each other. Silence for a while as they all envisioned this. "Guess it had snowed in the time we were playing cards." Silence again as all heads turn to hear him. Saying nothing, his vacant stare into the fire says it all, an orange glow reflects in his eyes. "Guess it had snowed...." he drawls on. "I found myself out in some field. The snow was around me, white and fresh. It was light out; there was a full moon, I see my shadow on the snow. I kinda come to my senses and was breathing hard. Now alone, I look around, turning to see if I could recognize the land. The snow is sharp, sparkles as I see my footsteps in it coming from the Pines to where I was. I hear something." He questions himself at this point; "I turn around facing the moon, see nothing but empty fields in front of me where I guess I had been running to? I am not thinking clearly because this direction was not where I would go, but I see who I think is my Father in the distance. The image is a blob - dark, black in the night air as it glides sideways left to right. This doesn't seem to be my Father as I look and see his walk is different. *That's strange how he's walking*, I say to myself. Getting closer, I know it's not him. I'm getting scared now as who ever it is becomes clearer under the moon. It's a man but I don't know him. He comes straight towards me so I step aside to let him by." Syd motions his stance. "He comes up right beside me and I don't see no face. He walks on, saying nothing as he follows my steps to the Pines. I stand there wondering. His blank face comes to me and I think *I probably couldn't see it because of the dark and the hat he had on.* I swear to myself this is what happened." Young Syd pauses to catch his breath.

"I stand there and wait till he vanishes into the trees, thinking, *why he didn't he say anything as we met?* Even a stranger will say hello if both are alone. I questioned this as I turned to go back to the path, not knowing what direction I was headed. I look up and see a figure in the distance and it walks in the same manner, not up and down, just sideways in a jerky motion. The walk bothers me, like a bad dream where things move around without reason." Syd stops momentarily and shivers.

"My skin crawls and the hair at the back of my neck starts to stick up. The figure comes closer and closer. Before me, again, I see a man but where there should be a face all I see is blackness that seems to move on its own. He whisks past me not saying a word and his wind following behind is cold as it lifts up the snow in a swirl. I look down and there are no footprints! I am so scared by now that my legs are weak, shaking as I try to run but stumble. I keep trying to run, but it's like in a dream and I get nowhere. I fall to the snow, weak; my legs won't hold me any longer. From the ground I look backward and see nothing, for a second I am happy." Syd turns his head, eyes wide in terror. "Then ahead I see for the third time the same man coming. On my knees I start praying as the black figure comes closer. I close my eyes, crying and bend my head down for the end. I feel his presence get stronger and know he is right beside me. I don't want to look, but something makes me open my eyes. I hear a grunt like a Bull and move my head to the sound. Nothing but darkness and I blink to see. Looking to a dull clapping noise right beside me on the ground, I stare. There, in front of me are the same broken hooves I saw under the table and as I look up I see his legs, the hair on them long and dirty. Then, I feel icy fingers on my shoulders. Slowly, a skinny, bony arm comes out from his sleeve, with a black crow's claw attached as a hand. It pulls away its coat. I don't understand my eyes.... I look for what should be a man but see two animal legs! And at the center where they meet here,"

41

Syd points to his groin, "is a face where it should not be. It opens its mouth and the red eyes roll back, a bad smell comes forward that chokes me. I shut my eyes and scream and scream and scream. I passed out I guess." Everybody's wide eyes are on Syd as his voice settles down, his actions becoming slower. He looks down as if to question the ground he stands on. Young Syd whispers as we all bend forward to hear him, "I can't remember what happened next but I awake two days later and my Father is beside me."

"That's right!" Everyone jumps as ole Syd sitting slightly behind, pipes up in his commanding voice speaking in Cree. *Ta-pway*! It is true, I dragged him home, stayed with him as he mumbled and screamed for 2 days and 2 nights in his sleep. After the Poker game when he left, I followed him, maybe half-an-hour later. Coming through the pines, I heard noises on the prairie, the field just beside us here. Getting closer. I recognize screams so I follow the steps that I see in the fresh snow. I run to them as they become sounds of pain. Far ahead I see two dark figures on the horizon, one down, the other standing. I bring my old legs higher and hurry as much as I could." He smiles here, running with his arms. This lessens the tension; everyone shifts their weight, relaxing a bit. "But looking up as I get closer, I see only one figure. Still running, I look all around as I search for the other, but - nothing. No one, ain't nothing there!" He states with a wave of his hand and broken English. "I come upon my son, he is on his knees crying like a baby. As I hold him, I search again, my eyes going across the flat land but it is empty except for us. Then my sight goes to the ground, I see tracks, big footprints of a Beast around where he kneels and they go off into the distance, where the dark pines grow. And I look closer

42

and see the tracks, maybe 30 feet away turn into footprints. Footprints of a human! But from where it came, was nothing!" Ole Syd stops here to make sure they are listening. His posture is frozen as his eyes survey the others.

His voice now in a hoarse whisper he says, "The tracks started there" he points to the ground, pauses. "How can that be? How can tracks begin in the middle of a field where my son was kneeling! Someone or some thing had been there…and the proof was there in the snow! I tell you my brothers, the Devil was there that night!"

"Jesus!" I thought yelling in my head. "No way am I going to be chasing women or drinking….**ever**!"
The story not only scared me shitless but struck a chord in me of what was right and what was wrong and that we will suffer or pay the consequences of our 'bad ways'.

A sudden gust of wind blew the embers high as a cold air descended. I could feel the chill on my neck; I shivered looking at the empty field in front of me, it looked blank and foreboding. I was a child then but still a verse recalled came to mind that my Mother had told me. The words floated before me, '*For now we see through a glass darkly*' and echoed in my mind like a prophecy. My comfort blanket was gone. I looked into the flames.

I knew the snow would be coming soon.

Chapter 6

Shelby, the name kindles fond memories, events. *Aaah*, the sweet times, nothing to worry about, no job, no responsibility other than getting enough money for the weekend movies. I had friends galore but Pug was always there; loyal, protective, steadfast like "Lassie" I used to think back then….or "Ole Yeller". We bawled, even 'blubbered' when we saw that movie, and then laughed hysterically when we looked at each other. We looked away but would start again when we heard each other snort or sniff. The Manager came down the aisle, shines the flashlight on us while some old lady in the aisle behind with curlers in her hair shushes us, so we were quiet for bit – till we hear her snort. Well that was it; we couldn't hold it anymore, breaking out in uncontrolled squeals. We were kicked out but the movie was over anyway. I still can see that woman in curlers with tears down her cheeks, her eyes glaring at us, her lipstick smeared from wiping it with her handkerchief.

Another time, we were fast biking, breaking every rule of the road as we sped down the sidewalk and coasted down the off-highway ramp. This was fun but dangerous, as our bikes gained so much speed we couldn't steer or peddle, but just hang on and hope that we didn't run into anything. This practice was also against the law and our constabulary enforced it. They, however, were nowhere to be seen on this particular day, so we peddled, walked to the top, then let loose. We streamed down so fast, the wind blowing our hair as we held on for dear life crouched to the handlebars. "The Silver Surfer!" we yelled. Then about a block away we see the Police Chief's car pull up to the stop sign. It seems to sit there forever as we streaked towards it, unable to do anything. Panicking, I slammed my foot hard onto the pedals for brakes. I hear screeching, thinking it's Pug screaming but realize it's my rear wheel making the noise. The Chief still hasn't noticed us and slowly takes off entering the intersection and "BANG!" I hit him broadside and Pug, my loyal 'never-part' friend, zips past me, disappearing into the dust, not to be seen for two days. I bounced off the front fender, flying right over the hood and into some bushes. I hear the Chief, "What the fuck!" as he climbs out looking around. He hears my whimpering and comes over. "Are you hurt son?" he hollers. Thinking I will probably go to jail, I start to cry, "I think my head is broken…." That doesn't sound right so I correct myself, "My brain is busted." That's not right either but too late, he's over me. To my surprise, he holds me then eases me back so he can look me over. No cuts, no broken 'anything', no brains hanging out and he says, "I think you're okay son." My bike was demolished, the front wheel bent beyond repair but I was happy – no jail. Instead he drives me home, tells my parents the whole story with some laughs in there. I couldn't understand why, what was there to laugh at? The next day, to my greater surprise, he brings me a front wheel and puts it on my bike. I never forgot that. That incident, one of many, had probably lent itself to my choice of a career in Law & Security.

Life was great then, with so many special events to relive and not a worry except to be home on time. I had noticed certain uneasiness at home the last week that bothered me. A secret being hushed or *'an adult thing'* we younger kids should not hear, I thought. I shrugged it off, not too concerned while I went to school having the time of my life.

45

We would get visitors from home; cousins, uncles, friends, aunties and those *first-timers* venturing off the reserve looking for a couch to sleep on in their search for a future. In those days, you needed a permit from the Indian Agent to leave the reserve for any amount of time. If you were gone more than 6 months, you and your family would lose all status, meaning you had no home. This is why every 6 months we would pack our bags, load the car and report back to the Indian Agency in Shellbrook. I didn't know this at the time, but would learn from my Dad, along with other things, like selling your own grain or cows, was against the law on the reserve without a permit (which was not easy to get). They gave you the third degree on what you needed to sell to buy other necessities like clothes. It was embarrassing, and my Dad wanted this practice stopped, so he began to get into politics. The odd time someone would stop over and they would go into the wee hours talking, arguing about 'how things should change'. I didn't understand most of this, being too young and naïve and really, not caring. All I wanted was my group of friends and to have fun, fun, and more fun. Everything would change that summer.

My Dad worked when he could - when there was work, and he did it with a passion. He always said, "Whatever you do, do it right and finish." I tried with great effort to live up to this and have it lead me through life, but I was always onto something new before finishing the old. When I got a good grasp on it, I quit. I would return periodically to some ventures, such as painting, which I kept up through the years, but never got back that passion I experienced at the onset. Dad came from the old school, that's how he lived and that's how he expected you to live. This would become an issue

46

throughout my teen years as the mind-blowing '60's came to our doorstep. My friends and I were getting the beat by the mid fifties and come the 60's, we were ripe for rock-n-roll. Our songs with Elvis, Chuck Berry, and Jerry Lee Lewis belting out the tunes were being replaced, modestly at first, but soon a new beat would arrive. Elvis movies were the 'thing' back in early Shelby as we gobbled up the tunes with our popcorn, then went home and played air guitar with some fantasy fights included for action. This was basic formula for Elvis movies; sing, fight and get the women. We could do the two but the third item was hard, if not impossible. We knew enough that anything like grabbing a girl and kissing her as in the movies was just out of the question. Before we get to this stage, we surmised we had to have what they had on screen – the songs, the cars, the hair and being able to fight. So we became experts, we thought, on these crucial elements of romance. We knew every song out there, all the car models, how to sculpt our ducktails and were experts at martial combat. It didn't work, something was still missing and I wouldn't find it this summer.

I remember one time we found my Mother's black hair dye so we slapped it on, combed our hair to an exquisite duck-tail, turned up our collars then went out to show off. Strutting along in our penny loafers, jeans with a fat cuff and white socks, we turned heads, '*Man, we were cool*' we thought until the rain started. Pug looks over to me, laughing as he points to my face, "You're getting black." he said. I look at him and he's got black streaks coming down his face too. "Oh shit!" we both say in unison as we look around to see if anybody noticed. Everybody does, including the girls we were trying to impress, so we take off running for home. My Mother was absolutely horrified, giving me a kick in the ass while she shoved Pug to the door and on his way home. Mom threw me into the bathtub tearing my clothes off which were soaked in black by now. The whole episode was so embarrassing; the street scene, the girls and now this - my Mother giving me a bath! Pug and I stayed low for a while not wanting to see anybody who may have witnessed this humiliation.

My Mom was quite forgiving…and forgetting. She didn't remember things for the purpose of holding them over your head to ridicule you into submission, as in *"remember that time"* was not a weapon in her armoury unlike our older peers who never hesitated to remind and demean us. She did have others like, *"keep doing that and the Devil will get you"* or *"the Lord knows what you are doing"* if I stayed in the bathroom too long. I often thought *'what the hell is He doing looking at me when I go to the bathroom? Why doesn't he go look at those people starving in India'!* At this time it was India that was the poster country for famine. I never shared the religious viewpoints of my parents; guess there were too many arguments I had heard over doctrine. But my Mom worked hard too at whatever she did. After school I would go to the Dry Cleaners where she worked - to get my 25 cents for my daily soft drink and chips. The temperature was unbearable in there and I could not imagine myself working in that hellhole. Sometimes in the summer, the staff would collapse from exhaustion, yet she stayed till she got laid off. We have photos of her at this time and I saw how thin and pale she was, then it dawned on me that it was the heat that had emaciated her. She took on any job to feed us and pay the rent though I didn't realize this till I got older. I guess we all do that to a degree, it's part of growing up.

They both worked hard to make a go of it; I never took the time to appreciate it.

All my uncles who came down to Shelby; some to visit, some to work, would exclaim how good we had it here. I thought so too, but being young and naïve, I refused to see the real picture. My Mom and Dad repeatedly having to look for work, renting basement rooms or dilapidated apartments that we could afford, and forever budgeting. All we kids cared about was getting allowances for pop, movies and fantastic presents for Christmas. A couple of my aunts and uncles did settle here with their sons graduating and even doing tours in Vietnam. Most other relatives who came did so for a short visit returning after a weekend here, maybe a week at most. I got to know my uncles and aunts in this manner and everyone would be sad when they had to part again. Sandy Lake, Saskatchewan was so far away. When we would go back to check in, we would travel all night arriving around 8 in the morning. My Dad would sign in then off we went to Mom and Dad's respective parents. It was exciting, an adventure, a great place to visit and I relished this time, but to live here? I never even considered it because the thought was inconceivable. Small town Shelby was my paradise, my home.

My aunties Lily aged 17 and Jane 16, my Mom's younger sisters, came down to stay with us for that life changing summer. I was thrilled till I found out that they were taking over my bed and I had to sleep on the couch, and adding salt to my wound, I learned my cousin, Kyle, would be coming soon after, which would then send me to the floor. I was pissed off and showed it, so they called me spoiled which made me even madder. But I couldn't say anything or I would get my ass kicked or get

49

slapped in the back of the head. I hated the back-of-the-head slap because it was always unexpected and sent you flying forward; never hurt, just embarrassed. I kept my mouth shut but the war was just beginning, I was going to get my revenge.

Pretty soon my aunties were making their presence known as boys became aware of a couple new faces in town. Informal visits by two neighbourhood boys became expected, to the extent that they were routine and considered real dates. Pug and I took this all in. This couldn't be better, it was more than we could ask for because right in front of us the whole mystery of romance, sex and womanhood was unfolding. We watched as they talked, how they acted in front of everybody, but the real show was when they were alone in the room, the house or the car. Pug and I took notes keeping a vigil on when the next occasion was going to be. Sometimes, we would invite our other friends over for a peek. Many, though, didn't see the importance or the need for such information and would walk off. The car was a great place to watch because beside it, where it was always parked, were some lilac bushes we could hide in as we watched. Jane and her boyfriend usually took the front seat with Lily and her 'Jimbo' in the back. Pug and I had to agonizingly sit through the most boring conversations before we would see any action, usually about 10 minutes. But sure enough, right on the minute, as we looked at Pug's Mickey-Mouse wristwatch, we could see a shift in their manner. It seemed to be an unwritten rule or code for dating, that on the 10-minute mark it was *down to business*. Immediately, it became serious, no talking while the radio played rock 'ditties' like *Leader Of The Pack*, *Great Balls Of Fire*, *Runaway Sue* and my favourite, *The Wanderer*.

All four were silent now except for some strange noises, we looked wide-eyed at each other and giggled. Pug pokes me in the side with his elbow so I cover my mouth. They sounded like they were eating at Dairy Queen with all the mmmm's and oooh's and sighs, so we crouched closer. We had crawled far enough that we were leaning against the car, on our knees under the window. The curiosity got the better of us; we had to see why all these noises were happening. Inch by inch we worked our heads upward at the side windows till we had a full view. They were kissing and nothing else, just a bunch of noise! We looked at each other, asking questions in our expressions when all of a sudden some guy yells behind us. We took off in the opposite direction of the voice, running blindly across a vacant yard where we used to hide and smoke. Bang! We ran into a wire fence we had forgotten about, the top steel cross pipe hitting my forehead and top of my nose. Lying low for a painful few minutes while the hurt subsided, we crawled out undetected, had a few giggles then we each went home. The next day at breakfast as I came downstairs from the bathroom, everyone around the table was talking about some burglar or 'peeping-Tom'. *That's a weird name*, I thought. Apparently, as I listened in to my aunties' hush-hush confession, the person who yelled at us last night had thought that we were strange perverts having some cheap thrills. Maybe we were, as I think about it now. As I neared the table they all became quiet, not a word as everyone stared at me... for the longest time.

"What?" I said.
"Where were you?" my Mom asks.

51

"I was out with Pug...at the mooovies?" I carefully added.

"Why do you have 2 black eyes then.... Braaan?" The question was dragged out to mimic mine. I had no clue what she was talking about.

"What do you mean? I haven't got black eyes!" I stare at her like a rabid racoon.

Mom gets up, grabs me by the arm and marches me to the mirror in the next room. I stare in disbelief while this other alien with 2 black sockets looks back at me. At first I panic thinking some dreaded disease had befallen me then I remember the fence. But I didn't want anyone to know we were sexual perverts so I said, "Oh that...ha ha," weak chuckling here as I try for more time to think up a reason. "ha ha....Me and Pug were fighting for the girls. You know, like Elvis and those guys?"

"What guys, what girls?" she snapped, fearing that I was becoming a goon at such a tender age.

"Those guys in the movies..."

"Who were you fighting? Which guys? Who gave you the black eyes?" she demanded.

"Nooo....I mean pretending, Mom. We were pretend fighting. Pug accidentally hit me on the nose. Really Mom. That's the truth." I said in a whimper, raising my 2 fingers up as the Scouts do in their pledge. Wow, didn't think I could lie like this. Everything went good, I thought, till I looked at my aunties. They had this look in their eyes that could kill.

"Were you being sicko last night... Braaan? Peeking in bedrooms? Peeping Tom, Peeping Tom!" It came to me then what this name meant. They accused, twisting their faces in disgust as they said it.

"NoooOO!" I said in desperation as my voice climbed. Losing all confidence, self-assurance, I blurted out. "Mom! Jane and Lil were kissing last night in the car!"

"They were kissing each other! Jane and Lil?" she screamed. I recoiled at that idea.

"Noooo…kissing Jimbo and some other jerk." my voice becomes strained. "And Jimbo was 'feeling her up'!" I didn't know what this meant but I had heard the older boys, especially my learned uncles, describe this and had a vague idea of what it was about. "He was doing this!" I hold my hand to my chest pinching my nipples repeatedly like picking up individual popcorn. At first the girls looked on horrified, then they started laughing; more like wailing. My Mom stares me down and I stare at the girls, anger in my eyes as they bend over in victorious glee.

"Jimbo is going to give you a 'big-stick"! I yelled.

Suddenly there was a total silence, like someone turning off the radio, then *WHACK*! I fought to gain my balance while flying across the floor, my Mom had 'back-head' slapped me. I must have flown three steps forward before regaining my balance.

"Don't you ever say that word in here again!" she screamed.

What the heck did I say? I asked myself, remembering all the times my uncles had used this word. I could hear my uncles saying, *I'm gonna give her a big stick*, and they would all laugh. I couldn't see the point, why would a guy want to give a girl one and why would a stick offend a girl? I had thought it was some bad joke they would make on a girl, or girls. Many a time I thought my uncles were idiots. And what's the big deal with wanting to give a girl some big sticks? I had thought, *Geez, why not give her a rotten apple or bad perfume; something bad that made sense, some thing a girl doesn't want.* So I thought, in my way, I was insulting my aunties, which I was, but not in the way I had intended.

My aunties gawked at me open-mouthed, at least they weren't laughing at me anymore.

"Get to your room and you're grounded for lying...and that...word!" That was it. I was defeated and knew it so I stomped off to my room. If I hadn't added the piece of "the big stick" I would have been okay, I think. I did get a bit of revenge though cause the girls were grounded for one night; I was grounded for a week. To top it off, we never did learn too much from these secret sojourns, recons, just a lot of moaning we would imitate later.

Chapter 7

Will became a regular resident of Seclusion after the Van Gogh incident, as he had always wanted – to be away from all the others. He was deemed too violent and risky for general population, so the "SW" (South-West) became his home, with many of his days being spent in the 'hole' that was adjacent and partial to this unit. We called, unofficially, this particular area Churchill (after a northern river). Inmates, residents here, were very long-term with many never seeing the world outside. They were too violent, too unpredictable for activities with other units, let alone the public. No interaction of any kind with social in-house or "joint" concerts, happenings, or special visits by groups that maintained a connection to the outside world was allowed for this unit of inmates. The risk and their impulsivity to violence made it impossible. They became forgotten in their crazed fantasy of what normal was. Mostly psychopathic killers, they thought differently than the regular inmate and often visualized literally their world in 'special effects'. People, they viewed, were not humans but denizens, demons of their mind, delusions of their illness. Treatment, therapy, counselling of this group was tentative at most times because you never had the time to sufficiently analyse what they were thinking, what they saw or what they were doing – never mind the 'why' of it. Constant security was the only continuity – *'protect your ass'.* You always approached with extreme caution, never knowing if they saw you as a giant Praying Mantis or some other insect to be terminated – or eaten.

In spite of these delusions and psychosis, they had a fellowship, special only to them in their individual hell. Reasoned by unreasonable minds, they shared kinship and friendship only madness could fabricate. Everyone was medicated here and they showed it with the incessant shuffling of their feet, choosing to remain clothed the whole day in their institutional pyjamas, topped by ivory white non-descript terry-bathrobes. Hollow eyes staring down or straight ahead, cracked lips from meds, pallor to the skin and unkempt hair made for a stereotypical image of an Asylum client or patient; except, these were killers, torturers, rapists, molesters. Their setting was a sterile anaemic atmosphere void of real colour; if there was colour it was a washed out pastel. Everything was considered regarding the inmate population's mental state and long-term incarceration, so that nothing architecturally, land and building design, décor or furnishing provoked them.

I looked around thinking this décor could drive me crazy.
When we brought Will here to Churchill, he was put into the cell next to Charlie, the kid who had skinned his parents over religious ideology. The two enigmatic killers seemed to hit it off, arguing very seldom, in their astoundingly insightful talks that ranged from dog to God. They sat inside the Spartan cell cross-legged on the bare cement floor, while they exchanged ideas and words. Under a dim ceiling light, they would talk for hours. Listening in now and then, I wondered how they knew what they knew. These two were not your crazy sub-human idiotic madmen of horror movies, but were the worst and most feared – the charming and calculating, manipulating kind. The kind who could charm your socks off, then strangle you with them.

Occasionally passing by while doing my rounds, I would stop and chat. This one time on a midnight shift Charlie calls to me.

"Hey Boss...Sam?" He now called me this on a regular basis. I had now been here at FPC long enough to be comfortable, more at ease with the abnormal.

I stopped, "Yeah?"

"I see you're an Artist," he states without hesitation or asking. Masking my curiosity, I wondered how he knew this.

"Yeah, you might call me that." I replied.

"Do you know the greatest masterpiece ...in Art...of all time?" he asks breaking up the question to emphasize its importance.

Not wanting to argue I tell him, "That's a matter of discretion based on what you know and what you like." Pleased at my diplomatic ambiguity I repeat, "Different strokes for different folks." Adding to this I state, "I suppose you mean the Mona Lisa?"

He smiles. I felt uneasy as his lips curled up showing his teeth. "Well, did you also know about the most famous unsolved murder of that time....in Los Angeles?" He knew he had my attention. "Did you know in the 1940's?" Charlie repeats the words mocking a Carney Barker in loud dramatics, "Did you know... in the early century throughout the world there was an Art movement called Surrealism; a kind of dreamscape or nightmare style of Art? Some of these turned to a more extreme movement called Dada where everything was Art and nothing was Art." He waited for my reply. I nodded in agreement. "Well, they had meetings discussing and debating the merits and values of Art. They had their heads in the clouds so full of their shit, and we thought of them as geniuses. Many wanted to be them, not so much for the Art but for the label or badge the public would put on them by belonging to this group. There were writers, philosophers, poets, painters and some were just people wanting to be part of this - *wannabes.*"

I'm getting a little restless, where is this going? I know most of this from Art history in my University days. Noticing my impatience, he steps up the tempo in his voice.
"Well, along comes this doctor, a Doctor of Medicine, Genetics who had an IQ matching Einstein.". I peek up at Charlie as his face fills the window. "His head, his ego is just as big as these other guys and he's a 'wanna-be' artist, thinking he could do anything they could do. So he joins and soon he's talking with guys like Man Ray... the guy who did the photo of a nude woman's back with cut-outs in black resembling a violin?" I nod to say yes. "They argue about sex in Art, influence by the Ancients and how the symbolism, the myths like the Minotaur figured in Art. The doctor questions Man Ray's art, especially the one titled "Minotaur" that has a man photographed with his arms up and over his head resembling the horns. He asserts he could without training or schooling, match what Dada was at the time and outdo any artist living."

Charlie is really into it dramatizing the story with animated gestures. He raises his hands to the dim light bulb above, brings them down again as if he was conducting an orchestra. I visualize a choir of Benedictine Monks chanting, harmonizing behind him. He rants on.

"You know the Doctor had killed before?" He answers himself. "Yeah...months before. Partly to cover a botched abortion but really it was for Artistic expression. A very young girl was butchered, her remains burned. She was declared missing and nobody ever suspected the esteemed doc," he sneered. "But...before getting rid of the little girl, he made some crude attempt at sculpting. Restricted by the anatomy, he removed the limbs and head so he could manoeuvre the parts. This all came from his discussion regarding Art, his assertion he could do anything the Dadaists could do and do it better. He had 'done' her for curiosity's sake, an experiment. He sat there after, without any guilt, looking at his work, feeling unsatisfied, analyzing his work. Something was missing. He would have to do it again and do it right. Images of the Minotaur head and horns came to his mind; the arms had to stay, they resembled the horns. He was an expert on the Minotaur, you know. Nobody knew more about this legend than he. He even had an exclusive "*by-invitation-only*" club, a Society of deviants dedicated to the Bull." Charlie relates this as a story or script being read. This has been rehearsed, I thought as he went on presenting a lecture as a Prof removed from the horror but with an intimate knowledge....and insight.

He goes on, giving me a sideways glance. "Soon after, the Doctor had intimate relations with an aspiring young actress - one of many! You know he treated unmentionable sex diseases of the famous so they all *came* on him, gave him favours?" Charlie smiles at his little play on words. "This poor young girl was just another object in his obsession to be the best artist. She was excess material, garbage, a human canvas to paint on and bring alive. He would show them what Art was!" Charlie becomes agitated. I look at him not saying anything. He's not talking to me I realize, he's presenting a case to himself for analysis, maybe judgement.

Charlie takes a short break here as he goes to the dark corner and comes back. "I was there," he mumbles, thinking as he grasps his hands tightly. He brings them up to his face and I can see the knuckles white from pressure. Abruptly, he regains control. Charlie turns to me, "So you know what he did?"

"I figure you are going to tell me Charlie." I waited for him. "So what..."

Ignoring me before I could finish, he retells the tale he has obviously memorized like he's doing a play, a soliloquy before an audience, "On the morning of Jan. 15, 1947 at the corner of 39th Street and Norton Avenue, the first spectators of his exhibit were a housewife and her 3 year old daughter. Later, a crowd would come with reporters and photographers, wondering, horrified at his work. Before them, on the grey frosted ground lay a pretty woman of dark hair. She had been cut in two with surgical know-how; the lower torso, waist to feet dismembered from the upper breast and head area. The pale bloodless legs lay spread-eagled and nude apart from the upper body. On top was his masterpiece or mantelpiece. Her vacant eyes black, stared back.... her mouth was slashed so it went from ear to ear; physically, violently painted with a surgeon's scalpel into a disturbing grin. The arms were set dramatically above her head to mimic horns of the Minotaur, her chest became the face of the beast, the nipples became the eyes. On top of all this was the head smiling grotesquely at what was below it...there had to be an audience"

He sounded like a news flash I thought, remembering those old news excerpts we listened to before the main feature began at the Roxy.

"Did you ever see Dali's *"Soft Construction With Boiled Beans"*? You'll see the man, woman in masochistic pleasure, pain, running across his face with a smile. That's what they saw on this fateful day, an exhibition, left for the Artists he so wanted to be part of."

He stopped, looking to see if I was taking all this in. I expected him to turn, curtsy and bow for applause. He bent closer, his forehead was pressing on the Plexiglas window. He whispered, "Did you know the Minotaur beast was a result of bestiality, an abominable sexual act? A bull was tricked into fucking a woman who had also been fooled. The Minotaur became an abomination not of his doing. In the Arts he was a depiction of forbidden sex, a sexual perversity, vitality but it is also ancient myth based on the actual practice of bestiality... did you know that?"

A deep voice behind says "Good story, eh Boss?" and I jump. It's Will and his window is behind me right next to Charlie's. Something tells me to check my keys...and the door. Instinctively, I check for the cell keys on my belt and slowly feel for the metal door latch while Charlie turns, smiles, then walks to his back wall. I find it and start to push down without making a sound or obvious motion. It opens slightly, a tiny gap appearing between the door and jamb. *God! The door is not locked! All he has to do is push on the door!*

Charlie looks to me, his head tilted with a smirk still there. "So there it was, the greatest work of Art.... The

61

Black Dahlia!" he ranted. "Not some image on paper but the real thing, Performance Art. The act of murder was a work of Art. That was the motive, the *modus-operandi*, so no wonder they could never solve it. The answer, the mystery was right there for all to see, but the detectives were not artists."

"Look it up – the Black Dahlia, if you don't believe…" he hesitates, staring into me.

The name strikes familiarity but my mind is not registering this as I realize my situation. I have this fear on my face and in my eyes that I can't show.

Charlie studies me, catches my eyes, "You're scared…but it's not the story. Is it?" He smiles broadly, knowingly, "Lose your self, Bran…forget something? You should turn the latch there, make sure everything is locked tight, Sam."

I fumble for words; anything to stall and give me time while I analysed what will happen next. Charlie's distant words haunt me now, "*Leave the door open…*" he said on our first encounter. I think back to our training, specifically details concerning seclusion. We had been locked-up as an exercise in experiencing what it felt like and it wasn't comforting knowing that inside, there is absolutely no way to get out without someone on the outside to turn the latch. I kept my composure and didn't do anything.

Thank God, I whisper in my mind. A nervous smile comes to my face and I start to giggle out of anxiety, a small laugh as I realized the consequence of my decision. It was a relief gesture like when you pass the cemetery at night. I thought he never caught on but he knew something was wrong with my reaction. If I had turned the latch to check if it was locked it then becomes unlocked and he could have pushed it open with both dead bolt and turnkey locks open. I called the Keeper over, our supervisor, explaining to him the doors had been left unlocked probably from shower time and I needed a second person there for security while dead-locking again. He shook his head voicing his disapproval of the last shift then proceeded to lock up. We went down the short hallway, to Charlie's cell door where he shoved the big brass key into the dead bolt and turned it. It was locked! He did the same to the latch key lock…and it was locked too! I saw it but I couldn't believe my eyes so I went over to turn the latch and it wouldn't turn, it was locked!

Charlie looks on sombrely, "What's up Boss? We going somewhere?" Nobody answers him.
The Keeper replies, "Nah, nothing happening…just checking all seclusion doors for my weekly reports."
"Well I can tell you that Bran here always double-checks Boss." Routinely we check all locks before the previous shift leaves, I hadn't that night. Why was he supporting me? Charlie smiles, waving as we leave.
The Keeper looks at me sternly, whispering, "What's going on Bran?" We walk briskly to the station.
"It was open, the deadbolt was unlocked!" I plead. The Keeper calls on radio for the 'extra' to come down for relief while he took me to his office.
"How many OT have you done in the last week?" he asks. Over-Time was serious here and you could virtually work 24 hours a day if you could keep your eyes open that long.
"Three." I tell him.
"I think you're overtired Bran and your mind is playing tricks on you. It happens, you're not the first one you know," he talks but I know 100% that door was open, unlocked – I felt it and saw the gap. I can't respond, as I

repeat the scene in my head. His words are distant, fading away while I replay the recording in my mind. I was sent home a few hours early to rest up, sleep, but the event would play on me for the next month. This really bothered me; not only my credibility as a guard, but as a responsible person I depended solely on what I saw as being real, being factual. It came to me then that this is probably what everyone here feels, our disturbed clientele. You can't trust your self and your senses; factual is fleeting. How is it that one simple mistake can break your tenure to reality, then everything else implodes? It unnerved me. We walk a fine line between our two worlds.

The previous event that had bothered me was almost gone now and I had relegated myself to the fact that I had somehow mistaken the door as open. Charlie had me fully entertained, so engaged in his story that my tired mind got the best of me. Another lesson learned.

The year was a haze rushing by so fast I had trouble to focus. Too much information too fast but we had to learn nonetheless and gain experience and the wisdom to use it. There was a lot going on, a lot of "events" and I remember vaguely the more interesting exceptional situations we encountered as the inmates' actions provided us with tales to tell later. I recollect one evening we responded to one of many PPA alarms. There was a full moon that night and it is an established fact that psychiatric patients, inmates, become influenced by the lunar cycles. We arrived at the 'sex' unit at full throttle and were ushered into the nursing station. The head nurse said there was a unique hostage taking being done in Rick's old room, the place of the Van Gogh incident now holding Bart.

We asked her, "Well, who's being held hostage?" She looked at us awkwardly, her head tilted to one side, "Bart's threatening his penis."

"WHAT!" someone yells. "You're joking?"

"No I'm serious. He's threatening to cut his dick off."

"Shit! Let him, who cares." says Bob who had been so concerned with Rick's balls before. Guess he had hardened up.

"He's got a knife for one thing – that, has to be retrieved. Another thing, and this comes from the Warden, patients shall be protected from self-abuse or injury. So we have to protect him from hurting himself."

"Fuck! Fuck the Warden and his hare-brained ideas. The guy's got a knife! Why don't we just wait till he gets tired or something?"

"What if he goes after one of the other guys? What if he kills somebody or himself? Do you want the warden on you if this happens?" We knew we had to go in; maybe we could talk him out of it.

Meanwhile Big Bill is mumbling curses on the Warden, "Fucking idiot Warden. Wish we had a real Warden." We prepare our battle plan to enter; the main heavy door is pulled open, rushing to his door we stop immediately at the sight before us.

"Oh my God!" Bob says in horror. He was the first one there but now holds us back with his arms spread out across the door. Standing there holding his penis, inmate Bart had the knife in one hand raising it to show he meant business. He brought it down. The suggested action and outcome hit us like a hammer.

We all simultaneously shouted "NO!" Inmate Bart stops. Bob was especially adamant, "No...please, please don't do that."

Bart was standing, sidestepping to his clothes-chest then very gently, he laid his penis carefully along the drawer ledge that was almost closed. The drawer had an extended wide ledge or rib so his dick could rest there without falling into the drawer itself, kind of like a miniature cradle or furrow. He turned to us, raised his knife, his penis in guillotine posture with the head waiting for the final chop. He brings down the blade and again we all say "NO!" and he smiled. He was enjoying the stage.

"Fuck this shit!" Big Bill impatiently swears and takes a step forward, kicking the drawer shut with his size 14 military boots.

"Ooooohh! We all moaned bending over. Bill had slammed Bart's dick between the chest and drawer. Bart opened his mouth but nothing came out. With eyes bulging out, mouth gaping, he sinks to his knees. The knife was grabbed, Bart was limp as a noodle; no problem arising and the incident was over just like that...within 5 minutes. Bart was taken to seclusion where he shared space with Will and Charlie, each in their own cell. For a week the unit nurse had to come in daily to switch bloody bandages and apply ointment over oozing cuts on Bart's penis. During these times he would have to endure profanities and ridicule from Charlie and Will, which we didn't try to stop. "Hey Noodles, Sausage Brains... come over here and we'll stamp on your poor little prick." One would comment, the other would laugh hysterically. It reminded me of an old Saturday morning cartoon I used to watch in Shelby, about 2 crows, 'Heckyl & Jekyl'.

Later, another 'penis' moment had endeared itself to our FPC Halls of Shame. We had troubles with a particular inmate, Mr Stool, who relished in utilizing our own directives, laws and by-laws against us. A very contrary individual, he used anything to screw us, *'beat the system'*, never minding if it hurt him in the process. He was prone to 'cutting', using whatever was available to cut himself, usually in the groin area. The rules stated that he could not have any utensils, tools or objects because of his condition. Another rule was that all inmate letters could be read before mailing. This angered him to no end and he became obsessed with repealing this rule attesting to personal privacy. Throughout the summer he mailed requests, sent notices, got organizations to advocate for his cause. Finally he got what he wanted, the right for him to send mail, uncensored, to the Commissioner, Director and Director General privately, that meant nobody could read what he sent in the mail. Brilliantly, now that he had them in his corner he demanded that the Commissioner give him free access to knives and razors, the old straight razors they use in horror movies, for his supposed handicrafts. These were refused, thank God, but in addition to the privileged mail rights granted him, the Commissioner wrote back and 'saw no reason why Mr. Stool could not have a Gillette disposable razor in place of a straight razor for his personal hygiene'. "Ole Stool" as we called him was in his glory. We knew what was coming and tried to change the Director's ruling, but our Warden wasn't too concerned either, so we just sat, swore and waited.

It was a weekend, nice sunny day and all the inmates were in a good mood. Just after lunch we get a PPA alarm in the sex units again. What did he cut this time we thought, his neck? Running into the recreation area between the 2 wings we saw one inmate on the floor, another was puking. We slow down to look around us.

67

The atmosphere was electric, so we walked on cautiously keeping a watch behind us. We got to Mr. Stool's door, there was blood all across the floor and he was fidgeting with something. He had an obscene painful grimace on his face but kept working at whatever he was doing. The scene brought back a snapshot of Dali's graphic painting, "*Soft Construction With Boiled Beans*" that Charlie had described. Entering the room, we saw what it he was so preoccupied with that he didn't even know we were present, watching in horror.

"What the Fuck…." someone says in a hoarse whisper. A collective gasp comes out.

His legs spread he had his hands on his penis; one pulling the foreskin backward, the other with a razor. He was skinning himself; his penis…like you would take off the fur of a weasel. He had grabbed his foreskin, pulled it back tightly then skinned it with that little disposable razor that the Commissioner thought was no problem. He hacked, flayed at the skin around his uncircumcised penis as he pulled the foreskin back to himself. With his hands all bloody we grab them and someone grabs his legs as he started to kick. He lay there; his limbs extended out in an X position. Sharon, the unit nurse came in, followed soon by the Doctor who seemed unperturbed by what was before him. Although horrific and disturbing, the damage done to his 'organ' was mainly cosmetic. The thought of what he had done, envisioning the act and unbearable pain was the real horror. So we carted him off to the hole with Charlie and company welcoming him with a nasty reception. Ole Stool knew his rights though, demanding to see the Warden 'pronto', to which the nurses obliged him

68

forthwith. They wanted the Warden to see the physical results of his political waltz with the Commissioner.

He comes down immediately through the main hallway door; wide steps with soles pointed outward, he looked like a cartoon character. "Okay, what's the problem here!" he bellows as he comes through us like Moses parting the Red Sea. We are all standing around motionless as Big Bill points inside the seclusion cell. The Warden walks briskly, turns, then buckles at his knees while his mind attempts to comprehend all the blood before him. No one offers any help as he turns pale, slowly turns away in disgust and throws up his lunch. The Warden left, not saying a word to Mr. Stool, but that was okay with him cause he got what he wanted, a reaction from the 'powers that be'.

We would get a follow-up to Ole Stool's creative dalliances with authority. In accordance with the Commissioner's ruling, he was able to send off another letter of protest, uncensored, to him and the Director General. In a week there was a buzz around the center so I asked what was going on.
"You didn't hear?" Murray my old friend asked.
"No…What?" I asked.
The Warden got supreme shit today from the Director General. Ole Stool sent a letter to him and the Director."
"So, I knew that. We all knew that."
"Well, did you know what was in the letter?" Murray has this big all-knowing smile.
"WHAT?" I shout.
"His foreskin! Ole Stool mailed his foreskin in a plastic handi-wrap sandwich bag!" We screamed like kids. "Imagine opening the bag and holding up this plastic

looking thing!" Murray is doubled over almost falling off the chair.

"Did he really do that, hold up the foreskin?" This is incredible, I think, as an animated comedy came to my mind. "Wasn't it bloody?"

"Stool had washed it before sending, cleaned it good." Murray explained impatiently.

"So yeah, yeah...he holds it up, the foreskin, actually rolling it between his fingers and thumb asking *What the Hell is this*?!" Murray mimed the action with his hand; a short pause followed to catch his breath. "And...and now he's got to have tests for AIDS and shots for Hepatitis!" Murray lost his hard fought composure, buckled over and fell to his knees off the chair.

.

We laughed all day, probably all month about that one. Perhaps this sounds callous, morbid that we would laugh, but that's one thing my people and we as guards shared. We used humour as a tool "to laugh it off". As long as nobody died, any incident or accident was fair game. That was one of the reasons I stayed there for so long - that similar slanted point of view and humour. If you were going to dwell on what occurred or what could happen, you would be crazy like the rest of them.

Towards the end of that year, I experienced my first institutional suicide; one I was directly involved with, there were many. The Keeper and I had been in the cafeteria scrounging up some grub for the midnight staff. We weren't supposed to be in the kitchen but the Cafeteria Manager was appreciative of security; it was good practice in being tolerant, 'looking the other way' so everybody got along. It didn't amount to much; we took bread, luncheon meats, veggies and fruit to munch

70

on through the graveyard shifts. Surprisingly it's the little things that mean a lot.

That one particular night we got a PPA alarm from the basement or 'dungeon' as we called it. This was 'bed' time for the midnight shift when each unit's lone security and nurse locked up the cell doors of all inmates in all the units. Done door-to-door, this was when things could get out of hand when risk of a riot or hostage taking was at its highest. This shift was also when we had the minimum number of security present, so until they were all in the cells, we were at attention.

Running down the stairs into the wing, we saw confusion and activity in a corner cell. The unit guard was holding someone in the cell closet while the nurse hacked at something above them on the steel bar that held the clothes. Getting closer we could see that it was string or some thin rope. Finally cutting through, the man slumped to the floor and the nurse positioned her self to do CPR.

The guard held up his hand, "Stop Mary, it's too late, he's cold." She felt his forehead and neck and he was stone cold. Where she ran her fingers across his neck we could see clearly that it was black and swollen. We identified after examining the crease in his neck that he had concocted his shoelaces into one long skinny rope that was sunken out of sight. His neck to his ears was puffed up and black as coal, literally. I had seen death before, but not like this, not so graphically in black. And there was a smell unique to death, a smell we came to recognize. He must have been hanging in his closet all day, a closet maybe 5 feet high. A stretcher was brought and we lifted him onto it, which proved difficult. When

71

someone dies, they lose all muscle retention, becoming a rag doll so that lifting them is a chore. After we got him placed on the stretcher, we took him to A&D, Admissions and Discharge.

We looked him over, finger printed him then called the Coroner because we had no doctors on the graveyard shifts. A tag was wrapped around his big toe, his name and file number on it, and he was officially discharged. The ambulance came quietly, took him away to the morgue where no one claimed him - that was it. He had been admitted decades ago, now we discharge him, no farewell, no commotion, nothing; just another useless item to ship out. That bothered me. The smell, the bloated disfigurement, even the color didn't arouse any emotion in me as did that fact. A person can go through life never having a life. Later, in retrospect, I began to look at time inside institutions as that - a lifetime without life not only for the inmates but for the guards too.

I would see 7 more suicides, 3 hostage takings, 2 more murders (one inside, one outside) and too many assaults to remember. It was the unusual 'events' that would keep me, intimate moments, memories shared with my colleagues. We became 'brothers' like the Indian War Societies of the Plains Tribes. We stood fast, solid for each other, like our life depended on it because it did.

Another memory comes back to haunt me, one involving a child's ceremony where I became 'blood-brothers' with an old friend.

Chapter 8

The Dance, the dance...finally the Dance! Those words were capitalized in my head. It was finally here! Before departure to the hall I dressed up in my finest; pants that narrowed to the ankle (so that we looked like we had super skinny legs) meeting huge leprechaun shoes coming to a point, a big wide belt and a purple vest finished the spectacle. This was the fashion, but not in Sandy Lake, not yet anyway so I took a second look and pondered. Times were changing, but in the reserve, we still clung to the fifties with *Bryl-Cream* ducktails, cuffed jeans and leather or denim smock jackets. I kind of looked out of place with my planned 60's fashion statement I meant to wear, so instead I wore my working cowboy boots complete with corduroy jeans and a smock. I was thankful because I didn't see any other boy or man there with a purple vest or those witch's shoes the Beatles wore. I'm sure I would have been singled out.

Everyone slicked their hair, primped their collars and checked the wallets to make sure they had money. My cousins and my uncles were all 'spruced-up,' talking and bragging about their anticipated dates with "Big Shirley," "Hot Anna" and whoever was "hot" at the time, so it went on and on. We knew (even to us at age 10-11), that most of this talk was just that – talk. Fantasy and bullshit reigned supreme in our teen years. But - this is whom we learned from in our innocent years, these experts with their "big sticks" who we came to question later in regards to their proficiency and conquests.

There was an entrance fee to the dance and those who had cars needed cash for gas – and beer. This is what many had been working and saving money for. This dance might be the only entertainment on reserve till Christmas, so people regarded this as the event of the year. Inside our reserve borders, entertainment was minimal, so we relished gatherings and the friendships made.

Arriving at the dance hall in our old 51 Fargo we called "Red Devil," we could see tents already pitched up, with smoke encircling the tops of trees that surrounded them. Those without cars came in their buggies drawn by a team of horses and some singles rode in on horseback. Families camping there overnight had kids and babies who were put to bed when the dancing started. Mothers with babies stayed in their tents while the fathers 'went out with the boys'. A slew of older cars parked around the hall in random order, cars of the fifties and forties - Fords, Chevys, mainly. The atmosphere was exciting and we jumped out from the back of the truck while it was still moving, eliciting a shout from my Dad. We paid no attention. Standing before the big red hall, "Den of the Devil" as some religious folks called it, we drank in the noise, the smell of campfire smoke and the electric scene around. All was abuzz waiting for the band to arrive, people skittering, scattering about in anticipation.

Close to half an hour later they arrive in their '62' Mercury, pulling an aluminium trailer. *"Wow, a new car! They must be famous."* I thought. A hush fell over the gathering then excitement sparked the audience to erupt, "They're here, they're here!" You can imagine my dismay when four old guys and one young guy stepped out with their instruments, one with a violin! I don't know what I was expecting, but it wasn't four ole geezers. I was totally ignorant of the music people favoured here in the backwoods, but with Ricky Nelson and the Everly

Brothers making the airwaves, I assumed it was going to be a rock band.

"What!" I said to myself surprised, staring at the sight before me.
My friend John, beside me, who was into Ricky Nelson big-time was also shouting in admiration, "It's Smiling Johnny & the Polka-Dots!"
"Who!" I asked.
'*What the hell was this*,' I said to myself staring at John jumping up and down, *The Twilight Zone?*'
"They're good," he said trying to reassure me, "You'll see."

The excitement overcame me and I relegated my self to a boring night of music but I was going to have fun, excitement, no matter what. As the sun broke the horizon that morning I would be in love with this music and still am to this day. It was the first time I had been forced to listen… and the violin wailing, especially in the waltzes, stirred me. There is something about the moaning and crying of a violin that shakes the soul. My aunties use to tell of a mythical '*Keeper of the Gates*' who succumbed to such beautiful music that the imprisoned dead escaped and lived again. I could see it now; I understood the myth and the power of music.

We watched while the band set up on stage, plucking the guitar and violin strings so they were in tune, "Twang, plink, plink," and soon you could hear a tune. A pause came to the tuning and everybody in the hall stopped what they were doing, you could hear a pin drop. "Ladies and Gentlemen, please welcome Smiling Johnny and his Bunch of dots!" The audience erupted then quickly quietened as Sydney our MC turned around. You could

75

hear some mumbling on the microphone, "What? Pokey? Poke....Polka? Okay, okay" He started again, "Ladies and Gentlemen, please give a warm hand for Piling Johnny and his Polka-Dots."
Someone disenchanted now, shouts out, "Get him off the stage, he's drunk!" Some others reply with a few soft boos.

Fumbling in Cree, Ole Syd now shouts in English, "Alright, alright, here's this guy," and points to Smiling Johnny who wasn't smiling anymore, "...and the Pokey-Dots!" In spite of the butchered introduction, the band struck hard on the strings and the music began. You would think a bomb had gone off with everybody's simultaneous yell followed by a flurry of action as all men on the floor scurried to the benches along the walls searching for the right girl or woman to dance with. Some shy refusals from the girls, but soon all had a partner and the floor was shaking, bouncing in rhythm to the music. The exhilaration took a hold on me standing there, feeling the ground throb under my feet. It felt good.

In the midst of the crowd from time to time I could see someone familiar. There went Moses, young Syd, then uncle Clifford...."man he 's a good dancer" I think, then in a second they're gone, lost in the crowd. Kelly comes up beside me, "Let's go outside." he says bending his head to mine. "Let's wait," I reply watching the dancers whiz by me, "I wanna watch this." About an hour passes and the sun goes down, replaced by a pleasingly cool darkness.

"Sam! Come on!" Kelly shouts my other name, which I prefer.

"Oh yeah...okay, let's go." We go outside and it's cool, the dust outside along the gravel road doesn't disappear as a car goes by, but hangs making low clouds. The moon starts to rise coloring the dirt clouds in blue, enchanting the view. This is a good night for romance, I remember thinking. Outside we could still hear the music but muffled in the background while close to us we would hear a sharp clang as some people said hello to each other with a beer-to-beer salute. There was no drinking accepted anywhere but on occasion, the people in charge looked the other way as long as the drinkers respected everyone else. We continued on you might say, 'making our rounds,' taking in the sights around us. It was a carnival atmosphere with things happening inside and outside, people mulling about, couples searching for a private moment to kiss and those sneaking beer to one another. Coming around the corner, I meet Sol and Jeremiah, the two workers my Dad hired for harvest, who looked 'pissed' already? The night was young and they probably wouldn't recall anything after midnight.

"Hey Bran, *Tansi*!" they said, "Wanna beer?" They shoved a brown bottle to me jokingly and surprising myself, I took it and had a sip. Both opening their eyes wide, Sol said, "Don't tell your Dad, eh? He'd kill us!" The taste was awful, bitter, puckering my lips leaving a sour tang that would stay all night. *This is what some craved?* I couldn't understand it then.

"Holy shit, man! Why did you do that?" Jeremiah turns to Sol with an accusing stare, "His old man will find out, eh?"
"Naahh, nobody will know. Right Bran?" Sol asks me, more a plea than a question.

With the dreadful taste still assaulting my taste buds I honestly say, "No, don't worry." In that moment I became life-long friends with Jeremiah and Sol.

They shook my hand repeatedly then took off to find more beer they had hidden, which they did all the time. This was common knowledge. A routine practice for them except they would get too drunk, forget where they hid it and cases of beer would go missing, which was a disaster. The next two to four days they would be in the bush searching for the lost treasure. You could hear them faintly in the bush,
"Find anything?"
"Nope. You?"
Occasionally they would argue in the bush, not being able to see each other, the two would shout out, "Nope. Jesus Christ, where did you hide them!"
"You hid them! Don't blame me, you prick!"

Usually, if we were party to these spectacles, we watched the tops of the trees swaying back and forth therefore able to detect which way they were going. Some days they would luck out, a scream would hail from the wilds, "Holy Shit! I found them, I found them!" Briefly, for an instant there was absolute silence and stillness, then from the opposite direction you would start to see the trees, bushes moving. You could see the charge; branches cracked, bushes shook, trees swayed like there was an earthquake and an occasional cry or grunt could be heard. It was like a moose barging through, and then suddenly, there would be silence again... with the odd giggle and a customary clank of two beers. All would be well until the next time.

We walked on. Far from the hall, we could see an old green car by itself. I looked to Kel, "Let's check it out." "Okay, let's go." he comes closer to me. Getting within hearing distance, we began to crouch. I didn't how that made our approach quieter but we did it anyway. Soon faint noises became clearer, louder. "Oh, oh, oh...." coinciding with a guttural "Uh, uh, uh...." The ole '49' Ford was shaking. We slowly inched our way finally getting to the rear side window. We never had actually seen the act, but an idea from the descriptions, stories we heard our older 'experts' relate. We thought this was it; we are going to find out the mystery. Holding our breath, we raised our heads to the windowsill. Across the rear seat stretched to the opposite window we saw 4 legs, one set with the feet down, the other with the feet up. The pair with the feet up was spread-eagled and it looked like the man in between was the mover with his feet down pressed against the side and the floor for leverage. We couldn't see too much in the darkness except his ass going up and down in time with his "uh, uh, uh". Staring hard, scared but not wanting to run, we gazed in wonder, spellbound by the action before us. His action became more excited, his tone more pitched. Suddenly he stopped. His ass pinching together you could see him push hard. She in response wrapped her legs around his, sighing in a moan. It lasted forever; the scene became etched into our being at that moment. In one minute we had learned what it was we had been wondering about for 2 years. We didn't see everything, but we analysed the act and concluded the end result. What was disconcerting later, while mulling over the ethics of our 'snooping' was that we had sneaked into a private, very intimate relationship. We snuck back to the hall and stood by ourselves for a minute, talking it over in amazement. We came to realize how classless our conduct was and made a promise not to share this story; being scared of retribution was another factor too. Had I become a *peeping Tom* as my aunties had disgustingly put it? Through the years though, I would find many who had similar experiences, which became their initiation into sex education. The later Sixties would get wilder and those hidden acts of love and lust would become common and open.

As an understatement, we had seen enough outside, besides the violin called me. Squeezing our way back in, snaking through the mob at the entrance, we popped right into a fight. Some guy bopped another before we could get out of the way and we were on the floor too. I looked for Kel to my left seeing this white guy instead which surprised me cause not too many came to a reserve dance from outside. Someone yelled, "Get up Charles!" and he was gone. To my right was Kel picking me up and dragging me away. Before the fight got serious, my Dad came into the circle that had formed. "Alright! Enough! If you guys don't stop you're out of the dance!" That put a halt to the skirmish immediately with the two, although the bigger guy said something stupid to my Dad. My Dad was 6' 2 inches tall, this guy was bigger. I could see the anger well up in my Dad's eyes. He went out the double doors with this guy following him, they both stopped. My Dad turned around and this guy hit him, a sucker punch. It didn't even shake him as he backed away from another punch the big guy threw. He missed wide and my Dad threw his left up and across. "Crack!" The guy went down like a sack of potatoes, laying face up with both fists clenched and in the air holding onto something invisible. He was out cold. This took about 10 seconds. My Dad told everybody to get back inside, "Get away from here. Go back in and have a good time everybody. Come on!" He went back in, started to dance and my Mom never even knew he had a fight. That was the first time I actually saw him fight and would see a few more. I never saw him lose a fight, nor did his brothers ever recount him losing in all the years.

We gathered back in the hall as the dancers carried on, not knowing or caring what had just occurred. Every dance had its fight or two, but nothing bad ever came of it. It seemed a 'right of passage' and every kid must have his day, so although frowned on, it was expected. The merriment carried on here and there like flashes or sparks in a shove but nothing like outside. "*Woo, that was fast. Pow!*" I thought, grinning.

Still smiling, I recalled the green car and the young couple inside when viciously I was pushed aside. Standing alone with my sweet memory, I failed to notice this older couple barrelling down my way, kicking up their heels in glorious neglect. Someone had just saved me. They whisked by in a wind of colours with a scent of "Old Spice" in their wake. I watched them speed around in a circle, passing all the other couples. The tune ended and they sat down huffing and puffing, the guy with a cigarette dangling out of the corner of his mouth. *They're having a great time*, I thought. In between them was a sealer of clear liquid, water I thought, that they took turns sipping. My suspicions grew as to its contents as each dance became more and more abandoned.

All of a sudden, the music stops, Ole Syd comes to the stage, "Everybody now, grab yer partners. We are going to do the Butterfly!" A wild applause, everybody scrambles to get a third dancer. The Butterfly is a dance

81

of three people; usually two men, one woman; the men take turns spinning the woman around in circles from one man to the next. The tempo is fierce; they hook arms spinning crazy then try to latch onto the other to continue, circle with one then circle with another. All are settled now, waiting for the music.

Ole Syd bellows out in broken English, "Okay, get ready your woman!" He announces then, "For dis dance we got someone new to play the fiddle. Peeesh welcome Charles, nephew to Johnny here." Sydney points to Smiling Johnny (who is smiling now). With that, the violin squeals, then this young guy makes the bow crawl over the strings in a moan. The dancers march in unison, high-stepping slowly, anticipating as the violin speeds up gradually, then all hell breaks loose when the fiddler hits a certain chord, stops, then furiously goes into a polka-type tempo. It was a madhouse! People flying all over the place, trying not to run into the others. The music was blaring, dust rising as the dancers twirled, precariously hanging onto partners then slowed to a march again.

I heard their laugh before seeing them again. Recognizing the old couple I kept my gaze on them. The guy was still smoking his roll-your-own cigarette, dancing with it dangling out and the ashes bent down almost falling off. She hung onto her purse as it flew wildly, dangerously, in synch with her twirling. He had his arm around her, as did the third man while they slowly raised their legs in unison, waist high waiting for the breakdown. And it came, throwing them into frenzy once more while they attempted control. She was getting a little 'tipsy' - you could tell from her jerky squirrel-like movements and she seemed to be having a hard time focusing her eyes. The dance returning to normal again, I

82

noticed the guy's cigarette was gone and he was lighting up another. They disappeared briefly behind the other dancers coming out like some cattle from a stampede. As they came around to where I was standing, I could see a faint ribbon of smoke coming from her purple hat. I thought I should say something but again they took off in a fury, twirling each like a top. The older lady being quite liberal in drinking whatever it was in the sealer jar finally lost her balance. The spinning mixed with the drink made her so dizzy that she went flying after missing one of the guy's arms. In slow motion she flew, her legs not able to keep up with her falling forward she braced herself with arms stretched out. She landed under the seat where the sealer was sitting, waiting. You could see a small amount of liquid bounce out from the collision landing in her hat. She laughed so hard that the guys had to lift her to a standing position. They continued whirling around in figure eights when all of a sudden, "Poof!", her hat caught on fire. The old guy screamed and hit her on the head with his hands. She glared at him, not smiling now; and then belted him with her purse, her hat in full blaze at this point. The other guy grabbed her and she screamed, both falling to the floor. Someone finally put the fire out. Getting to her feet, she grabbed her tattered burnt hat that was still smoking, put it on, hooked her arms to the men and danced away, laughing. Everybody was laughing and the short interruption didn't stop the dancing.

After the Butterfly dance ended, all came over to make sure she was okay. She was fine and having a ball. Remembering them now, I realize they were not that old, just old to me at the time. They lived by their own rules, never hating or hurting anyone, but didn't give a shit of what other people thought of their 'accidents', their lascivious behaviour. The same could not be said regarding those other 'holier-than-thou' couples who condemned such merriment. Preaching the Gospel in daylight but when the night came you could see them lurking in their true colours screwing the congregate. Religion is fine; just don't rape me with it.

The evening turned to morning and before we knew it the day was breaking. We walked outside for a breather. The dust clouds still lingered, hanging over the gravel roads stretching to the hall now. Crispness was in the air with a sweet smell of dead foliage mainly the scent of Cranberry. I loved the smells at this time of year. Taking in the tranquillity of the sunrise, smoke around the tents, I breathed in deeply saving everything for my future. The music, the dancers were winding down with sleepy-eyed waltzes. I went inside to see who was left, leaving my friends on the entrance stairs. There was Brownie sleeping with his head propped by his arm, elbow on the stage sitting with a smile on his face. Glancing back towards my friends, I see my Mom and Dad sway across the floor to the *Isbister Waltz*. My heart skipped a beat, wondering why they looked so beautiful, my Dad holding Mom, both smiling together like it would never end.

I felt happy, content but a bit of sadness crept in as faces of my old friends popped up from my memory. There was Mark, Allan, Danny, Eddy, Ricky and Pug....'*wonder what they're doing right now?*' I contemplated. "Definitely not out at this hour!" I whispered to no one. I was beginning to like it here but still, I wondered what I would be doing if I were back home in Shelby, which I still called home. That emotional shadow swept over me again. Leaving the hall, I was tired, but it wasn't so much physical as it was mental. We should be going home.

The violin played an encore, I recognized it as The Ranger's Waltz and heard ole Syd say, "Good night folks, drive carefully and God bless us till we meet again! Good bye to Smiling Joey and his Many Dots!"

I didn't think Smiling Johnny would be back.

Chapter 9

Pug and I decided to go to the football game that Friday night. Dillon's brothers were playing and were known as all-stars, all-American. Besides, this would be our first game and maybe, just maybe, the older girls, 'our girls' would be there cheering. Two of our crushes, Linda and Mary Jane, were freshman and now junior cheerleaders. This was a pre-school exhibition readying the team for the regular fall season. Arriving after a good 2 miles on our bikes, we met Dillon and the 3 of us meandered about, watching the crowd. The stands seemed too far away so we planted ourselves close to the team opposite and across from the stands, beside the cheerleaders. This was off-limits, but nobody was paying attention to us. The game got underway with a whistle, the fans coming to life under the field lights. The game began; back and forth, grunting, grinding, swearing while we toddled cautiously through the players off field, on the sidelines. It was intimidating, strolling apprehensively through this labyrinth of giants, yet comforting at being accepted into this fellowship, tolerated was probably a better word. The excitement of being in their company soon wore off, our attention diverted to the scantily clad cheerleaders on the same sidelines. The game became boring; the crowd noise stimulating us a few minutes ago was now a faint din as the girls enthralled us with high kicks and non-stop bouncing. We commented, admiring the athleticism of such moves, the high fashion of their outfits and the moral fortitude they brought to the team. Completely immersed in their performance, we forgot that the action around and apparently barrelling down on us was a juggernaut of flesh and bones.

Suddenly, the air became electric with screams, our vision distorted with flashes and darkness. For a split second, I saw Pug flying, *"Hey, that's cool,"* I thought with streaks of colors surrounding me, and then darkness and a crushing feeling. I felt entombed, couldn't move anything; a blackness engulfed me. Panicking, I tried to scream but nothing came out. I had never been so scared before - it was a feeling of helplessness and absolute paralysis I could not have imagined. I would never forget this feeling and never would I wish it on anyone else. I began to hear voices, feeling movement around me, but the paralysis stayed. Soon I could see the stars, the stadium lights above and a whole bunch of helmets.

"Are you okay?" someone asks. I nodded vigorously my wide –eyed expression betraying my terror. I clamoured to my feet, wanting, needing to get away. But, glancing to my left, there was Pug lying motionless. Players and coaches rushed to him, a first-aid female attendant frantically feeling his neck and head. He didn't respond, his eyes remaining closed, still, frozen, as my panic returned. The ambulance, siren blaring, drove up beside us and stopped with the mechanical scream fading to nothing. Two male attendants lifted him onto the stretcher while the woman held his neck. *This was serious,* I thought. This bed-on-wheels always reminded me of death. They pushed him into the ambulance back door and without thinking I started to climb in.

One of the attendants roughly pushes me aside and I yell, "I gotta go with him, he's my friend!"

Disregarding my plea, they close the door when one of Dillon's brothers shouts, "He got hit too! You better take him for a check-up."

87

Staring at Dillon's brother, it struck me, *"where was Dillon?"* Off to the side, Dillon stood with his other brother, fine and not a scratch on him. I guess he had been paying attention to the game and got out of the way sensibly. They let me in, seating me in the corner as they worked on Pug. My apprehension rose as a premonition set in. Arriving at the hospital, they ran him to a separate room; a nurse wheeled me to another for examination. I waited while they attended Pug; shortly thereafter, a doctor came to me inspecting my eyes, assessing my reactions to certain prods and poking. I asked for Pug, but the doc went on, not saying anything. Finally, putting down his stethoscope, he asks what happened, listening carefully to my words as he made me follow his finger.

The Doc sits back, "Okay, I think you're fine, nothing I can see."
I knew this already asking, "What about my friend Pug?" I was scared for the answer. "Pug?" Is that what you call him?"
"Yeah, we've always called him that." I didn't elaborate, not wanting to waste time in a long spiel on why we gave him that nickname.
"Well I think Pug is going to be alright. He got knocked unconscious and has a bump on his head, but yes, he's going to be okay."
"Can I see him?" I begged.

"Sure but make it short. His parents are coming in to pick him up....and he's got to stay home for a day. No running, no excitement!" the doc hollers as I run off. I get to the door fast, sliding my feet on the glistening sterile floor as I come to a stop. There's Pug, small in this big white bed and the room smelling of antiseptic all over the place.

"Geez man, you scared the shit out of us." I instructed him. He smiled in that pug face upturning his nose and wrinkling his face when words were at a loss. "God you shouda seen it, everybody was like "WHOA!" when you were dead there on the ground. The whole town knows you're here. You'll probably be on TV, maybe even Ed Sullivan!" I added.

"No way!" he exclaims' "Cool, man."

"You flew like 100 feet in the air, man. Like a bird!" I animated his flight. The elevation would get higher and higher as the tale was retold. "Then you came down on your head. Splat!" I hadn't seen the actual landing but this must've happened, I assured myself.

"Cool." he says, taking my words to heart.

"And then you were like, dead, there on the ground! All these guys come over; the players, the coaches, the ambulance...even the cheerleaders, man! Craayzeee, man! You shoulda seen it, man!"

"Craaayzeee....Neat-o." Pug props himself up with his elbows. Mentioning the cheerleaders had sparked his attention.

"Then loading you into the ambulance?" I inform him, looking to him, "Linda came and put her hand on your head." Linda was his favourite of our crushes.

"Really?" he asks in astonishment. I was lying outright here but I thought this would really make him happy, make him feel good. It does. "Wow," he whispers in contentment.

"Then they brought you here." I ended with a toss up of my arms.

His parents came shortly after with a million questions and concerns. Receiving the full diagnosis, they were reassured of Pug's good health and luck, and Pug was sent home with a prescription in case of possible headaches. Momentarily, like Andy Warhol quoted, we were famous for 15 minutes!

I walked back to the field to retrieve our bikes and after two hours, I was back with Pug's bike. His home was a two level white house with dark green trim and the roof broken with dormers and green shutters on the windows. It was on a heavily treed crescent, quiet and serene. Think of the "Ozzie and Harriet Show". Pug's bedroom was on the main floor with his window on an outside wall so sometimes we talked in secret if he was grounded or sick. I ushered his bike to the backyard beside his window and tapped ever so lightly. Immediately pulling aside his curtain, lifting his window he pokes out his head.

"Brought your bike." I show him.
"Great, Thanks." he rests his head on his arms on the windowsill. "Crazy day, huh?"
"Superrr!" I start out then cover my mouth quickly. One thing we did have in common was strict parents. The similarity ended there with location of our respective homes, the space or lack thereof, and the amenities included. You might say I was from the other side of the tracks and poor but didn't know it – neither did Pug. There was an actual railway that separated our neighbourhoods. We were just too young to know or maybe too innocent yet to be corrupted by society's classes.
"Super-duper day" I whisper. We giggle, talking about the events of that day wondering what tomorrow would bring. Soon we weren't saying anything, just sitting, wondering and being happy. Friends don't have to say

90

anything to communicate; sharing a common experience silently can say everything. After a few minutes, I stand up to the window, my chin resting on the windowsill, looking at Pug eye-to-eye not 6 inches away. "Well, gotta go."

""Okay, see you Daddy-O" he slurs too lazy to lift his head off his arms.

"After a while, Crocodile." I add slipping into the dark.

"See you later Alligator," he adds but I'm gone already.

I got home later, lazily biking the long way down Main Street, taking my time. I came to our driveway noticing my Mom and Dad sitting out on the porch stairs. They were silhouetted at the door by the orange glow of the light bulbs. They looked at me, saying nothing as I came to a stop in front of them. "*Am I that late?*" I asked myself, "*Are they mad at me or something?*" One foot on the ground, the other on my bike pedal I ask, "Something wrong? What's up, Mom?"

"Sit down Bran." she quietly said. She didn't act like this usually. She was solemn, frozen in posture, no gestures with her voice cold, calculated. "Got something to tell you." I didn't like it. I only heard this tone when someone had died. Then, without telling me she asks, "How do you like our old home? Sandy Lake? "

"It's nice…but this is home," I corrected her. Confused, I refused to see the context here, of where this was going.

"Well Bran, Sandy Lake really is our home. We came here to work, to try and make a better life." The fear started to well up in me. My stomach was churning, my heart in my ears. She paused for this statement to sink in. "Things haven't been too good."

91

"Nooo, everything's good Mom. Right Dad?" I look to my Father imploring his aid. He stares at the ground, at his shadow cast by the kitchen lights behind.

"That's not true Bran." Shifting his weight, still staring, he says sadly, "Right now I don't have a job, Mom's paying for all the bills."

"You'll get a job Dad!" my voice peaks.

"Maybe, Bran…. but I always get laid off. I'm tired of never knowing, I'm always scared of losing what job I have." I never knew my Dad to be scared of anything.

"I'll get a job!" I blurted out.

"Bran, be serious." he said sternly, "You have to go to school, you have to finish so you're not like us – always broke and always looking for work."

"We have to move Bran, we can't afford to live here," she said those terrible words I had been dreading. That sentence, those words, breaking up my world. "Look around you Bran, look at this shack. Look at our car!" noticing my shoes in the light she points to them, "Look at your shoes. The soles are coming off!" They were, the soles had been coming apart with gaping holes along the side. I look up and for the first time I realize the condition of our small house, the color-faded car, no grass and the dirty streets around us. Another insight hit me. This is why my friends' parents never came here to visit. All of a sudden, I felt dirty, betrayed and so alone.

"Dad's got an offer from Indian Affairs to start something back home."

"This is home!" I yell cutting her off.

"BRAN!" my Dad shouts and I knew to shut up.

"I'm not going, I'm not going," my voice broke as I started to cry. I seldom cried. I spun my bike around,

92

ashamed of my crying, mad at my parents and sped down the street. I rambled through the streets, avenues till I got tired then sat on some isolated sidewalk, crying my eyes out. I must have been there for two hours completely unaware of anybody or anything when I heard a loud car puttering and then pull up beside me. I didn't care; I just sat there, my head on my arms, my arms crossed on my knees. I had taken off my v-necked t-shirt to cry into and wipe away the tears. I felt a rough hand heavy on my bare shoulders while someone big sat down beside me on the sidewalk edge. Nothing was said for the longest time as that car stammered, coughing as it waited.

Moving his hand to the other shoulder to embrace me, my Dad whispers soothingly, "It'll be alright Bran. You'll see. You'll make other friends." My Dad wasn't one to show his emotions, his affection, so this little act started me crying again. This time though, I hugged him. I was mad, I was sad, I didn't know how to feel because I loved this man but he was tearing apart that world I built and loved.

I didn't see Pug or anyone the next day, Saturday. I was too depressed to see or talk to anyone and Pug did call numerous times but I had told my Mom I didn't want to speak with anybody. When the phone rang, I took off out of the house. I guess they had delayed telling me from concern of my reaction thinking it better to wait till the last day. They began packing that Saturday. We were leaving Monday.

Finally on Sunday evening I biked over slowly, crawling to Pug's house. I took in everything around me, seeing for the first time the big beautiful elms, aspens and neat rows of Caragana hedges protecting each household. The smell of pavement, asphalt encircled me, reminding me of the fair coming that I would miss....and school. Coasting along, I absorbed my surroundings; noises of traffic, clanging of the railway cars, far-off voices all filled my ears as music. Yesterday I wasn't mindful of such sweet sounds that made my world. I met a couple friends along the way but with a cordial wave of the hand, I went on, not stopping or wanting to talk. Entering his driveway, I parked my bike beside the hedges out of sight. I wasn't going to talk to anyone else if Pug wasn't home. I snuck back behind the attached garage crouching to his window. I tapped the closed window, immediately sitting down on the dirt waiting for him to open the window. I wasn't ready to see him face-to-face yet. Nobody answered while I fidgeted, restless and apprehensive for him to open the window. I calmed down, my ears picked up familiar music coming from his bedroom. I knew he must have been lying down with the record player on beside his bed. I remember Pug playing this LP record before which had been a Christmas gift 3 years ago. It was a collection of slow songs, tunes, lullabies his Mother had given him so he could fall asleep. He still listened to these even as he got older; no one knew this except me. He loved a couple songs - always playing and replaying them, specifically one tune he always hummed that I recognized called, "All The Pretty Little Horses". I sat, listened with tears welling up, trickling down my cheeks. I didn't want this; this moment is what I had been bracing myself for, rehearsing all of last night. The song ended finally. My eyes red, my throat sore from holding back outright blubbering, I jumped as a voice overhead yelled, "Branson! What you doing down there?" He called me Branson the odd time.

"Shhhh!" I whispered loudly opposite to him. Aware of my running eyes and nose I sat there biding my time while I composed myself. Choking back the lump in my throat I lowered my voice, "Someone might hear."

"So? It's early…. What's wrong with your voice?" he asks pausing briefly looking down on my head.

Choking back again, I think of reasons, but nothing comes out.

"I phoned you three times yesterday. Why didn't you answer? Were you sick?"

Sick? That was a good idea, "Yeah, sick," I repeat "Think I got a cold or something." I was starting to get a hold of myself now. I stood up, my profile to him, asking, "So what you been doing today?"

"Nothing," he says, adding, "I've been waiting for you. Today and yesterday!"

"Sorry, Pug." He angled himself, studying me and I knew he knew something else was afoot. So after some small talk that dwindled to nothing, we both stared at empty space sharing the awkwardness of our solitude.

Breaking the silence he asks, "Are you mad at me or something?"

"NO! No, no." I adamantly declare, scared that he would think so. Previously unsure if I should tell him the truth or just leave, I knew from what I felt right then, that I had to tell him. It wouldn't be right to leave without a forewarning, to leave without a good bye. In my innocent reasoning, I had almost concluded our friendship with not even a word. I couldn't imagine me doing that, what was I thinking. "You'll always be my friend, no way would I be mad at you." I hesitated, the lump was crawling up my throat again as I swallowed. "We're moving." a long silence followed.

"What?" he asked.

"We're moving."

"You mean to another house…in town!" he states, not asking, while he brings his feet up and kneels on his bed. "No….away from here…to Canada." the words crawled out in patches. Total silence now as he searched my face for a joke. "No joke." I put in, seeing his disbelief.

For the longest time we stared at each other contemplating what this meant to us.

"You mean we're not going to see each other ever again?" Pug is dazed by the question he asks. Repeating the question he answers himself, "You mean… we're not going to see each other again." I just nodded. He hops off the bed and through the window, now standing beside me. We both sit down below the window, contemplating the reality of that statement. I don't know how long we sat there without a word. Arriving at the same thought, we stood up simultaneously without talking, then walked to the street in front of his house. We ambled, shuffling our feet to the corner and sitting down cross-legged on the curb. Killing time, we picked up whatever was around us tossing small pebbles onto the road, watching as they bounced along. The silence said it all, we didn't need words to know what we were feeling.

Out of the solitude, out of the blue Pug pipes up, "Did you know Jerry Lewis married his first cousin?"

"Nooo," I said, genuinely shocked, "Jerry Lewis the funny guy?"

"Nooo, no, no," Pug corrects me, "The Balls guy?" I shake my head. He grabs his groin, "The Balls Of Fire guy?" Then he bellows out, "Jerry Lee Lewis!" laughing at how he got me. I put him in a headlock, laughing with

96

him. The wall of silence gone, we began talking like nothing was amiss.

"No kidding? Jerry Lee Lewis married his cousin? That bums me out." I ask.
"And, dig this, she was only 13. Only 13!" Pug hollers.
"Crazy - sicko!" I exclaim sharing his disgust. "That's like marrying Mary Jane or Heather! That's about their age, ain't it?" I add in awe. We both stop a few seconds to visualize this.
"Cool!" we both say together laughing at our joke, poking pretend punches at each other. We joked for the next hour, the jokes getting less and less funny as we strived to keep a happy face. The atmosphere got sombre and we were back to a hush with a few worked jibes thrown in here and there. Impulsively, our talk turned to the more dark side we feared mentioning. Subsequently, in that mood, the deaths of our idols; Eddie Cochran, Jimmy Valens, James Dean came up in conversation as we muddled through our emotions, yet staying away from an actual statement.

"Hey, remember Eddie and that song he sung?" Pug was snapping his fingers trying to recall.
"Summertime Blues," I instantly say pointing my finger at Pug.
"Yeah, yeah. God I loved that song." He starts to tap the beat waiting for the lyrics to come.
Then he starts to sing as I beat the sidewalk curb in time...
Every time I call my honey, and tryda getta date..." Pug looks to me for my intro as we had practised; he continues singing playing an air guitar,
My Dad says...

97

Right on cue I jump in with a deep voice,
No way son, you gotta woka late

We knew that whole tune. We had tried others but that one we had mastered. Our friends often asked or 'requested' this song, which we obliged with staged humility.

Then Pug says, "You know he died last year? Got killed in a car crash." The solitude again as we mired ourselves in muck not knowing how to get out. What we didn't want to acknowledge, my departure, kept creeping into the conversation, so running thin on other topics we just sat there throwing stones again. Soon after, his Mom, having lost Pug momentarily, finds us at the end of the street.

Being an adult, she could read us like a book, "What's going on guys? She knelt beside us, "Something is wronnnng..." she poked Pug with her elbow.

"Nothing, Mom...nothing." he replied in a tone nobody could confuse.

"Alright," she says, "Something's wrong so c'mon, let's hear it."

"I'm moving," I said dejectedly, "to Canada."

There is a brief pause while she analyzed the both of us. "Okaaaay, so what's so wrong with that?" I look at her with venom in my eyes. "Noooo, what I mean to say is, think of it as an adventure. Everybody moves sooner or later." I wasn't listening. "Besides, you can write to each other, maybe even visit each other during the holidays." This perked us both up. Sensing she had our attention, she goes on, "I would be excited. I'd be making new friends, seeing new places, exploring, maybe even discovering strange and wonderful things."

She made us feel better, pretty soon we were all walking back to his house. Maybe it won't be so bad after all. We can visit whenever we feel like it, write letters everyday till we visit, maybe find or make things I can bring back. Yeah…like an explorer coming home bringing presents and gold. With that fantasy embedded, I got on my bike saying 'Good Night' to Pug who had the same pleasant thoughts.

I reminded him I would be back early in the morning because my Dad wanted to be on the highway by 9 am. I got home, surprised at what remained of our house. There was nothing except two mattresses along with the pillows and blankets. Everything, all the furniture, was loaded onto the truck that we had borrowed, along with clothes, shoes, small breakables stashed into our new 1960 'winged' Chevy. Wow, my Dad waited till that Saturday to trade in the old 1947 Ford wanting to keep it as a surprise. He arranged the sale last week but didn't have enough money for the plates till Sunday so they held it for him. We would be travelling in a new car! Well it wasn't quite new being two years old but to me it was new and smelt like it. I felt a lot better after Dianne's (Pug's Mom) talk. Her positive remarks ringing in my ears, I was eager for my journey into the unknown.

That morning, fresh, excited I hurried to the bathroom for the necessary business, washed up and combed my hair making sure it was perfectly flat. I had a dry military flat-top now, replacing the antique greasy duck-tail, things were changing. Soon this would change to a crew cut where the top remained flat but the sides stayed long. It was 7 in the morning and I dashed out without any breakfast; there was nothing but cereal anyway, which I hated.

"Be back by nine!" my Mom shouted after me.

"Yeah, yeah." I shouted back, too much in a hurry to argue the time given. Recalling the night before, my senses tuned in again to the surroundings. Mindful of leaving all this, it didn't take long as the damp pavement, aspens, and manicured hedges dulled my enthusiasm. By the time I neared Pug's, I was in a sour and sad mood. I knocked on the door then turned around and sat on the steps, waiting for the answer. He opened the door without a greeting, planting himself next to me. I could detect the sombreness that seemed to radiate around us.

"Well, guess you're going now, huh?" Pug says.

"Yeah...soon..." I droned like one of those ridiculous sci-fi robots of the movies.

"But you'll come and visit, right?"

"Oh yeah, yeah....and write," adding as an afterthought, "lots of writing."

The air was tense, neither of us wanting to break down into blubbering fools which would have surely occurred if we hadn't kept our 'manliness'. We took a walk, sauntering to the same spot on the corner doing the same thing; meaninglessly throwing small rocks. Pug says matter-of-factly, "We're just like brothers," then asks, "huh...Bran?"

"Yup, since grade one Pug."

"Wow, that's a lonnnng time." dragging the word he looks into the distance. "That's far out..." he keeps staring, thinking. He pipes up, "We should make it official Bran!"

"What? What do you mean?"

"Since we're brothers, let's do what your People used to do. Like in the movies. You know...let's become 'Blood-Brothers'." He lifts up, tilting his body; he reaches to his

100

back pocket pulling out his Swiss-knife that had everything in it except a gun. "I'll cut my hand, then you cut yours, then we put them together and shake. Dig it?"
I'm taken aback momentarily calculating my next move. I wasn't scared of blood but getting cut terrified me. I visualized guts coming out of my cut hand. Before I can form an argument, his excitement charms my doubts so I consent.
Feebly, in a faint voice I consent, "Okaaay."

Right before my eyes Pug opens his hand slicing a small cut into his index finger tip. Blood oozes out, a few bubbles in it. He hands me the knife, "Okay, your turn." I can't back out now so I take the knife pressing it to my finger. I try but can't do it. He mistakes my expression as pain but I was grimacing in anticipation.
"See, wasn't bad, huh?" Pug says grabbing my hand. I nod in agreement clenching my fist in pretence. He pulls it to his, not looking for the cut and presses his palm to mine. We look at each other sharing an intimate moment then he moves his hand to mine in a handshake.

"We are blood-brothers now, forever." he holds my hand tight, a small drop of blood spattering onto the cement. He doesn't know I haven't cut myself and the blood dripping is his alone, not mine. He relaxes his grip then runs to his house. I wondered if he was going to come back when the door flew open. He comes running back, gauze in hand which he promptly wraps around my hand. "There," he says as the cotton soaks up the blood, "Nobody can ever break our bond." Pug smiles, pleased with his action but I cringe. I couldn't tell him the truth. His heart was so into this selfless act I didn't want to hurt his feelings or let him know I was a coward for pretending to do it. I had been silent through this whole 'brother' ritual.

Continuing my charade, I made small talk, then ran out of things to say as did Pug while we awkwardly wasted that precious time. Separation, leaving forever, was what we were thinking but not talking about. I made the first move, standing, walking to my bike. He followed dragging his feet, trying to slow the inevitable.

"Why don't you walk with me Pug? I ask him, "As far as the tracks anyway, okay?" He nods his head not saying anything now. "Bring your bike." I tell him.

"No, too much trouble," he whines with that cute doggy-look of his, "I wanna walk anyway." So we rambled onwards walking and talking not saying anything important. Seemingly in no time at all, we were at the railway tracks, even though it was probably the slowest journey we had ever walked.

Stopping, I turned to him, "Guess this is it, huh?"

"Yup, gonna miss you Branson." his voice starts to break. Looking to his eyes I can see tears welling on his lower eyelid but not quite big enough for tears to drop. Pug is biting his lips. My eyes well up as I see this then I bite down too to stop my lower lip from trembling. Suddenly the country song my Dad listened to, '*Stop Them Trembling Lips*,' came to mind and I began to laugh thinking of it. Pug starts to laugh at me, the tears now coming down our cheeks. We quickly composed ourselves, wiped off our wet cheeks with our short sleeves and snorted up the snot dribbling from our noses.

"Gotta write… right away, soon as you get there Branson!" he scolds me.

"I will, I will….for sure. Soon as I get there." I extend my bandaged hand. He grasps it, shaking with all his might as his blood smears both of our hands. "Gotta go Pug!" I pleaded as I began to choke up again. He lets go, raising his bloody hand in a timid wave, with a forced smile. I wave back; smile, in the same gesture turning away.

Hopping onto my bike I murmur, "See you later, alligator."

He responds with a mutter, "After awhile, crocodile."

On my bike pedaling away I shout, "See you soon, Baboon!" Looking over my shoulder I see him smile.

Pug shouts back to retaliate, "In your dream, Gene!"

I start to pedal faster across the tracks; he's still standing with that stupid little wave so I slow down, not wanting to go. Circling, I wave back. He puts his hands in his pockets, turns slowly, walking with his head down.

I shout again, "You're the best friend! Ever!"

He halts for an instant, then taking his hands out of his pockets he runs as fast as he could. I stop, watching as he got smaller and smaller, running down the street. I don't hold back the tears while I pedal furiously away from this moment.

Chapter 10

Ten years had passed since my first day on duty; I was now a veteran - a 'lifer,' living the curse other veterans had warned about. The atmosphere still gave me a 'fix' - the action, the unexpected, fuelled me like a junkie. Having adrenalin rushing through your body and mind was a cheap high. The comradeship was there, sharing the "sticks-n-stones" and bullshit the bureaucracy and inmates slung at us. Doing 'life' with the inmates, you began to think and identify with them more easily than with the armchair wardens and Napoleon wannabees in Ottawa. Abnormal incidents and events became normal, almost dry and used in their repetition so we maintained the humour that bound us in satirical sometime morbid drama we constructed for our amusement. In addition to the normal abnormalities of FPC we had each other to 'screw' around and none were more vulnerable than the rookies. Always, as custom dictated, there was some sort of initiation for the rookies who came in fresh as a baby's bottom from college with high expectations and an empathetic philosophy.

I had received mine 10 years ago. Through a forged memorandum, on a graveyard shift, I was instructed officially to broadcast the weather to all stations through our control center. The control center had communication and video with all units and stations inside and outside. I was suspicious, seeing that "the weather" had been occurring all day and evening before we even got there. Nobody I knew had broadcast the weather during the day shifts.

"Why would you want to know what the weather was like while working the midnight shift? For those working outside, they

already know how the weather was." I mused, scrutinizing the signed memorandum given to me by the Keeper who was Warden on midnights. I figured this was just another flaky idea administration had come up with or maybe it was someone's 'brainchild' from Ottawa. *'This is stupid,'* I thought but I did what I was told, broadcasting the weather twice nightly from control – at 2am and 5am, if we were not busy. Holding the mike, I would go through the whole 'bit'; clear, rain, barometric pressure, pollen and what time the sun rose. No forecast, nothing of what the weather was going to be in the next day or days; just for the present early morning. I did this for a week, growing more and more suspicious, as I thought of the scenario and of fellow guards commenting on the great broadcast, saying that I was a 'natural.' Apparently, everyone "tuned in" at these times to listen. The shift directive, the memorandum was an order, so I felt compelled to do so, although my reasoning dictated otherwise. I can imagine them now, all gathering around the 2-ways for that early morning broadcast – something out of the 50's and "Howdy-Doodey". I finally resolved to end my brief stint as the "Weather Man" by saying farewell on the last night of our 7-day shift.

I began with the usual greeting "Gooooood Morning FPC !" then proceeded to do a 'news special' regarding my broadcast. I reported that, "Just got this after the magic hour. Ottawa has terminated this program because all the inmates are sleeping or should be sleeping. And if the staff need to know what the weather is like, then just look outside or stick your head out the window." I deliberated on my planned newsflash beforehand, expecting a reprimand from Admin but nothing occurred, so I knew this had all been a scam and I was Joe Schmo. I sought to get even with the perpetrators and I would. Revenge would come premeditated or at impromptu times when opportunity rose its ugly little head.

I recollect one specific opportunity when my colleague 'Stokes', one of the original initiators or instigators, asked me, "Bran? What Indian name would be great for a dog, a Husky dog?"

Having Native ancestry, everyone concluded I could speak the language - Plains Cree. I did know some but my vocabulary consisted mainly of swear words learned from my teen years in school where it was 'cool' to swear undetected by the teachers. I contemplated the opportunity rising itself as that humbling initiation event came back to mind.

"Hmmm," I racked my brain, thinking to myself. "There's *tah-kiy* meaning penis, *Chuk-sees* meaning 'little prick'.

But there was one word real dirty in my youth, so dirty we seldom used it. The word was shortened with enunciation changed or 'slurred' for quickness in speech and meaning. The word was "Mush-a-wahn" meaning intercourse but a dirty description of the act; more like fucking as opposed to making Love.

At last I said, "I got it! *Tay-mus-a-wahn*! But you can use "Mushawahn" for short."

"Yeah? Sounds great....and it's got that 'mush' in there which sounds good for Huskies."

I nod, thinking of more bullshit to give him; this was my day. "Yep, that part comes from the Eskimos, eh?"

"Really? What does it mean?"

"Great Leader-Of-The-Pack." I hold my head high stoically with my arm across my chest.

"Wow! That's perfect. The dog's a puller....part Husky and Labrador, eh?" Stokes is proud of himself, smiling, "And that "MUSH"... fits right in."

I had totally forgotten about this dog-naming, when one day Stokes marches to my post, the station where I was working at, slaps his hand down onto my table. "What the fuck did you tell me, you son-of-a-bitch?"

"What? What do you mean Stokes?" And then I remembered and had an idea what was coming, but I played innocent, raising my eyebrows and hands.

"You know! You know what I mean, you bastard!

"Whaaat?" feigning innocence I ask with a smirk.

"That name you gave my girlfriend's dog!

"Your girlfriend! Your girlfriend's dog?" the plot thickens. "I gave you a name for YOUR dog, not somebody else's'!"

Ignoring, he rants on, "Do you know what happened? She takes the dog to the store."

"So?"

"So!" he's buggy-eyed now, "So he runs away... she's calling for him."

A scene starts to envelop my imagination, "Sooo? What happened? Nobody knows what the name means."

"Yeah, well it just so happens there's a bunch of Indians there in the parking lot! They know! She's yelling 'Mushawahn...Tay-mus-a-wahn'!"

Oh God, this couldn't get any better but I begin to fear for my health. I couldn't help but smile.

"Oh yeah, this is funny. Smile you prick!" he glares at me "They started to laugh too."

I couldn't hold it any longer, breaking into a muffled laugh, my hand covering my mouth, "What did they do?"

"Well lucky they didn't oblige her!"

I bellow a laugh then attempt some control before he does hit me. "Okay, okay. What did they say...or do?"

"One of them comes over and thank god he's civilized enough to tell her what that means. Then she turns to me and hits me, punched me right in the gut...hard!"

I scream, laughing hysterically not caring if he does hit me.

"Go ahead, laugh you son-of-a-bitch. I'm gonna get you for this," he warns as he storms out, "better watch your back."

By week's end he was telling the story as entertainment, especially at our alcohol fuelled 'debriefing'. After a few beers, he would start to embellish, imitating the expressions of the bystanders...and hers when she realized what she had been saying in the parking lot. God we laughed at that. None would ever ask me for an "Indian" name again.

Charlie and Will were being their usual selves, assaulting inmates or just flipping out to get some quiet time in the hole. I would sit and listen to endless cell-to-cell conversations but wondered how they would actually act if those walls were not there. Will was Native, spiritual and in the sex offender unit but his assault victims were mostly pedophiles, those who had sexually assaulted kids. There was a code even within sex offenders. Charlie was Polish, educated, well read, hated any religion and had a particular hatred for Pedophiles. They seldom were in the same room together. Sitting there conversing within their domain was Will in his reserve, Charlie in his preserve, each bound by their culture, beliefs, values and morals, denouncing authority. They had two things in common which was rebellion to the powers-that-be, and mutual respect for the other's space. Two lives, two cultures existing side by side with their borders up. Maybe that's why they got along. I looked at my life wondering what, who was I. These cells, the reserve both with the institutions around that bound them, felt comforting, secure in familiarity yet demeaning. There were many here who didn't want to leave. Meagre in the condiments of life it did have shelter; security, which was good enough for many who called this home. Guard and inmate alike find it hard to leave after a 'stint' of 10 years. Myself? I was a loner, maybe a drifter just stopping by for a visit – *"here for a good time, not a long time…"*

There weren't as many PPA alarms as there used to be back in the early days. But every week some oddball was admitted from some other penitentiary that couldn't handle them or maybe didn't want to. Not all were killers, violent schizoids, or pedophiles. We received all kinds, from those requiring an assessment from courts to those suffering from compulsive/obsessive disorder to manipulators to 'escape artists'. Nobody had ever escaped from the FPC; Charlie and Will knew this from experience. Charlie made it to between the barbed fences then got 'zapped', Will tried leaving with the visitors but specialized detectors around the perimeter and buildings picked him up as soon as he hit the 'boundary'. Inmates, upon being admitted into their respective unit, were supposedly given microchips embedded into their vitamins never knowing. Think of the barcodes on store items only these were so small the eye can't see them. We used to tell them that if they even made it outside the primary fence they would be micro waved, which wasn't far from the truth. This was a super-max although not too many stayed, being Forensic meant treatment or analysis for most, not permanent housing. Since any inmate from a burglar to a serial killer could be admitted

109

because of mental disorder, the prison had to have the security to deal with the worst. Charlie and Will both 'lifers' would in all probability be moving into a 'terminal' institution that housed 'dead men', those imprisoned permanently till they die. Both had gone for a visit to one particular dead 'joint' but sent back for more treatment. Maybe they were thought to be salvageable.

I asked both about what they thought of their future. Each didn't care, brushing it off as an inconvenience. They lived day-to-day without a future, never planning for the next year or for family. This, I was taught, made an inmate dangerous; what's to lose – your future? If you're doing two life-terms what is another murder going to get you? What are they going to give you… another life-term?

"I can't even think of that. What future?" Charlie once said. "It's like asking me what color is red if I was blind from birth. This is all I know, I've been here since 18. Before that I was in 23 hour lock-up in Juvenile till I became an adult then came here."

I asked about what he had done and how old he was then.

"I was 13 going to be in grade 9 that September. I was starting to see girls in a different way. You know what I mean Boss? Mom though, on Grandpa's orders, wasn't about to let me run wild with those lascivious women even if she had to lock me up. This, coming from a mother who played with her son in sexual games, played with his 'winky'."

Charlie got agitated fast, dramatising the words. I told him to take it slow, not to let the anger get the best of him.

"I got tired of her locking me up for her enjoyment. It never used to be like that you know. Never. I was happy with Gramps in those early grades but later I was sent back to my Mother for further education, which my Grandfather dictated. It was not until I began changing physically, when she changed too. She kept bathing me, bathing with me," Charlie grimaces, "and after I'm 10, she's still bathing with me. She used to tease my cock with her feet till I got a hard-on. You know what it feels like to get turned on by your Mom?" He stared to a dark corner. " I became 11 and no longer a virgin. By the time I was 12, I was a man experienced in all ways of the flesh but too young to fucking even go outside on my own! So, I left for awhile, ran away till Gramps died." He takes a breather thinking. "My Dad, who wasn't really my Dad – a stepfather, wasn't any better, never fucked me but he used to put his finger up my ass! When he came home drunk he'd ask me to come over and sit, if he wasn't beating me. He'd pull me up onto his lap then the fucker would do his thing. God I hated that! Give me a licking. Give me a beating any day before that!" He looked to me then, hollering, "FUCK! Fuck, I wanna kill someone… Right now!"

"Cool it Charlie, take it easy…" I knew he was on the edge. If he had been out of his cell he probably would have killed me. Usually we could talk him down but what was coming out was unprecedented. He had never voiced his pain like he was at that moment. He had told his story before but in monotone with no emotion so there were questions as to its credence. What I had just heard came from the heart, from the soul. A few minutes passed by while he paced restlessly.
"This is good Charlie…. good that you talk about it."
"Oh, you're a fucking psychologist now? Suck my cock!"

111

A couple more minutes his pacing slows. "This went on till I got too big. I grew up fast; I did exercises since I couldn't go anywhere…like I do now in my cell. By the time I was 13, I was close to 6 feet…with muscles. One day after a bath by mother dear, she went into the bedroom waiting for her 'Little Johnny'. I had had enough. What my Mother was doing was wrong and I knew what I was about to do was wrong too but it didn't matter. I go to the bed, looked at her naked body, the body that had given birth to me and all I could see was a damned bitch, a fucking whore! I drove my fist into her face, breaking her nose. **Crack**! She lies there holding her face, whimpering. I took the sheet, wrapped it around her neck and choked her till she wasn't kicking anymore."

I waited. "And your Father, your step dad?" I ask.
He smiled pleasantly.
"I put Mom down on the floor, on the carpet and waited for Dad to come home. I was hoping he was drunk. It would be fitting that he was drunk, huh?" A pause, "So Dad comes home and guess what? He's drunk! Fantastic! He plops himself on that favoured big-armed armchair sitting…waiting for a drink. I know the routine but instead of a glass I bring the baseball bat. He yells out my name "Lewis!" and I answer him, "What.". He looks back at me, I'm standing there, nothing on and he gets this weird look on his face. He turns his head to get up and I slam the bat into his skull. Whack! He's down and out!" Charlie does an umpire's gesture for being 'out', slaps his hands to mimic the action.
"I whack him again and again….till some grey stuff is sticking to my bat. So I'm finished then drag him to the bedroom…the same bedroom where Mom is in. I take off his clothes and lay him beside Mom. I figure they

should be together. I sat there for a while then this great idea, an old memory, comes to me. I run to the garage, get a razor, you know, those utility knives? I skinned both of them, hair and skin. I put their skins, or rather *their selves*, on hangers and hung them in the closet. It wasn't perfect you know, but you could tell where the pants were and the where the shirt should be. Gramps had taught me." He smiles at me, I smile back not knowing if I should believe all of this. "You don't believe me, do you?" he asks. "Go, check the files, there should be some photos in my file." I told him I would.

"You ever kill anyone Boss?" I told him no. "Well...you will." he says matter-of-factly.

"I don't think so Charlie."

"Oh yes you will, mark my words Sam." I hated when he called me that because only my closest friends called me Sam. "And you'll do it in cold blood, because you had to."

"Like hell I will." this got me pissed off and I showed it. He began to giggle as I turned walking away. I had heard enough.

"Hey Boss, something else...'bout my parents." I stopped. "Did you know we used to have a big dog? A big Dane?"

"Yeah, so? What happened to it?"

"I skinned that fucker too."

"Why?"

"He used to fuck my Mom."

This sounded familiar, then a flash came to me. He mentioned bestiality in his previous rant on the Doctor and the supposed masterpiece of Dada Art.

"Yeeeaah, you remember the Minotaur," he whispers, knowing what I was thinking. "Good, good...you were listening, maybe that's what I am – a Minotaur. Not with

113

a bull's head but a monster bred in Hell between my Mother and a bull; a perversion, an abomination…"

I cut him off, "That's bullshit Charlie and what you're telling me is bullshit. Blame somebody else for what you are. Right? You're just trying to convince yourself and the head-shrinkers here that you're not that bad and that you deserve a chance to get outside."

"Hey boss, did you ever see me being mean just to be mean? I don't bother anybody, I don't look for trouble, I don't scam the nurses…"

"Charlie, why are you in here, in the hole? Soon as you get bored with unit activities or someone pisses you off or you think some rule sucks, so you do something to get in here. You never face the problems, you never face yourself. Jesus Christ Charlie you not only killed your parents but you skinned them! You just finished telling me that, you just confessed! Then you wrap it nicely so it looks good, so that you look good."

Surprisingly he murmurs, "Yeah, sounds pretty fishy, huh? Sounds convenient that they should be such bastards. But you know that's the face they put to the public. They were God-fearing bible thumpers helping the poor, the destitute, but nobody saw them as I saw them… no one will believe me, not even you Boss," he points to me accusingly, "I figured you better."

"Better? If I believe you, I'm better? Come on Charlie don't con a con. Sometime that's what you need, a person who questions you, someone who doesn't take all your shit. For fuck's sake man, own up to what you've done."

"Yeah, you're right. Don't believe everything I say."

"I don't."

There's a long pause, thinking I somehow reached him through his delusions, I slowly walk away then he stops me again.

114

"Wanna know something else Sam? The Doctor? He was my Grandfather, my Mother's Father...and my Father!" Charlie giggles uncontrollably slipping to the cold cement floor.

I walk off briskly, feeling like I just got conned or was party to someone's dirtiest secret that made you want a shower. I now needed the whole story, the real story. I needed to know if my instincts were correct and I was being conned for a setup or if he was actually telling the truth – which would be horrendous. It took a scant few minutes to get hooked, to be obsessed with his story that, before, I really didn't give a shit about. I wanted his full history not only for the files but also for my curiosity - how he knew me.

I didn't know it then but it would take a few years to know the whole truth and learn the full story.

Chapter 11

I graduated in 1968. I absolutely loved this era, sharing my life with friends from Sandy Lake and Canwood, growing up, meeting lovely girls. I was a kid in a candy shop, the world was our oyster and we picked the pearls – we loved to fantasize. Delusions like this and even hallucinations during this time of turmoil were quite common. There was Maureen, Lila, Judy, Therese, Gail, Rita and that dream girl I would come to marry, Claire. I met her in my last year and it was instant love. I knew this was the girl I fantasized about in my dreams, that surreal image I imagined, that face I always looked for. People really do get that feeling you read about in romance novels; that this is the one, that she is your soul mate. Gone were the daydreams of Mary Jane and Heather MicGregrrrr...still loved to roll that name off of my tongue though. When I got my license and my first car, I was a terror; don't know how I survived those years, just lucky I guess. We went *Helter-Skelter* with the Beatles, rolling with the Stones and *Running Through The Jungle* with CCR as this music blared on our 8-track stereos speeding down gravel roads like something out of *The Road Runner Show*. Amidst plumes of dust in our wake we abandoned caution, daring the Devil. He almost caught us 3 times as I crashed my cars with one particular rollover that did fish-tails for 700 feet, then flipped 13 times. At least that's what the RCMP deduced from their investigation. We all flew, four of us, out of the car into the ditches - no seatbelts used in the sixties. Nobody was hurt other then being unconscious and we partied the next night. God, what idiots we were then! And this behaviour wasn't just restricted to cars, but to girls and life in general. That age, being a teenager and that era of the Sixties, where all reason and sanity seemed

116

to be absent. A lot of hormones from growing up along with new and accessible drugs of the time, kept that era crazy. Maybe there's a connection here between insanity and growing up; you either figure it out or you go crazy trying to.

I had quite a few girlfriends in my teen years just like any other normal guy. We strutted, veritable wolves on the prowl with a brain about the same size. If you had a car, especially a muscle car, you had it made. You could be the geekiest ignoramus but if you had a GTO you were never alone, maybe not a stud but always a crowd with you. Even today the same law applies, *he who haveth car, haveth girl*. We would congregate our rumbling beasts in the tall dark pines, drinking our **Boh** and **Blue** and bragging about our conquests. Embellish is a better word because the reality was more words than action and you could tell who lied by their content. The eyes would be darting back and forth, watching to see your reaction, fidgeting as if he was on death row. The 'real deal' would be a confident guy not saying much, with eyes looking at something we couldn't see. A guy getting that lost look of contentment and pleasure in his eyes was someone to be worried about. As a friend, you might be losing him forever to a woman; think of a wolf being groomed, cultivated with its devil-may-care attitude replaced by the ignorant bliss of a Beagle with a vacant stare – domesticated!

The pines, the Pines….so many stories of friendship, love and angst. Sitting around playing the guitar, telling stories, or just making out, this was the place to be in Canwood. Canwood itself was a small town somewhat like Shelby but smaller with grid streets but it did have a main street that we cruised. It was really the only street to have any interest because on it was a bar, three cafes, grocery store, your proverbial three country hardware stores and a poolroom. There were three service stations on the beat too and a health clinic where our lone doctor plied his trade. You might say this was a farmer's town; basic needs with its nails, lumber, gas, milk, medicine and an outlet for the farmer and his wife to go to when more bored than usual. But it had pavement, stores, streetlights that had me feeling more at home, secure. If you have ever lived in a city then left it for years, you know what I mean by the smell of pavement, asphalt that clings to your memories. We, most reserve students, were transferred to the school in Canwood after my first and only year at Sandy Lake School. It was the period of assimilation where federal policies were legislated to get people off the reserve, permanently paving the road for maybe no reserves at all and no rights for the Native People. The Treaties made in the 1800's said we would get free schooling and health care, providing we give our rights to Canada and stay in little sections of land called Reserves. We never wanted these Treaties; they were forced on us while we starved as a result of all the Buffalo being 'culled' from an order of the Government. People should read the real history. The whole of Canada for small rectangles of land we couldn't step off of unless we got permission – like a prison. If you were lucky enough to have some cattle and grain, you could not sell either unless the government said you could. You had to get their permission to do so. And taxes that everybody screamed about us not paying(?)…the only time we didn't pay was when we were on the reserve - where there was nothing to buy. Off the reserve when we were allowed, we paid just like everybody else. So about this time, the 60's, all children on reserves were moved, bussed to the closest town for schooling

118

especially high school. To me this was fine, in fact, it was a pleasure to get out of that tiny wooden school where three grades were in one room. During that period it seemed we were in someone's house, the teacher's house where we took classes then had a break to go outside. Because I didn't know anybody I wasn't thrilled about going outside where I was alone. It did toughen me up though; having to stand up for myself in a world where I was the minority. Some fights, arguments, and my attitude of not giving up or slaving to the master got me through this period and by the end of that first alien school year I had friends, albeit most were relatives. My uncles, especially Hank made the difference by watching out for me while I forged my personality, my maturity as I dealt with the obstacles. They didn't fight my fights, but they didn't let anyone else get in or gang up on me physically or verbally; I could handle a punch but words can be more painful than a fist.

Doing a year of school on the reserve toughened me, prepped my entrance to high school that I looked forward to. Everybody else was petrified attending high school outside the reserve, which escaped my reasoning - I looked forward to it. Why would they be so scared? Then I remembered how I had felt when I returned to the reserve from Shelby. It's all relative, leaving the confines of your security, leaving what you call home. They would be undergoing the same confusion and doubts that I had experienced. I fit right in comfortably in Canwood, but some of my friends and relatives would not last the year giving up on school all together. Here I thrived, felt closest to home, taking a fancy to the 'white' girls walking the halls. This aspect was new, weird, intimidating to my friends and was all they talked about. I'm sure the 'white' girls talked about us too, some not in a good manner. I had girlfriends in Sandy too with a couple relationships that became serious in the later grades. All this ended when I met my future wife on one sunny autumn day. I had just turned 18 and was driving school bus while attending to make some money as I finished my senior year and to pay for my car, a green Pontiac. Not a muscle car but no shy-away either, mainly wheels I could afford after rolling my old Pontiac the year prior.

She came walking by my bus where all the kids lined the walk and boarded. I was wearing a Fedora I had recently purchased to be 'cool,' when she caught my eye walking by. She had the perfect posture carrying herself proud, golden hair glistening, a smile that melted my soul and her body I fantasized pictured in Playboy. I couldn't believe I never saw this girl before! She briefly looked at me smiling, probably not at me but at my Fedora. That was all it took; I was hooked, obsessed with her, watching her every move the next two weeks.

During school I saw how she walked, how she talked as I would get closer just to hear her voice, her laughter, closer to feel her presence. She had a regal air about her, not snobbish or overtly proud, but unmistakably there in her own glow. I found out she was in Grade10, who her friends were, her brothers and where she lived in town. By the time these 2 weeks had elapsed, if she came within touching distance I crumbled, actually feeling weak as the blood left my body rushing to my head. I absolutely would lose myself, which was unthinkable before. She was absolutely beautiful! I was a charmer, not great in looks but words were my tool, I took pride in the art of conversation, confident and being interesting. That all vanished when she came near, freezing my vocals so I could hardly breathe, my face turning red, most notably my ears. Oh how I hated it if I got embarrassed and my ears would turn red, not just pink but red like Rudolph's nose. This is what I feared as I imagined my ears turning scarlet red, sweat pouring down my nose, and a tiny little squeak coming out as I tried to introduce myself. God! It would be like Mickey Mouse on Helium! I wrestled with these thoughts mustering words to say, sentences to sway her when I got the confidence that had abandoned me. I dwelled on this daily, torturing myself. Finally I resolved that today, this Friday, would be the day. I am going to ask her out. This thought…. this resolution, came at noon hour and I suffered the whole afternoon after. Typically, routinely she came by at 3:45 so by this time I was a total wreck having sat there for 30 minutes rehearsing my lines.

I recalled that unforgettable moment. I was sitting tight hanging onto the steering wheel with white knuckles waiting for her to come around the corner. *"Here she comes…fuck!* She's got a guy with her! Oh God what do I do? I can't lose her now! No way, no way!" I said to myself panicking. *"You gotta do it – now!"*

She came closer, closer with that son-of-a-bitch Casanova beside her. I was mad and terrified. I stepped down the bus stairs, determined to say something before I lost her for good. I propped my body with my arm on the door, angling my posture with my two feet crossed, one over the other like Sinatra or Tom Jones would do, I imagined… the coolest pose, stance I could think of. She comes closer than usual, a mere 2 feet away by the time she is right beside me. I smile at her; she smiles back as I tip my hat being so slick, so cool.
Then I said "G'nee eh…" She looked at me puzzled.

121

"*What the hell was that?*" I asked myself "*What the fuck was that! G'nee eh?? Jesus Christ you're so stupid!*" I yelled in my mind. I didn't even know what I said, it was supposed to be, Good Day or Good to see you but it got choked in my throat. "*Oh God, shoot me, let me die, banish me to Siberia*" I cried as I rethought the words and how I had sounded like a squirrel. She walked on, her head down as her shoulders shook. Her laughing was obvious.

I went out that night and Saturday but not to Canwood. I picked up my friends Shaky and Kel and went to Shellbrook, Mont Nebo and even Leoton where I got stupid drunk. After about 14 beer, 3 AM in the morning, I started bawling with Kel and Shaky both wondering what the hell was wrong with me. I blubbered unintelligibly about my incident as they comforted me with their hands on my shoulders and more beer. Come Sunday, I was so sick but "Who cares?" I said in private, "Let me die, I deserve to die, I'm such a fucking idiot." I groaned, "Ooooohh how am I gonna see her tomorrow? Well, it's over. That's the end. She's probably porking that ugly prick she was with anyway!" I reasoned in despair. But then immediately I was sorry I would even think that about her, the most gorgeous angel in the universe! "Sorry, sorrrrry…" I groaned out loud this time. "Oh God, God, God….what do I do? Maybe I'll enlist and go to Vietnam or join the Foreign Legion. Maybe I'll get killed and then she'll be sorry. *Snap out of it Man, you're acting like a kid!* I reminded myself but continued, *Okay…maybe I'll get my legs blown off and she'll take notice.* Then I thought how I would make love to her if my legs were totally blown off or my arms – or God forbid, my balls, or my Manhood! I visualized this. It was too scary, so I turned my mind monitor off and returned

122

to what tomorrow was to bring, my dilemma. *Well maybe I'll just go logging way up north.* I ended my self-torture.

I probably slept 3 hours that night, waking up periodically then staring at the ceiling till my eyes closed again, thinking all this time of my beloved. Towards morning as the birds started chirping in the dawn, I slipped off to another short sleep. Disjointed images, voices came to me as I looked for the source. The voice was familiar, enchanting as it turned to laughter. I ran to it through a maze of dark faces around corners, shadows I stepped on as a painful sluggishness developed in my body I couldn't overcome. Something sped by me. A shadowed apparition I could not describe passed by and in it's wake a cold smell of death enveloped me and I knew it was going to where I wanted to be. I struggled, willing my legs onward, faster to overcome this beast before me. As I got closer I saw its footprints in the murky alleys of the maze. A low thunder filled my ears and as I realized they were tracks of cloven hooves a ghastly smell struck my nostrils and my throat became constricted from the stench. A fear tore at me, a premonition of horror I had never felt. I breathed hard, strained my muscles and forced my legs even faster gaining upon what demon I was pursuing before it claimed what I desired. Soon in the black dust I saw the dim outline of hooves kicking up, my eyes stared at the melancholic repetition of the trotting hooves. I heard someone, something and was torn back to the fear. Echoes of the hooves brought back the horror I knew awaited if I did not get to the voice in time. In a last attempt knowing that beguiling voice, with a face, was around the next corner I jumped into nothing searching for something physical to grab onto and pull down. My fingers grasped a round long object as I felt the

123

roughness of tree bark and the coarse hair of a horses' mane. We tumbled, a heavy weight played on my chest, a breath bellowed onto me that churned my stomach and left me weak and defeated. I looked up and peered into dull black orbs, the eyes of a bull. Flaring nostrils wet with mucous dripped on me as it snorted in laughter, "Ha ha...where you going....Sam?" I began to shriek and behind my scream I heard that laughter I was chasing. Somebody else was wrenching my arm.

"Wake up, wake up Branson. What are you doing?" someone said as I hung onto the metal posts of my bed still squealing in terror. I fought off the hands holding me, slowly coming back to reality. "Take it easy...easy. What were you dreaming?" my Dad asked.

"Holy..." I was going to swear but realized my Dad was there, "Geez Dad, had the weirdest dream of a monster I was fighting. Think it had horns, I still feel them." I clenched my fingers then rubbed them together to erase the feeling. "It was a man, a cow or something with hooves...and it smelled really bad. If evil has a smell that was it." I told him as he smiled. That felt good. Even in my teen years I felt secure with his reassuring smile. After a minute or two he told me to memorize everything I could, write it down.

"Dreams have meaning. In time it will make sense in what it means, what they are telling you." I brushed aside what he was getting to because my Mom and Dad were strong believers in dreams, prophecy and warnings. I knew what it was; it was my predicament in what to do today so I could salvage what I could with Claire. Nothing else had occupied my thoughts since the disaster last Friday.

I laid back down, relieved, comforted in my reality around me. The blanket, the pillows, even the cold steel of the bedposts I had been strangling, felt so pleasantly real...so nice in their factual existence. I grabbed the quilted blanket, rolled it and brought it to my chest.

"Like a baby rolling his blanket," I whispered beginning to get disgusted with myself. I reminded myself in anger, *Jesus Christ, having nightmares! Over what? So I bombed out Friday, was a total idiot - big hairy deal. Get a hold of yourself!* I got out of bed, made the fire, put on the water kettle for coffee and got ready for the bus run. I reassured myself of my determination but a nagging thought hung with me, *What if she refuses me? Piss off, don't think like that!* I retorted to my inner voice with more anger. I refused to wonder about it any longer. This weekend had been a cabaret of self-torture; getting stupid drunk, blubbering, self-pity and a God damn nightmare to top it off. But still, I wasn't at ease and the doubts came back as I began my morning run to school.

I drove into Canwood, unloaded the kids and was about to close the door when a pleasant voice called "Whoa! Wait." I took my hand off the door shift looking to see who was talking. Coming into full view between the folding doors was the most beautiful face. It was Claire. I was stunned, speechless again. "I didn't see you in Canwood this weekend. You all right? Not sick?" she asked in abbreviated English. I shook my head slowly, not believing she was talking to me, let alone inquiring about my health. "I wanted to talk to you and you weren't around. We're having a party at Donna's and wondered if you wanted to come...if you like?" I nodded again slowly, not quite registering what was happening. "Well it's at 9 this Friday. Bring your friends if you like. OK?" I nodded again as she smiled. "OK, see you then." I nodded again. God, I couldn't believe it! All weekend I was in self-mutilation, torturing myself about what to say to her so she wouldn't think I was some retard. So she talks to me and what do I do? Nod my head like some idiot bobble-head dog you see in the rear car windows and say nothing. Nothing at all! Not a single word did I utter, I realized, reliving the scene in my head.

What a Bozo! I was now disintegrating into a mass of despair when the light went on like you see in the cartoons. Wait…wait. Didn't she just ask you out for this Friday? "Yeeeeaaah." I said out loud. Then it hit me! I became ecstatic clenching my fist, remembering Muhammad Ali standing over Sonny Liston who he had beaten the second time for the Heavyweight Championship of the World…. "Yeah!" I yelled. I was entranced, hopelessly bewitched.

For that week I was in limbo, a mental zombie. It's amazing that I never had an accident, with all my focus gone, nothing there but an empty head with some songs replaying over and over. Tunes I associated with good Karma stuck to me that week; "Get Together", "Crimson and Clover", Credence Clearwater Revival's "Candle In The Window" played in my mind like a stuck jukebox. Cranking up the volume on my 8-track, I screeched in accompaniment to these songs day-after-day in blissful ignorance of my flat vocals. Didn't go anyplace that week, just waited - and waited and waited. Just about drove my parents crazy with my singing as I think back. Shakey, John and Kel were coming with me; Kel was bringing his guitar along just in case we ran out of things to say which I could see happening here. What was I going to say, talk about… or do?

"How about them Chicago Blackhawks?" or "What kind of power-saw do you like?" I know it was stupid but that's what you think at that age, the worst possible scenario that can and probably will happen. At least we would have something in common to comment on or participate in like a good ole 'sing-a-long'.

Man, that Kelly was good with the guitar, making it come alive as he got into fingering, stroking the strings, creating the mood, feeling the songs and making you feel them. He reminded me of Waylon Jennings with his long hair, rough looks and a cowboy hat he sometimes wore but he sounded like John Fogerty of CCR with his nasal growl in the slower songs, nasal because Kel had his nose broken a few times. He was a scrapper but usually lost to too many beers. He could have been big in music if not for the beer and no mentor to guide him, but back then, who did? Kel was also our beer-slinger, not old enough but looked it so he was able to buy the suds for us and we spared nothing for that weekend. By Friday we each had 24 beers; that was 96 amongst the four of us, the 4 musketeers. Early Friday, we loaded up the beer and guitars. The Pontiac was sitting low at the back with all that beer and the 4 of us when we cruised into Canwood. None except Kel could go into the bar so we cruised down Main Street for a few minutes. Nothing there, nobody yet so we stopped at Ole Pete's Poolroom for a couple hours wasting time and bothering Pete.

Ole Pete was a cantankerous ole fart but lovable too. I see him still; sitting alone staring at the floor, his home made *stogie* hanging off his lip with the ashes bent, hanging ready to fall and the smoke crawling up across his moustache. His white moustache yellowed at the corner by years of smoking so it looked half white, half yellow. Occasionally, a column of ashes fell silently onto his knees or his belly depending on how he was sitting. He always wore white shirts with grey pants that

127

matched the worn, weathered wooden benches that surrounded the pool tables. He seemed oblivious to our commotion till we broke some rule, then he would awake vampire-like and yell, his cigarette standing at attention, ashes blowing as he screamed the rules like they were Gospel. Sometimes he would scare the shit out of us! I think he would've made a good evangelical preacher with his booming voice.

Finally the time came. We hopped into the car as it groaned to our weight. We approached Donna's house with apprehension, I wasn't the only one nervous. We inched the car up the driveway and parked silently – waiting. We must've sat there for 10 minutes at least till someone says, "Aren't you going in?"

"You go in!" I retort.

"You're the one who's got a date." John says. "Yeah!" someone else says.

"Jesus Christ, why is it me that has to do everything?"

"Get going! You were blubbering about her last week you pussy!" Kelly says. "Yeah!" someone else echoes as I look in the rear-view mirror to see who it is.

"I was not!"

"Yeah you were. Bawling like a baby, your beer was dripping off your chin." Kelly smirks and the others laugh as he takes on a high voice wiping fake tears from his eyes, "Don't leave me little Beaver!" he wails away. I punched him with the back of my hand right into his stomach. This took away his moment as he grunted and doubled over in the front seat beside me, him now the 'butt' of renewed laughter.

Soon I was laughing too, a little more at ease. "Alright, alright, I'll go in!" Opening the door, I saw the girls coming out of the house, seemingly alarmed and anxious.

"Let's go, let's go!" the five of them said as they crammed into my Pontiac. There were 9 of us now as they exclaimed, "Donna's Dad is coming! Hurry, let's get out of here, step on it!"

"I thought your Mom and Dad were gone?" I asked looking at Donna.

"They were supposed to be but I just got a call, they're back already! Something must've happened, I don't know....let's go!"

"Where?" I asked as I put it in reverse and the car jolted backwards. I thought *there goes my universal joint* but it grabbed easily as I backed out of the driveway. Turning around, looking backward through the back window, I came face-to-face with Claire sitting on the edge of the back seat a scant 6 inches away. No time to get scared, no time to prepare so I bent forward and gave her a kiss....and that was it! I heard a few "Oooo's" and all the stress, the anxiety was gone as we smiled at each other. "Where are we going?" I asked trying not to be so apparent in my pleasure.

"The Pines." someone said as the others chorused "Yeah, the Pines!" We found the approach the smell of Pine welcoming us as we entered into a warm dark canopy made of overlapping branches,. A few more feet and we could see the remains of an old campfire so we stopped and all piled out setting our little space around the ashes. It didn't take long and we had a campfire going. Everyone paired off and those finding themselves alone sat together singing the tunes...or the blues. Before we knew it, the beer had run low so Kelly, anticipating a longer night and more people to come, did the rounds for a collection of cash making a fast run to the bar before it closed. The bars here, in the sixties, quit serving at midnight and closed off-sale at 1am. Kelly returned with a 24 pack and we continued into the wee hours. After a couple hours some of us went into the woods to gather more deadwood for the fire, so I excused myself. The real reason was I needed a leak so I ventured further in, a short way from Claire and did my business. I stood there feet apart peeing on the moss when an image appeared to my right.

I didn't recognize the figure so I shouted out, "Who's there?"

"Whatcha talking bout, it's me – Shake."

"No, not you. Somebody over here, do you see him?"

"No. I'm finished, gotta get back to my woman." He joked in a low voice. "See ya, don't piss on your moccasins."

My eyes returned to my right again and the figure was closer but it was smaller. *A kid* I thought wondering what the Hell a young kid was doing out here. He took a few steps towards me and there was Pug! Except he was young…hadn't grown!

"Pug, Pug?" I kept whispering but there was no answer and the figure moved on not seeing me or acknowledging me. The spectre scared the shit out of me, so I ran back through the bushes to the glowing campfire slowing to a walk as I neared it. I didn't want anyone knowing I just got scared shitless in the woods. I hopped onto the tailgate Claire was sitting on.

"You look like you saw a ghost." she leaned backwards at my glance.

"Promise you won't tell?" I asked her. She nodded. "I think I just saw my old friend Pug… from the States." I said as calmly as I could, then asked out of impulse, "What time is it?" I needed to remember. "It's now Sunday, July 21st, right?"

"Yeah, right. It's 2 am, 2:01 to be exact. This is a joke, right? You trying to spook me, Sam? Who is Pug?" She already knew my nickname, I liked that, Kel or Shake must have told her.

"Yeah, you caught on, thought I would try and scare you so you would come a little bit closer to me." I gave her my best smile, it seemed to work as she nestled her body to mine grabbing my arm with both of her hands. The scene lingered though, still frightened at what I saw...and if it meant anything.

I gave her a short history on my years in Shelby and who Pug was. Retelling the tale of the end of our friendship endeared itself to her romantic side and she sidled even closer to me. I playfully shouldered her with a mock check as we smiled at each other and the phantom I had perceived was gone. Nothing else mattered at the time except us.

Claire and I sat closely together, our bare arms touching, shivers running through us as we found our hands clasped together. Everything happened so natural that night. We kissed, sang songs under the Pines while the flames flickered and our shadows danced. The beer flowed as we cranked up the volume on the car stereo, some dancing, and some singing off-tune to what was playing. More friends, classmates came to our campfire which became more visible through the night; funny we never had a forest fire in all the parties we had there, guess we knew what to do even when we were drunk. We talked through the night, a kiss here and there but no frenzied lust or groping you see in the movies. Everything seemed so natural... soul mates. That was the first night of our life together. I never forgot that feeling, that second kiss under the stars, on that magical evening many years ago – my nirvana.

Contrary to stereotypical portraits of sex and drugs of that age and that time, our relationship was quite 'old-fashioned' maybe because of our small town upbringing and definitely a reflection on our Parent's expectations. Back here in the northern woods there wasn't that much to rebel against. Oh we had fun, we weren't drugged out and deviant sex-crazed like Charles Manson but yes we had fun…. and sex.

That time…. was the best time. The Pines was more a feeling than a place and the Sixties, more a Spirit than a time. I wished Pug had been there to share it.

CHAPTER 12

I had been at FPC now for 14 years and thought I would never say this, but I was getting tired of it – bored. Same ole same ole came in and went out, revolving doors. There was still the rush in responding to an incident or PPA, personal panic alarm, but most often it was false or minor. The atmosphere here was gone; where you could cut the air with a knife because it was so tense. Most liked it that way. There was still the odd event but not like the ole days when we were running to-and-fro every day like it was normal. Never mind exercising to stay in shape, just go to work. Management and the system was still a joke so we had that to kick around. The monotony of routine got to you. Everyday we would bitch about this or that; didn't matter, we just had to bitch about something so that it seemed we were in the know and had control. But we didn't know and we knew it. Really, we were at the mercy of everything and everyone around us, which was probably the real reason we became so cynical. Knowing your situation but unable to change, just waiting like an inmate on Death Row. I became more and more aware of this negativity, the cynicism, as the years went by but I never saw it in myself, only in others until my wife mentioned it and asked me why I was drinking so much and the kids asked why I was so grumpy. It came to me, bit by bit and I finally realized that I was becoming institutionalized, trapped like everyone else and unconsciously mad about it - stagnant and brewing like a batch of bad moonshine.

We had had numerous suicides through the years, not all were inmates. We also had murders inside and out as a result of inmate-staff relationships. Walking out the door at shift's end doesn't mean everything was left behind.

We carry out what we witness inside; sometime that gets too heavy. So to decrease that load of shit, we devised de-briefings to vent ourselves with beer and talk... and they got wild. It got so we only went to work to collect the shit then unload it at a de-briefing; well, maybe not that bad but it seemed so at the time. The humour we used to use for venting was gone now.

One thing didn't change; there was Charlie and Willie, still there and doing segregation about every 3 weeks. Both, over their time, had left for a 'break' to other centers in Quebec and the Maritimes, but never for too long. We teased them on their 'vacations' and alluded to their longing for FPC. The fact was, in their sentences served they probably had been out of FPC a total of only 4 or 5 times. The regular Penitentiaries, the Maximum Institutions would not have them at any cost. Those two, unpredictable as they were, were still part of the routine we all knew. Everything would follow its due course and happen like we all knew it would. Just as the sun rose every morning we knew these two would be in *Seg* together, talking, chatting, having tea, every two weeks or so. "Flipping out" became normal and routine with duration in the seclusion cells of the Seg wing lasting a week....maybe, if they were not inclined to stay longer. All it took to book another week in Seg was to swear at the staff.

Willie had come from a poor family as opposed to his friend and colleague Charlie who came from wealth and authority. Being raised on a reserve then scooped up for compulsory residential schooling a thousand miles away, Willie was a victim of social upheaval that moulded him into his present character. Mellow one moment, tearing at the walls and anyone close, the next. His parents were

134

dirt poor. A third-generation after the Treaties were signed and everyone was imprisoned on Reserves, his parents were just learning to be farmers or ranchers.

Loving their kids like everyone else, Native parents of that era had to contend with something unbelievable that the general public would never have put up with. They had to deal with government policy of amalgamation or extermination of the "Indian People". Starting in the early Century through to the Seventies, the Government and the Churches developed a system to do this. It was called *'integration and civilization of the Indian People,'* which we later referred to as Cultural Genocide. Residential schools were set up across Canada to educate the Indigenous People and there were no consultations, nor were there any options. Through legislature, the youth on reserves had to go to school. These schools were built regionally, not per reserve, with many Residential Schools far away from their homes. They were built big, imposing and administered by the Church, mainly the Catholic with their Priests and Nuns. From the age of 6 to 16, it was deemed unlawful to not be in school. So every year in the fall, cattle trucks would come around to each reserve scooping up all who were of this age. There was usually a gathering place where they would load up the kids into the back of the trucks but some would hide. The authorities would check their list on which families had children of this age; every reserve had what they called a Band list with all families entered. Reserve was the geographical location; the families who lived there were called the Band or Bands, a reserve could have more than one Band living in it but usually the Reserve was named after its principal or largest family. So it was determined who was missing, then they would send out a search team to find their homes, round them up and pack them in like cattle, for a long, long drive to their respective schools. Some kids were persistent, creative in where and when to go, when the trucks came around, running into the bushes or forests where they hid out till the trucks left. Sometimes, the even more persistent 'Rounders' would wait for supper when the kids would be so hungry they would cautiously venture out, only to be seized by the waiting men. Then you had those like Willie who escaped all by staying in the bush for a day or two. He managed to miss capture a few times but eventually they found ways to outsmart him and he, like the rest, succumbed to a life away from parents and home for 10 months of the year.

Many would die in these schools from Influenza or Pneumonia and there were instances the parents didn't know till the summer when they came home and their child was not in the truck. Student life in Residential schools was not pleasant where all culture was to be eradicated beginning with the language. Students were punished severely and physically if they spoke their Mother tongue; long hair and braids were cut to a bowl or brush cut, they were dressed in institutional uniforms and they were subjected to a demeaning, corrupted version of their history and culture. Adding to the atrocities, many of the Priests sexually assaulted students. This happened over many years through generations, until some brave enough came forward and revealed the truth. The scandal transpiring over generations, broke across Canada and many Priests, authorities fell like dominoes. Still, into the eighties, the Churches refused to acknowledge or offer apologies to those victims. It wasn't till the nineties when other Canadian and American religious institutions similar in 'providing for the youth' fell in the wake of truth and the media flood-gated the public with this news. Consequently investigations, reports and charges were laid. Only then did the Church and Government acknowledge the wrong they did but it was too late for many. Willie was one of them.

Scarred, humiliated, degraded by sodomy at the blessed hands of the righteous, Willie was broken for the rest of his life. In his quiet brooding moments, he would recall those events exploding with ferocity nobody wanted to witness or bear. To get into disassociation or Seg, all he had to do was think back to those times, do some damage physically or verbally and he was whisked back to his second home, seclusion cell 132. He needed the silence and solitude the Hole brought him, as did Charlie. Two people so different in upbringing and culture suffered and retaliated from the same causes and abhorred authority in general, a logical result in my opinion. Willie, in seldom, quiet interludes, would talk about his schooling that inevitably would result in him becoming agitated, so we didn't pry too hard. But on occasions, he did reveal some of his demons, those memories that tore at him.

Once in his gloomy recluse sitting on the cold cement he blurted out, "Fuck off!" I went over took a look inside and saw he was walking wall-to-wall whispering angrily, "Get out of here you fucker, you cock-sucker." Waving, clenching his fists he strode his cell easily in two steps as his gait became faster. I thought, *oh oh, here we go again.*
"What's up Willie?" I asked not expecting a response.
"Fuckers are at me again..." he replied drawing it out.
"Who Will?"
"Those fucking pricks that used to fuck me!" he shouted stopping to look at me.

137

"Who are they Will, who are you talking about?"

He wrestled with the question, wondering if he should answer. The passion at the moment got the better of him though, he couldn't stop. "The Priests, they're in my head. I can hear them!" Clenching his teeth he bellowed, "Get out of here, leave me alone!" as he craned his head to the ceiling. Moments passed, I waited for the physical violence, the banging on the door. Instead he closed his eyes hoping to shut out the demons and sank to the floor in a hushed cry. A whimper from a man this big, this violent, didn't seem to fit. I stared at the picture before me. In a small voice he said, "Please don't – pleeease." I didn't say anything, I didn't want to. He seemed to be reliving a memory, a nightmare as he sat there broken. I stood there not wanting to go away, the seconds turning to minutes feeling like a lifetime as I waited. A big sigh came out of him, *bad air being purged* I thought. He stood, raising his body slowly till he was looking down on me. His eyes were different, softer while he studied me. He inhaled deeply then exhaled the words of his revulsion that he never shared.

"They used to call me, wake me after everyone was asleep. The Nun would come over, shake me and I knew where to go." He paused seeming to watch a video unfold on the wall. "I went into the Father's personal bedroom. I didn't want to but I had no choice…just like the others. He was waiting. I went to the desk, bent over. He came behind, lifted my nightgown…then fucked me. I can't count the times he did this, sometimes we had to blow him off cause he couldn't get a hard-on. Fuck I hated that!" He looked away. "This went on for four years, then I escaped, walked for six days." He stopped, held his breath like he was holding his tears then turned,

138

walked to his urinal in the corner. He stood there silently.

"Go on Willie." I whispered. Another awkward suspension while I wondered if I should talk or not.

In his own world now he stammers, "You know what though, you know what? You know what was the worst? When I found my home, found my parents and told them? They wouldn't believe me! They said, '*A Priest would never do something like that,*' that's what they said to me – to me, their boy!" He yells to the wall, to someone in the past, "Your blessed Priests are a buncha ass fuckers!" Willie turned to me then, didn't say anything, just looked to see if I was listening. I nodded. We both stood there for about 15 minutes, no words. It was close to 3 in the morning and Charlie next door hadn't said a word or interrupted in any way. I knew he was awake and it dawned on me that Charlie had purposely been silent out of respect for Willie to tell his story. There was a bond here between the two.
"I believe you Willie." I told him as I honestly did.
"I do too," Charlie interrupts, adding angrily, "Fucking religion and ass-fucking Priests!"
"Thank you," Willie said with sincerity. For the first time I saw Willie relaxed, at peace with him self. I was about to return to my station when he added in a monotone, "That was the last time I saw my parents. The next day I walked again, this time for two days towards Alberta where I knew my Uncle lived. Finally found him...stayed there for three years then started working.
After a pause I asked, "Did you ever marry, have any kids?"
"No, couldn't. I couldn't or maybe I didn't want a woman after what happened to me. Hmmm, never

thought about it cause it just never happened. Probably too drunk all the time anyway."

A wall seemed to disappear; Willie was open, talking freely. "You know my Uncle was really good to me. I think part of the reason why was because he lost a son, two sons"

"Yeah, what happened?"

"My Kokum told me this, she stayed not far from him. Around 35 years ago, my Uncle got word from the Indian Agent that his son was sick at the residential school. So he hurried, got his horse and was about to ride the four days it took to get there. At the last minute his oldest son offered to go, so Uncle thinking the boy could ride faster, let him go in his place. This was in the winter. He was gone for a week then Uncle starts to worry and sent out a search party. After many days they found his sons, both frozen stiff under some snowdrifts, the horse standing over them, waiting. The reins were still in the hands of the eldest lying there on the frozen ground and his younger brother was nicely wrapped up on the travois being dragged. Guess the boy was already dead when he got there, so he wrapped him up and brought him home. They ran into a blizzard and the boy not wise, maybe not caring, continued and finally fell and went to sleep. That is how they found them.

"Wow, that's so sad."

"Yeah…but things like this always happened. Nobody listened, nobody cared. Some put up with the shit but others fought."

"You one of them Willie…a fighter?"

"Guess so. Look where it got me though. I never bothered that young girl like they say I did. I was carrying her home because she was lost. Some prick sees us, tries to take her away and I give him a good licking. That's it, nothing more, now I'm here for 12 years, for abducting a child. Why? Because they believed the man! Not me – or the child who told them the truth." Willie rethinks his recent charges, "Started out for 12 years, now it's what... life?"

"Really?" I ask. I had read the file on Willie and they had him down as a molester, a Pedophile. "Holy shit Willie you should get a lawyer, fight this because you're labelled a sex offender. That's why you were in the Sex unit Willie."
"Aaah, I've tried but the fucking lawyers won't work on it. Too much work they say to get the evidence, too long ago."
"Yeah but in the meantime you're marked. Do you know that? Inmates in the other units would love to 'hit' you and get some honour points for it."
"Let them come, been through it many times. Tell the truth, it feels kinda good to get that excitement…and to lay a shit-kicking on those bastards. I pretend they're the Priests. It feels good you know." He looks at me, smiles. Never saw Willie in such a jovial mood, well jovial, in relation to his normal glaring self.
"Still, you should get a real lawyer, get some recommendations and talk to someone. Walk out of here before they carry you out in a body bag Willie."
"Mmmm maybe, having fun right now though….and don't know if I want to be outside. Fucking terrible out there!" he dramatizes in good nature.

"You said it Willie!" says Charlie right beside us, laughing, having a great time. *Maybe there was a time when 'Good-Time' Charlie was happy* I thought to myself. I believed Willie; not totally, but the part of him abducting a child for sexual purposes? I didn't believe that. I had seen so many inmates mislabelled from a one-hour interview to assess their category for incarceration and treatment. It was a joke at times. Charlie? He was a manipulator who loved to play games. He was intelligent, maybe a genius as his results had shown when they had tested him, and dangerous, unpredictable. Willie was up-front; you knew when he was mad and ready to blow a fuse. The diagnosis for Charlie was a 'Paranoid Schizophrenic" with delusions of persecution. 'Irreversible and long-term' it stated in his file. In his own words though, he saw them coming, manufactured his psyche, getting them to assess, diagnose the label he wanted. This way, being hopeless, they didn't bother him and the other inmates feared him. We told the Psychiatrist this but '*no*' he knew what Charlie was. He was a murderer, absolutely; perhaps multi or serial but we knew he was not mindless or delusional. Charlie had his wits about him; he knew exactly what to do and calculated obsessively in when and where to do whatever he dreamed.

I started to my station to do my hourly rounds. "See you boss," Willie says. In the background not as loud Charlie repeats, "See you Sam." After all these years that still bothered me. How did he know my nickname that only my on-reserve friends knew? He would never tell me.

Across the hallway I heard a call for security to go to Admissions. I heard something about '*deportation to Montana*' then '*click*' it was over and I resumed my rounds. We had special clearance to hold anyone for the U.S.; as a Federal multi-max institution, we were the only facility able to accommodate such requests from the courts or international affairs.

142

Midnight shift over now and home at 7 in the morning I climbed into bed, the conversation with Willie fresh in my mind. I wondered on what dreams they had, Willie and Charlie, when they went to sleep.

Chapter 13

I had to get away, do some thinking. The routine was becoming overbearing, redundant and I struggled to go to work. The excitement, the rush was diminished; the good times had gotten old. I needed a spark to go on…or quit while I was ahead. I didn't want to be that grumpy ole stereotypical guard we imagined and laughed at so many years ago. I remembered that one special day on my 10th year anniversary at FPC when I had these same thoughts and did the same thing – went to the Reserve, to think. After thinking I returned to my home in Saskatoon, back to work and did another 10 years. I hope I wouldn't do too much thinking on this 20th anniversary.

On the highway getting closer to Canwood, I recalled that fateful hot day some10 years ago.

I was on my way back to my Reserve hoping to stop by and visit our **"Best Bar"**, *our only bar* in Canwood. I had just finished a 7-day work schedule with added overtime and needed that familiarity an old place of acquaintance and its residents bring. This was the summer (not winter) of my discontent. I had been a Maximum Security guard for a lifetime now, 10 years, dealing with disturbed inmates that no other penitentiary wanted. I was in need of that familiar humour we took comfort in. I knew I would find it back on the Reserve. Deprecating, sometimes depressing yet comical, the stories retold here were typical even conventional of what happened on reserves. Humour was a tool that we used to make the best of a bad situation. It saved our sanity amidst a world gone mad with its governmental rules, regulations and Religion imprisoning us on a piece of land. Within these confines we had our own world. We lost our selves for a time but laughter; the humour would always bring us together – even when we were apart.

So I sat there with my solitary lonely beer feeling restless as the dog day dragged on and nobody came. The beads coming off the cold bottle collected at its base, making a pool as I fingered it. Finally the pub door opens and in steps a dark figure outlined by the glare of the setting sun. His features slowly begin to emerge through the dark silhouette and I soon recognized the face. It was Solomon!

Solomon was one of twelve children, all of whom were named after some biblical figure, as was the custom back then, especially for those parents who had found the Lord. In this case Solomon and his brother Jeremiah never quite lived up to the wise men they were named after.

Proceeding in, he glided smoothly yet cautiously through the blinding sunlight like a revelation. Stopping momentarily he cranes his head, squints his eyes then marches across the threshold in bold calculated steps to make sure he didn't trip. Solomon parades through, sidestepping the tables and straight to the back where I sit. He comes closer, sees me in the dingy dark through a cloud of smoke, smiles, and sits down. He's got this big smile on his face like that cat in *Alice in Wonderland*.

"*Something's up.*" I say to myself. Already I'm on alert cause he's smiling too much, like a salesman selling vacuums.

Amid the din and muffled sounds, Waylon Jennings is wailing out *Amanda* on the corner jukebox. Dressed in a plaid lumberjack shirt and tattered blue jeans Sol keeps

145

inching his chair closer to me like he's got a secret. Finally he sets a base, his chair next to mine.

"Watcha doing here?" he asks.
 "Came for a visit. How are you doing?" I ask.
"Pretty good. How bout yourself?"
"Good, good." I say while he smiles away.

We sit there, both of us smiling, nodding our heads, as we look each other over. It had been a few years since we had seen each other. He was a little older than myself so we weren't in the same crowd. He and his brother used to work for my Dad at times mainly to get enough money to buy beer for the weekend.

About this time my eyes adjust to the halo, the glare of the open bar door surrounding his silhouette and I notice a couple butterfly bandages on his head. The smell of beer hangs in the air along with stale smoke and you can hear the clink of bottles echoing behind as Wilbur the bartender stocks his shelves. I motion to Wilbur with my fingers spread like a V to bring us two beers as he glances sideways at my bottle and me. Communication without words, you learn sign language fast in a bar especially when you get 'loaded' and words don't come easy.

 "What happened to your head?" I ask as I pointed with my lips.

Most Indians will point with anything but their fingers because it was deemed rude, unless they're politicians; it's a cultural thing.

"Oh...got shot in the head." he says matter-of-factly.

"You got shot?" I whisper loudly as I squint to see, the light behind still blinding me. "Jesus Christ! Shouldn't you be in the hospital, man?" I ask him.

"I was." he tells me, "Then I got thirsty, so I checked myself out. Besides I wasn't in too much pain or anything...and I could see all my fingers ... and my toes too!" He laughs, I don't.

"What the hell happened?" I ask in astonishment.

After the beer arrives he relates the story. He takes the dripping wet Pilsner and after a long swig he places it down gently. He caresses the bottleneck as beads stream down and over his fingers. A far away look settles into his eyes.

"Well...." a brief pause as he recollects the facts, probably with some difficulty, "Me and Jeremiah, my brother?", he kind of asks nodding with his chin pointing and puckered lips to make sure I know who he is talking about. I nod in return, he goes on, "We were drinking all night. We had hired Moses to take us to Mont Nebo for a couple cases of Pilsner earlier that day. Get ready for hunting, eh?"

Moses used to work for us too and he would frequent the bar of a small village called Mont Nebo close to our reserve. Population there was probably 60 but they had a bar. We, the younger crowd, would often remark on *'Moses going to Mont Nebo for a few beer'*, relating in jest to the Biblical stories where Moses parted the Red Sea and Mont Nebo being where he ascended to Heaven. The coincidence of name and place was too good to pass up.

Sol continues, "By early morning we were out of beer but feeling pretty good as the sun came up. We start

147

talking bout what a nice day to go hunting, of how many Elk we could get."

"You know," he turns to me remembering, "The season had just opened for Elk?"
He exclaims and looks at me to make this point as if it's logical for what they do next.

"So we decided to clean our rifles, get them ready. We're sitting there and Jeremiah's just finishing oiling his gun. He's got it on his lap, pulls back the lever, cocks it, and I was just gonna ask him if he checked the barrel when "BANG".....and everything goes white. Not black like they say", He looks at me as if he's the expert now, "but white, real white."

He's looking up at the bar ceiling now gesturing with his hand in a half-circle, eyes half-closed, no words. I look at his glazed eyes and wonder if he's OK cause he's too silent for a bit. Maybe he's got some internal bleeding or something I'm thinking but he starts up again in low gear. He comes out of his temporary trance slowly at first, and then escalating his narration, he relives the moment.

"Next thing I know I'm on the floor looking at the ceiling. I hear Jeremiah screaming, see a flash or blur as he runs to me. I feel something running down the side of my head, around the temple", He raises his hand to his temple, "and I touch it and there's blood! It comes to me, I've been shot in the head!"

"Jeremiah stares at me with bug-eyes, kind of scaring me", he continues, "Well now I start to go crazy thinking I'm gonna die and I start screaming. My bro flips out too

148

and we both run out the door and about 20 yards away there stands Uncle Luke (after the Apostle). He's not moving or anything, just standing looking at us. Guess he was wondering what the hell's going on here, one guy goes this way and the next guy coming out goes the other way - both screaming. By now I'm scared shitless and run off to the bushes. All that beer didn't help either I guess", he says profoundly as he thinks about it. "Anyway I take off, just run, gotta get outta there. Don't know how long I ran but I end up in some willows, sat down and you know... just waited for the end to come."

He says this stoically as if he was some great warrior. I'm smiling to myself.

He goes on, "I was sitting there, blood all over me when I remembered I had toilet paper in my pockets so I reach in my pockets, take out a whole bunch and start packing it in my head to stop the bleeding. I keep a lot on me in case I have to go to the bathroom when I'm away from home, eh?" He nods at me to acknowledge this wisdom, which I do, I've been there.

"I could feel where the wound was with my fingers and it ran down the middle of my head so that's where I put the toilet paper." He motions with his hand sliding down from the top of his head to his hairline. "Finally," he says, "I begin to hear voices a long ways away. I'm kinda dizzy, just like I'm gonna pass out, eh? I'm thinking, those must be the angels coming. The voices get louder in my head. All at once, like through a fog; a nurse, a dog, RCMP and my Chief come galloping through the bush."

149

"What! What the hell is going on? I'm talking to myself, trying to make sense of this," he explains to me, "cause I was sure Angels were coming."

"I guess Uncle Luke had called the Chief who called the community nurse then the RCMP who happened to be in the Rez. That's why they were there real quick and together."

"I look up, I see their mouths moving slowly but I can't make sense of what they're saying." He takes his Pilsner at this point and half-empties it. He catches his breath, repeats, "they weren't making sense.... so I said nothing, besides I didn't know what to say so I just smile at them. The RCMP is holding this huge dog that wouldn't stop yapping, the nurse is holding up 3 fingers and your Dad (Chief) is shouting at me. I'm mixed up, can't say anything, can't think, so I figure; I'll show them how I stopped the bleeding. So I pull the toilet paper from my head that is soaked with blood, held it out and showed them. Well, all Hell breaks loose, eh? The nurse screams, the RCMP faints landing on top of his stupid barking dog that takes off dragging the cop along cause he's still hanging on to the leash....and my Chief's eyes are popping out!"

"Plop!" he says as he describes with his arm how the poor officer fell then waves it like a snake to imitate the dog's actions as he pulls him along. A devious smile comes to him as he reminisces fondly on this picture in mind. Getting buggy-eyed again, he looks at me.
"They thought I was pulling out my brains!" he hollers in a gleeful wonder smacking his knee. His smile gets bigger as he studies me then erupts in maniacal laughter. It was like an artist putting the final touches to

150

a masterpiece. He signalled the bartender with a "V" for another round, pointing to me for the cash. I would buy quite a few that night.

"So they put me in the ambulance when it got there. One of the guys asks me how many fingers he's holding up. I tell him, I was never good at Math, eh? so he asks me again which pisses me off."
"Then I ask him, '*Don't you know? Why you asking me?*'"
I'm just about falling off the chair at this point.

"Your Dad yells at me now to smarten up or he would kick my ass but I'm not joking, eh? Never went to school or learned to count, always depended on my smarter brother for that. So anyway your dad tells them to take me to the hospital. Bout this time I can hear some crying in the bush thinking maybe it's the angels again. Meanwhile as they look me over they say **'I was still in shock'** but I misunderstood this. Well, you know, my hearing was not too good after that gun going off beside my ears so I thought they said '**I was going to pot** 'eh? You know, going to die but in a slow way?"

I was getting weak from laughing. "Yeah, yeah...." I said urging him to go on.

He's smiling from ear to ear as he knows he has me. "Well this crying keeps coming and I'm looking to the sky." Then the Chief says," He's over here."

Sol looks at me, "Wow, I thought, the Chief is talking with the Angels."
My knees are almost on the floor now as I try to contain myself, my stomach muscles getting weaker.

151

"Then this big noise like thunder comes and I get kinda scared again. I look to the noise and here comes Jeremiah flying through the bush. Ugliest angel I ever saw with his broken nose and 5 teeth." he says to himself in disappointment. He adds from memory, "Two molars on one side and three front teeth. Anyway he's a bawling, tears all over his face. He reaches out, grabs my hand thinks I'm dying too, eh? Well we were hugging each other, blubbering away when that stretcher I was on breaks. Jeremiah lands on me and he's big, eh?" I knowingly nod.

"He almost crushes me and knocks the wind out of me. I'm gasping for breath and Jeremiah is just wailing away like ole Waylon and Willie. He thinks he has really done me in. Finally I get my wind and can breathe again."

My ribs are cracking, I am laughing so hard.

"So I tell him. *Jeremiah, it's all right. It's not your fault*, but I was lying, eh? That bugger…it was all his fault. But I tell him, *you can have all I got when it's all over, when I die…won't be long now."* Sol does some dramatics with his forearm to his forehead, continuing,
"*Really?*" My bro asks. "*Even that black velvet Elvis painting?*" He stops crying at this point which kinda pissed me off. He wants that painting that bad…just a second ago he's bawling because I'm dying?"
He recollects fondly trying to understand. "But you know, Jeremiah really did love that painting. He would imitate Elvis and sing, *"Love Me Tender"* but he's got no teeth, eh? Some words he sang I didn't know what the Hell he was saying."

"Then he asks me!" Solomon shouts, "With tears still in his eyes, *what about that moose rack for the guns?* I coulda killed him then. I'm on my deathbed or death stretcher and he's asking for material things, my things? So I reach up, grab him around the neck and start choking. He's making these weird *'eek eeeeek'* sounds when your Dad grabbed me. The Chief shakes me hard, yelling *"Stop it! Both of you! You're not dying - you buncha idiots!"*
"And you," pointing to Jeremiah he says, "Get out of here, I'll talk to you later."

Jeremiah apparently persists, staying around and asking about the head wound but is assured by my Dad there was no permanent damage

Sol quotes my Dad imitating his actions with a pointed finger, waving his hand, *"Buncha idiots! Bastards! Drinking, fooling around with guns...Jesus Christ! What the Hell do you expect?"* My Dad never swore, Sol was improvising here.

"Then you know what he did, what Jeremiah did?" Solomon tells me, "Just as he's leaving he asks, *Say Chief, can you loan me a twenty?* Your Dad lost it then. Jeremiah sees his eyes starting to bulge out, knows he's about to get a shit-kicking and starts running. I think he's still running." I was in hysterics visualizing the scene.

The next day I asked my Dad and he said, "Yeah, it's all true, I was there." He shook his head in dismay and disgust as he told the story in his words. It wasn't humorous the way he told it. It's funny how the same picture looks different when it's in another frame ... but I still laugh remembering Solomon's version.

153

The eventual sad conclusion to this story followed years later. I met Sol again. It was 11pm Tuesday on a moonlit night.

The troubled seem most vulnerable in the graveyard hours when the full moon does have strange influences. The thought of going to sleep alone or the dark walls that close in on you…or the lifelessness a cell bears, all these play on you. There is something about cement and steel that is so rigidly cold. Maybe it's the warm memories a full moon brings on bitter nights, which break the will.

Doing the required count before locking up, we were called to the basement unit we called the 'Dungeon'. This unit held those under longer-term assessment, waiting for parole or for more psychiatric reports. A nurse motioned us over to the station while the unit security locked up the inmates.

"We're locking up before I take you into the West Wing." she had said. "I didn't want the others to see this and get all agitated before lock-up." She stood there emotionless staring at the dark orange door #131. The inmates knew something was afoot but they walked into their rooms, no problems.

After the count was done she ushered us back into the wing and to the door. We looked in as she whispered past us then stood there. Under the dim glow of the cell light she removed the sheet, sterile and crisp with starch. A dark face made darker by the whiteness of the sheet slowly came into focus. There below me lay Solomon. I never knew he was here. Guess he had been court-ordered to FPC for a Psychiatric review. What a shock, I couldn't believe it and just stared blankly! An old friend before me, his clouded eyes staring vacantly back at me. He lay there cold as the cement floor, no smile with a self-made noose that hung around his neck like a beggar's necktie.

I found out later through my Mom, Sol never did get over his addictions, his problems. His life surrounded alcohol, the only thing that gave him pleasure. It came to own him as he later stole, fought for it and suffered the change in his self. Good ole Sol became something else. That cheerful demeanour, Devil-may-care outlook drowned in liquor in his later years. What remained was a man older than his time, cynical with sarcasm replacing the humour he once had. I relished the laughter we had shared, that 'feel-good' atmosphere he created out of situations gone bad and that smile that said, "Everything is going to be alright." He killed him self with a cheap felt blanket each Pen issues to inmates. He had cut it apart, specifically the sewn hems with a dull edge scissors borrowed from a nurse, fashioned it into a hangman's noose then hung himself from the embedded steel coat hanger. His considerable weight did the rest by tightening the knots, locking them together like they are supposed to. Once tightened, there is no release without being cut down.

I imagined the time in doing this would have been slow, lingering... more than enough time to remember things. Did he remember the good times as his life faded away? Did he remember his brother?

We carried him out, quietly, then finger-printed him, took photos and that was that. No words, no concern, just a routine born from repetition, done in silence.

155

I never told anyone I knew him.

I bypassed the bar in Canwood this time around and went straight to Sandy Lake, saw my Mom and Dad and chatted. My Uncle Buddy was there visiting, so later we travelled into town and got some beer. Inside the bar, by coincidence we meet - guess who? Jeremiah! We invited him to tag along and he was more than happy to oblige our invitation since he was broke – as usual.

Feeling nostalgic, we went east of town into the Pines where we made a campfire and talked of old times, the good times. Sure enough, the shotgun story came up, this time with Jeremiah's version. We laughed like it had happened last night – the story had become legend. We reminisced around the fire; the moon over the Pines looked down on us, our faces glowing orange before the fire and our laughs carrying through the dark forest.

Chapter 14

I got back home, my city home with my kids and wife, preparing for another week of torturous boredom and routine. We worked in a 7-day roster with each consecutive roster being different – days to afternoons to midnight. I had traded my afternoons with Murray for Midnights thinking if I'm going to be bored it might as well be a quiet boredom. Besides, I coached soccer too, my only passion nowadays was to watch my son play and *God* could he play. I had seen thousands, coached hundreds of players but he stood out shining like a star. *Might be a pro career here,* I often thought if he could just focus and stay away from negative elements? My daughter, the oldest, was more like me although she would deny this vehemently. She was stubborn, self-determined, tough but sensitive with an eye and a hand for Art. In fact, she was fast becoming better than me in the application and techniques. The youngest and probably sweetest because she came later was my 'munchkins'. She was still pre-school, dependent, who made us feel still wanted. The other kids were getting older which made me feel older, so questions started to arise in me about this job and *do I want to do this for 35 years* to get a full pension. *An inmate doing a 'double-murder' will be out before me,* I shook my head at that thought. I got my reading material along with some art paper and pencils together for the midnight shift. This is what kept me awake – also made me feel productive but my Keeper probably wouldn't agree.

I came onto the grounds a little earlier than usual. It was a beautiful warm summer night, the crickets chirping away to the background harmony of the frogs behind the center where the river and marsh lay. The moon was

157

declining in brilliance after its full moon phase but still casting night shadows around me. I walked into a harsh glare of florescent light, clanking sounds punctuating the silent halls. Nobody around as everyone was in their units getting ready for lockup and lights out. My boots creaked on the polished concrete. I looked around remembering the first time I entered these walls feeling like yesterday, yet a sensation of eternity pervaded.

"Don't know…" I whispered to myself thinking of the next 15 years. A 'clank' startled me as I came to the unit door. Control had been watching me waiting till I got there, opening without my having to press the button, a little favour. I waved to the camera thanking whoever was there behind the big-brother lens.

"Have a good night." someone said over the intercom.

"I will." I replied realizing it was Murray. Good ole Murray, we'd been friends since I first got here. I was suddenly aware I'd miss him and many other 'colleagues'. The halls, the station, the unit were all dark by now, my gait slowed to a crawl. Without hesitation, we locked everyone up then after double-checking I sat myself down and went through the log. Everything seemed fine, normal, no incidents worthy of attention except for an asterisk noting; *order in for deportation of inmate Charlie Fuhr*.

"What!" I asked myself, questioning, "Deportation?"

"Oh you saw it?" a female voice ushers, "Not too loud, don't think Charlie knows this yet." It was Kayrin my unit Nurse.

"How can he be deported? He's Canadian."

"Some new documentation came in, you should read it." Kayrin goes to the back, another room where the nurses kept all files. She returns with a box filled with letters,

158

legal papers and annotated investigation notes. "Some Marshal will be coming to escort him back."

"Marshal?" I question the singular. "You mean Marshals."

"Not according to the signed permits for transfer." she adds also amazed.

"Jesus Christ, are they fucking stupid!" Incredulously I try to fathom all that's going on here. He has to have citizenship in the States! He's a multiple killer; he's violent, schizophrenic, manipulative. One person is escorting him all the way to the US? "What the Hell do they want him for? He's been here for what, 20 - 25 years?" I ask.

"Dunno..." she bends over my shoulder stacking the files in front of me. In Canada we are not privy to certain aspects of client assessment, diagnosis but here was everything in one document, nothing was censored or placed in other files for confidentiality. Apparently the US system didn't have the same confidentiality rules between inmate clients, security and Psychologists as we do. I rummage through the files quickly, picking at the documented evidence. Calming down, I begin to make sense of his family history in chronological order. All the shit he told me was beginning to have some truth to it! But, some gaps, interludes remained and relationships were vague.

So his Grandfather was a Doctor, I said to myself as I leafed through the documents. And here was that rumour of bestiality and the grandfather's statement of incest with his daughter (Charlie's mom), which he had confessed to, and later confirmed by protected witnesses and by his own documentation. He asked for a Priest on his dying bed. The Priest, whose papers were later to be found in

159

the Diocese of Los Angeles, documented this and other information. Guess the old man laughed when he saw the Father's face turn pale as a sheet on hearing his confession. While the Priest insisted the confession was genuine and soul-searching, the pessimistic detectives thought otherwise. They believed there was more to this, that Dr. Fuhr's activities continued and Dr. Fuhr's confession was just a last attempt to put an end to further investigation. There were previous crimes tied to him that were unsolved and a lot of prominent 'friends' whose history with the Doctor could be career ending or extremely embarrassing at the least. It was all contrived, as was his life.

Where did he come from? There was no lineage, no ancestors to backtrack only his legacy in this century. His earliest appearance in name comes in a New York Prep school yearbook dated June 26th 1916, three years after this, an announcement of his thesis and Doctorate in Medicine and Biology from Cambridge. A similar, maybe abbreviated name of Charles Fuhr PHD shows up in an Art exhibition catalogue in Los Angeles titled "Death of DaDa" 1923. Through the 1930's to 40's there are continued short and indulgent blurbs on him attending functions around Hollywood. Following 1947 there is nothing, not even listed as father in his daughter's marriage announcement of 1959. Charlie was born 1950 with *"no father"* stated in his American birth certificate. In our records he was born in 1963 in Canada. This was impossible because his parents were killed in 1963. Somehow, and because of this brazen mistake, Charlie vanished all that time – till now.

A whole four boxes of copied letters, official church correspondence arrived after our Psychologist at the time asked for whatever history could be accessed from the supposed family Charlie claimed he had in California. The request here in Canada inadvertently led to a trail the L.A Police had been searching for years. This was documented proof, Charlie wasn't lying just as he had maintained all along. I hurry through the evidence compiled. Shockingly in the forties, fifties and into the sixties there was a cult in L.A dedicated to the Bull, its arch leader and founder being Charlie's Grandfather, Dr. Claymont Fuhr.

They built a religion around it, this reverence to the bull, analogous to the Apis Bull Society of ancient Egypt. The Apis, the chosen Bull was a god to be venerated for his excellent kindness, virility and for his mercy towards all strangers. Apis was the most popular of the three great bull cults of ancient Egypt (the others being the bulls Mnewer and Bakha). Unlike the cults of most of the other Egyptian deities, the worship of the Apis bull continued by the Greeks and by the Romans lasting until almost 400 A.D. There were girls; adolescent virgins who were recruited then served as Queens for a decade till they were adults.

Adding to this Egyptian deity legend the Cult founders, many of whom were artists, included their fixation with the Minotaur - a beast born of woman bred by a Bull in Greek Mythology. The L.A. Cult actually recreated or staged the Legend by getting female volunteers to copulate with a bull. Staged in ceremonial splendour participants performed acts of the mythical tale. A hollow wooden cow was constructed, as in the Myth, for the honoured maiden or queen, to climb into in order to deceive and copulate with the bull. The offspring of their coupling was the monstrous Minotaur.

161

Taking the myth word for word they actually re-enacted the whole saga with special attention for the care, safety and security of the woman. The recipient or Queen of the bull's virility was held in high esteem and for the duration of her pregnancy she was given any luxury, all the opulence accorded to a Queen and any vice she may wish. Of course there was the medical, biological fact that a bull or any other animal could not sire an offspring with a human woman. The Cult Patriarch, original founder Dr. Lewis Claymont Fuhr remedied this problem. While preparing then assisting the recipient for the copulation act he would include his semen with the semen of the bull. The act was consummated, where the Master under an enforced cage that resembled a cow guided the Bull into the Queen with his small dissolvable bag of sperm. No one knew or was ally to this fact thus giving credence to the Cult's supernatural powers as offspring were born. Master Lou C. Fuhr of the Cult, had on his deathbed, recanted the previous statement of him being the 'father' and swore the fertilization of beast and woman was successful through DNA splicing. Recipients subjected to the act recall collectively and unanimously they believed in their souls they had experienced a supernatural revelation of pregnancy during the consummation. Others claim it was an unholy union and that Dr. Lewis C. Fuhr was indeed Lucifer or – the Devil. Some 200 Queens became mothers but only 12 of this number would give birth to a normal and live infant. Most others were miscarriages, Molar pregnancies and deformed fetuses with some of these living briefly in pain and torture. Charlie's mother was a volunteer, a Queen, on numerous occasions finally becoming expectant with him. Charlie's rambling, so-called delusions now made sense.

"Un-fucking-believable! The Grandfather, Charlie's Grandfather impregnates his daughter. Charlie's Dad is his Grandfather! Jesus Christ what a bunch of sick bastards!" the words escaped me as Kayrin looked on.

"I know! Sick! Just when you think you've seen it all, something like this happens – in real life." She continued in consternation, "What about the kids, the family after? God, who would want a legacy like that…."
My attention turned to Charlie on that question. How could you NOT be infected with a perverse anger at the world with this in your mind?

I got up slowly, shuffled to the doorway…stood there. I turned to go to the seclusion wing.

"What are you doing Bran?" Kayrin looks with a scowl. "Don't go there." I walk to Seg not knowing why but feel I have to. "For Christ's sake don't say anything or all Hell's going to break loose." Kayrin shrieks in a whisper.

"Don't worry." I assure her.

I continue but with no reason. Entering the dark hallway I suddenly remember a time long ago when I was 5 or 6 when we were at a fair and there was this dark alley within another huge wide tent lit by lanterns. The dull orange of the light silhouetted what was behind those canvas sheets. Stationary statues, fixed figures, some seated moved in rhythm to the stale breeze that moved the canvas walls so the shadows cast danced in unison. This was the sideshow of freaks. The similes on the wall terrified me yet I moved on spellbound to see what was on the other side of the canvas sheets.

163

Today, this walk, this hallway, was reminiscent of that night long ago where I saw things I never imagined, frightful realities of nature that had shocked me.

An uneasiness followed, the hair on my arms bristled.

CHAPTER 15

The memory disturbed me. I came to Charlie's seclusion door with its little hole for a window, expecting in my fantasy to see a Minotaur standing above me, its breath blowing the dribble from its nose. A horned Beast on human legs I imagined. I shook the apparition away, inched to the window cautiously peeking from an acute angle now too anxious to stare directly in. The anxiety turned to fright, terror when my eyes couldn't distinguish anything in the dark – nothing! I turned my body then looking full-face, nose to the pane, my eyes scanning the room – nothing! I instinctively feel for the doorknob, find it and slowly turn it. It's unlocked. 'What the fuck...' I step back. Looking around in slow motion, my senses sharpen, every nerve anticipating something. My ears burn as I hear a 'thump'. I freeze, then another thump...then another. At the far corner of the hallway still dark with no lights I hear a footstep, a shuffle. It dawns on me then, why are the lights off? I take another step back. My heart is in my throat. I swear I can smell something now, it's that close.... I feel a hot draught of air on the back of my neck.

"Bran, Bran!" a jagged whisper echoes. I jump. At the same time a soft hand grabs my arm and I smell a faint perfume. It's Kayrin.

"What the hell you doing?" I ask, mad at her for scaring the shit out of me. "He's not there Kayrin. He's gone, Charlie's gone."

"What do you mean – gone!" She looks at me scared.

"What do you mean, *what do you mean*'....he is gone, Charlie is gone! Holy shit! Better stay with me, stay behind me. Gotta call control, get the guys over here....fuck! Shit! I left my radio on the desk! You got your PPA alarm?"

"No."

"What do you mean 'no'? Fuck sake Kayrin, you're supposed to wear that all the time!"

"So where's your God Damn radio!"

"Never mind." I look around again, my eyes focusing in the dark. I back peddle to the doorway then into the security station. *We're safe!* We locked the station door then Kayrin looked to the door of the back room with the files. I knew what she was thinking as she looked at me. Tears in her eyes she asks, "Did you close that door?"

"Nooo…"

"Oh God, we're locked in with him…"

I grabbed the two-way radio on my desk, turned up the volume and whispered in, "Security needed, Code 55 in Churchill." Code 55 was a "Missing" person emergency bulletin used only if you thought there was an escape, possible hostage taking or abduction. I repeated this three times looking 360 degrees, both of us backed to the locked security door away from the backroom where we thought Charlie was hiding. I reach down, took the ring of keys from my belt fingering for the right key to this door. It took an eternity as I fumbled for the correct key out of the16 huge brass keys dangling there like Gypsy baubles. *Found it!* I quietly inserted the key twisting it slowly and deliberately as the dead bolt retreated into it's housing. It unlocked with a soft 'clink,' both of us turning our head to the Nurses backroom door, still closed. I opened our door, closing then locking it again from outside the station. At the same time Security comes crashing in, five of them with shields, Mace and batons. No firearms because of the potential catastrophic results, only ERT (Emergency Response Team) had the authority to use them and they were

166

probably on their way now. On a Code 55 every emergency resource responds automatically unless they are 'called off' by our Control Station. We point to the filing room. They surround it; kick it open – nothing there! The Keeper comes in, motioning me over. I give him a quick de-briefing and he gathers the squad together. Seclusion, segregation wing is searched along with all closets, crafts room, the makeshift painting studio and music room. All items are checked off to make sure he hasn't got a weapon. Willie is questioned but he's confused as to what was transpiring.

All doors are checked and locked again with the wing now inaccessible. The squad moves into the actual 'patient' Dayroom unit with an individual room check. All are accounted for except Charlie's cell, which is empty, as it should be since he was in his Seclusion cell. When he goes to Seg, security locks up his room in the unit till he returns from seclusion. Nothing! All inmates are rustled from their beds and made to sit on the floor, as their cells are searched one-by-one, thinking maybe he had bunked with someone. His room is opened and they look hurriedly, nervously under the bed. Now I can see that everyone is alarmed, an anxiety pervades the room. The ERT arrives and set up operations essentially taking command of everything including communications. Kayrin and I are questioned, interrogated again, this time aggressively. A bulletin is issued to the Police, RCMP, news media along with the required corrections authorities and FPC staff who were present on the previous shift. All units without exception are searched and locked down; the whole institution is shut down while all areas such as the cafeteria, laundry, A&D, Visits and even admin offices outside the walls are searched, then stripped of any possible hiding spots. As the sun

167

rises, the center with its staff and inmates are in turmoil. Nothing! Incredible, shocking, disbelief as the teams are made to search again. This Institution was deemed inescapable; many had tried but didn't even come close according to our officials. We knew better. Now approaching 8 in the evening with all possibilities exhausted, the Warden decides to feed the population before they riot, which was a definite probability. All inmates in all units had been given crackers, cheese and milk put together by the nurses, the kitchen and cafeteria staff had long ago departed. The order was issued with subsequent staff called in to make the meals. Extra security was brought in on overtime to deliver impromptu meals to each cell individually. My station, Churchill and *Seg* was the last unit to be fed.

The guards, two at a time, along with a nurse, opened and closed each cell. After the allowed 15 minutes, the trays and emergency issued spoons were retrieved, the 'Meds' were handed to each as all in Churchill were prescribed drugs to maintain or contain them. The staff on overtime was not familiar with Churchill, but they went about their duties as ordered, cell-to-cell. I had decided to stay in Churchill when not being interrogated. Arriving at cell #196, they unconsciously unlocked it. I was watching from within the station, wondering why they were opening Charlie's vacated cell when I see the nurse drop her tray of Meds as the door opened. The three of them retreated, synchronized step by step, their eyes fixed on something. All Hell breaks loose; the ERT also witnessing this, rush in pushing aside the staff. They stop too, jaws dropping. Regaining his composure the Leader barks some indistinguishable commands as they swoop in. In less than five minutes that felt like one hour, they came out clamouring around somebody in a

168

body belt with shackles to his feet. They whisked him past the station and I saw it was Charlie. "How in the Hell…" I started to say when he side glanced at me - and smiled.

He was interrogated along with the 30 or so of us over the next two weeks. They locked him in on a 24-hour order and removed everything from his pillow to his toilet paper. With a full investigation now required, we were instructed to report in triple file everything that transpired, as did those staff on overtime that were there for the duration. I completed my report that took me another 2 hours and included about 10 pages of information pertinent to the case. I completed another round of questions then was released pending more queries as needed, warning that I was to be silent.

The exhilaration, excitement and anxiety drained from me. In a second, I was wasted, weak with exhaustion. The clock said 11 pm so I had been awake for over 24 hours. I had to be back here at 5 in the morning to meet the Deputy Commissioner so I decided to stay. Although dog-tired, I couldn't sleep, the adrenalin still pounding my heart. Don, my Keeper, told me to wait in the Officer's mess "Sleep if you can, I'll wake you when the DC gets here." I nod my head but knew I couldn't sleep. I sat there in the mess watching the news special as they broadcast the 'escape' of a serial killer and successful recapture. Everyone could sleep at ease now. The event unfolded in my mind as I listened to the news report. Thank God he didn't escape, I thought out loud, "…but where did he go? I looked into his room, the squad looked and the ERT did too – twice!" I whispered to myself, barely audible in the quiet secluded room. Nothing made sense as my thoughts became

169

disorganized, slow, and lazy with fatigue. I didn't want to think anymore.

"You know my Mother never sang me a lullaby?"
I jump, spinning my head to the voice.
"Yeah, you know that Sam?"

Charlie asks, smiling, standing naked. I notice a blue color to his body, a drab lifeless blue like he was dead. I leap from the couch looking around me for familiarity, reality, then I look to him again - he was gone! I ran to Control, banging on the door. They open, angry at my loud intrusion but I push in anyway going to the surveillance cameras that monitor the seclusion cells.
There he was, sitting naked in his cell, "He's there… he's still there." I repeat softly.
"Yeeeah?" someone questions my reason. "He's not going anyplace now."

I started to shake then. The Keeper was called along with a nurse and after a short talk she gave me a tranquilizer that helped immensely. Pretty soon I was feeling normal again, if you can call it that. I assumed with the Keeper's coaching, that I briefly fell asleep and had what they call a lucid dream, a dream between REM and being awake. I could sense from Don that he was beginning to question my mental state; I didn't blame him, this was the second time I had claimed there had been an 'unnatural' incident. The picture of Charlie not being there, his absence, the cell being empty, kept replaying like a premonition. An old saying from my youth resounded again, *"You can lock up the Devil but you can never hold him."* I met the Commissioner in the morning, retold the incident, but contrary to normal procedure and stated misgivings from our Warden, the Commissioner asked

170

for my input, my opinion. I related to some issues but asked if I could think about it and get back to him after some rest. He obliged, telling me to write them down. I went home, told my wife nothing, then crawled into a nice comforting bed. My eyes closed but for a while I was conscious. *"Something is not right."* I drift off, the sub-conscious cautions, *"Something is missing."*

As the investigation revealed, it was determined that Charlie had been transferred to his home cell by the day shift immediately after the documents and the Official Order for Deportation arrived at our unit station. This Order and debate on how to deal with it coupled with the newfound archival documentation *'created a connection of activities that resulted in a conundrum,'* as the investigative panel put it. What they meant was everybody fucked up because they *'didn't do what they were supposed to do when they were supposed to'* as we put it.

When he was moved from Seg to his home cell, the move was not recorded or logged for the next shift nor was it relayed to Control; subsequently, Charlie goes missing from Seclusion. When Control staff changed over and no communication shared, the next shift paid little attention to the seclusion cameras that recorded it as being vacant - until I had sounded the alarm. With no quick debriefing, the new shift figured Charlie's seclusion cell was vacant because he was in his homeroom inside Churchill Unit. There are no cameras in the individual homeroom cells.

But still there is the fact that the squad, the ERT and I searched Charlie's cell. There is no place to hide in these 8x12 foot cells.

A few of the guards are getting spooked, especially the ones who actually did search the room. Consequent to

171

the newly discovered history of Charlie and family, the rumours start to circulate that there is a supernatural element at play here. You wouldn't think educated people, well-informed staff would believe in such superstition or black magic.

Roots run deep as do still waters, those dark whispers we heard as a child still ring in our ears.

For the next 2 weeks, the investigation consumed everyone, officials came from Ottawa bringing their experts, the voracious media was updated, pacified with a communications expert handling the Press. An engineer was brought in to review any and all old blueprints. The whole institution staff and inmates were pissed off with Charlie since, in effect all activities and programs were curtailed or postponed. He didn't give a shit though. He enjoyed the commotion and attention as they tried in vain to find out how he escaped detection in our cell-search. He wasn't talking. At the end of it all the officials determined it was us who were at blame deducting, to which I painfully agreed, that he had to have been in his cell all along. There was no other conclusion. But with a whole myriad of staff; nurses, security, ERT in question they put it down as 'systemic' in procedure. No one was fired or suspended, instead we all underwent a review and awareness of security, log entry and reporting. Others looked at it with suspicion and all wanted Charlie out on the next transfer. His Order for Deportation to the US was put on hold for a couple months while the institution returned to 'normal'. During this short interlude, we found out there had been another pair "skinned" in Montana years ago and through intelligence sharing via the government's new electronic mail, it was discovered that Charlie had connections to this case. His

172

grandfather, as stated, had been there briefly so this coupled with the unique similarity of the crime, Charlie's signature or *modus operandi*, meant he could be involved. Or, maybe, he had copied from the original – the Master.

One positive result came of this episode and that it was deemed crucial that two people would escort Charlie in transfer, the FPC and Corrections Canada would not release him until this demand was met.

Chapter 16

The two months waiting for deportation became a flurry of activity, with many incidents arising from this one episode. The increased activities resulting from this also spiralled the Churchill residents into a frenzy. Seg wing and the seclusion cells were taken over by Charlie's resident colleagues. By month's end every inmate in Churchill, Charlie's 'den', had spun out and been placed in seclusion cells. Charlie and Willie, subsequently, were sent to their unit home cells while we dealt with the influx of admittances to Seg, but having Charles in the dayroom also had a negative effect particularly now with his reputed and newly affirmed powers.

During this period there was an unusual amount of outbreaks or disturbances. One particular inmate, *Abe,* feared Charlie with a passion envisioning him in awe as the vengeful angel, Michael. We called him Abe, short for Abraham, which was his real name. Abraham had killed two Nuns after fantasizing about them for two years. He knew them from his community Church groups where they organized and kept a shelter for the poor. Abe was a recipient of their benevolence and returned the favour by raping then killing them.

He called his hands the 'hands of the Devil'. He had torn up most of his right forearm methodically with his teeth and now had begun on his left. Every time he masturbated he would proceed to punish himself by tearing away the forearm muscles of his arm to the extent that his bone would show, all done in guilt with self-retribution. Having not much left on this arm to chew on, he now concentrated on the left arm. It was

174

getting so bad we had to straightjacket him so he couldn't do more damage.

I asked him once in the many times of his reckoning, "Why don't you just quit jerking-off?" He didn't say anything for the longest time. I thought this trite little statement had slapped him into some mode of normalcy when, to my disgust, I came upon him again with fresh bandages covering most of his forearm.

"What the Hell did you do Abe?" I asked in a huff.

He looked at the floor, "I didn't really do it you know....jerk-off?"

"So why the bandages?"

"I thought about it," he said softly.

"What! Jesus Christ, Abe, all you have to do now is think about it and you're guilty?"

"Well yeah, Bible says even if you think about it then you're sinning. Thinking is like doing the real thing Boss. I read it. Charlie told me what I was thinking when he was in the dayroom." It seemed Charlie was at play here. He enjoyed upsetting the unit sanctum and what better way than to instil guilt and paranoia.

"Christ Abe, everyone here knows what you're thinking. That's all you think about is women and whacking-off."

I looked at him for a long time and the realization came that no matter what I said or did, it was fruitless. I raised my arms up in defeat, walked away shaking my head then a thought came to me. "When did he tell you this Abe?"

"When all you guys were looking for him."

Another inmate we called Ben sought to fix his personal problem at this time too. For years he had been bi-polar suffering the extremes of depression accompanied with delusions and hearing voices. I had escorted him many times to the "room" as everyone called it with fear in their tone. He would undergo ECT or electro convulsive

175

therapy by way of a cheap looking gizmo they hooked to his head by means of a pair of headphone looking 'things' attached on a huge clamp. The doctor would place this arcane instrument onto his temples, then a wad of rubber encased in gauze was stuffed into his mouth. There were two dials; one for power, the other for duration. Ben knew the routine, never putting up a fight, always calmly positioning his self the way they needed. Then the doctor and the security present, no nurse, would flip the switch. Ben would straighten like a two-by-four board, moaning, "uhmmmm…" that slowly died out, then his body seized into a pretzel. His limbs came up; bent at unnatural angles then froze in that contortion like it was −40 below. For a minute or two he was a solid piece of stone, resembling those gargoyles on church cathedrals hunched on the precipitous balconies, a blank lifeless stare in his eyes. Soon the muscles eased, his body slowly relaxed to a normal state. We would wheel him to his cell, help him onto his bed and he would sleep for hours, his body exhausted. Once awake, he was always 'chipper', upbeat, never remembering the pain but then ultimately as always, he relapsed. He began to hate the routine knowing the eventual outcome so one evening he concocted this idea of self-treatment. Inspired by no less than Wile E. Coyote whom he had been watching, he set forth his *'no-return Acme guaranteed'* therapeutic regimen.

We were in the nursing station and it was an exceptionally boring day. The Nurse noticed Ben in his odd activity through the last hour, which was unusual in manner because Ben was usually not doing anything. "Ben is up to something. He's not his normal self today." Normal… meaning abnormal for Ben. In his normal abnormal condition, he was for the most part in

176

his dark room conversing to no one there, if not screaming at staff. I nodded not really listening.

Suddenly there was huge *"CRACK!"* The walls thundered so loud it shook our station. We stood, immediately glancing about for a clue of what just happened. One of the inmates in the dayroom pointed to an area in the far corner. Behind and under the day room table was someone lying motionless, a waft of smoke rising from his head. I rushed in while everyone skedaddled to the cells, choreographed in precise movement and timing, you would think we had practiced this. Skidding to a stop I saw who it was, it was Ben. I could see the smoke rising from his frizzled hair, the black powder around his mouth.

I thought, '*Christ, he shot himself…where is the gun?*' His hand out of sight I stepped on his right arm jutting out from under his midsection, thinking he had the gun there. Kneeling, I felt his neck for a pulse - there was one. There was no evidence of blood so I turned him over, cautiously pulling his arm out at the same time. No gun, no blood. The smoke was still drifting off his head and his eyes were bulging out bloodshot, blinking rapidly with pinpricks for pupils.

"Ben! Are you alright, can you hear me?" I shouted into his face.
By this time other security and nurses had arrived, apparently it was not just us that heard the racket. Ben's mouth was open, his black tongue hanging to the side.
Another nurse opened his mouth wider pushing in a depressor, "He's burned! She exclaimed, "He has burns all over inside!"

177

Placing the oxygen over his mouth so he could breathe, they lifted and carried him to a stretcher then wheeled him off to the infirmary. Bob was the first to observe long black marks of smoke on the wall close to Ben's cell. A little more scrutiny produced the culprit, a pair of slender aluminium rods melted out of shape. The black smudge on the wall was where the electrical outlet was located. He had taken his radio and broken off the antenna into two rods that he placed in his mouth. Next he crawled to the outlet, antenna in mouth and through patience and trial he finally got the rods into the receiving socket. During this time there were two inmates sitting, watching the whole show clueless of Ben's intention, until the thunder and lightning struck with Ben flying back across the floor, the two observers scrambling to their cells. That's when we came in.

The next week he was back. You couldn't believe the change. Although his tongue was still slightly swollen, his speech was clear in its content and semantics; he made sense.
"So how's it going Ben? I asked amazed he was alive. I expected upon learning the cause of his accident he would be brain dead…or just dead. I imagined his brain frying like an egg on a hot skillet.

"Fine," he says, "…fine. Couldn't be better, never felt this good since I was a teenager. Charlie said I would be better someday."

Murray and Bob joked with him and he retaliated with wit and humour. He surprised everybody in his conversation, reason and ability to sustain a long conversation with no meandering. Within the next month Ben would be released, a free man and one of the very few to walk away and resume a 'normal' life. But then he was never an inmate, was never charged under any law and was there because the psych wing at the Hospital couldn't handle his outbursts. Ben was admitted due to extenuating circumstances...the Hospital and staff didn't want him. So after pre-scheduled tests for such rare admittances were given and passed he was released. He never came back.

These events were just two of a long list of unforgettable occurrences we called the 'Churchill Bazaar', a tweak on bizarre. There was the now regular, routine 'slamming-of-his-dick-in-the-drawer' Bart who had learned from our impatient supervisor, Big Bill, on how to administer the worst pains to his self. Bill, as noted prior, didn't have the tolerance in extending negotiations or mediations with inmates; he was becoming wearisome on diplomacy. We all were, at this period, not abundant in *'positive patient relations'* as the institutional bureaucrats wanted.

There was Dennis who murdered his teacher in his graduating year of 1982 and kept the body in the trunk of his 1968 Mustang for months. Only after blowing out a tire and opening the trunk for the spare tire did one of his few friends discover the body still wrapped in the original 3 bags of plastic Dennis had used to hide the smell. . In his violent hatred for authority, any kind of authority he had a particular distaste to those who interviewed him. He initiated two attacks on our Psychologist and Psychiatrist leaving an imprint of his teeth on both of their arms. Lately, he also had developed a fondness for ears, probably learned from the connoisseur who mangled the Doc's ear – the Van Gogh incident.

179

There were the "Boner Boys", a dangerous pair of sex killers. From their behaviour, character and thinking you would never think them as dangerous and volatile. For want of a better name to describe them I called them the 'Boner Boys' after a memorable occasion of my adolescent years. Giving the duo a name, a name based on personal humour sounds macabre, maybe disjointed but bestowing comical names to our clientele was typical of our dark side. It was also a means of NOT giving them a respectable name, they didn't deserve it – yet.

These guys took special interest in showing off their 'instruments, organs, rods' to the nurses. They seemed to have perpetual 'hard-ons' (maybe symptoms of medications) and shared the intricacies on how to achieve desired results and long-lasting memories for after-hours entertainment. They knew from experience the best effects came from those not cognizant of their habits but those who were green or 'virginal' provided the best results. They got their 'kicks' from the shock of the spectators. Many temporary or practicum nurses were fodder for deviant displays of sexual fantasy. A person can't list the endless acts recorded, many funny, some stupid and others just plain sickening. They were in Churchill since the sex offender unit expelled them because of the disruption they brought to that wing and were deemed untreatable.

Then there was the escape artist Marvin a.k.a. '*Whodunit*', so-named after the smarter Houdini. He had prosthesis, a fake leg, but we never let him have it. It was the weapon he had used to kill his wife in an argument over a dinner of cabbage rolls. He had beaten her unconscious then stuffed the leg down her throat .In an

180

attempt to escape Marvin had made it to the second fence where the Patrol Guard had shot off his 'dummy' leg with a shotgun blast not 8 feet away while he dangled atop of the fence shaking in shock as the electricity coursed through him. The leg had gone flying like it had wings.

Whodunit was always searching for not-so-ingenious ways to thwart the officials, mainly in escape attempts or fashioning weapons from available materials. In his repertoire of gadgets were shanks made of woven burned straws, tooth brushes, sharpened shoe arches, dried branches, chicken/beef bones...and so on, some actually dangerous. Prior to Charlie's disappearance *Whodunit* had attempted an escape by painting his own body so that he resembled an officer. We had a temporary studio, a hobby room with all the paints where they could, during 'activity hours', paint whatever they wished. It could have been successful, but he was a terrible artist not to mention that everyone knew his face and body (naked or clothed) – and he had that one leg missing. The colors didn't match, he had the wrong symbols on, had a painted on cap that looked ridiculous and was skinny, bent over with that one leg missing. Coming out of the studio it didn't take long for security to notice him whereupon he was promptly escorted to seclusion. No mention was made of this; it was just another stupid episode that happened, not worth the time and ink to report on. What this obscure forgettable incident did do was make security and other personnel more laid back, blasé in regards to escape attempts, nothing to worry about. Following Charlie's brief disappearance *"Whodunit"* visited the Medical Doctor that same week mentioning to him, "I saw Charlie in the dayroom when he was missing." The Doc wrote the statement down in his log but never relayed it to anyone. It didn't sound important.

To add to the turmoil, we had another artist, *Paris*, pronounced *Pa-ree* who utilized unique media to express himself. He had been a Psychologist turned self-proclaimed Pastor who killed his wife and two kids. He had received word from God to kill his 'sinners' and dispose of them by cutting them up into pieces and throwing the remains into the McKenzie River of B.C. close to where Charlie had lived.

Mimicking the Dada movement of the 40's, Paris used his own excrement, body waste, toenails and blood to visualize his emotions. Why was there such a preoccupation with Art amongst the crazy? He was quite proficient during this Bazaar so we called it the "brown period" of his artistic career. This was the most loathsome activity at that time with many guards phoning in sick if they heard they were stationed to Churchill on the roster. When Paris was into his work, you could smell it a mile away down the hallways…nobody came around. We, or whoever had the misfortune to be there on Midnights when maintenance staff and janitors were not present, had to move him to seclusion then clean the mess on his walls with hose, water then disinfectant. If this was not done soon enough, we would have inmates waking up, complaining of the smell then we would have the whole unit banging and kicking their doors. Mr *Paris* frequented many a beating from his resident patrons especially Charlie, critiques that we did not interrupt. His exhibitions became less frequent.

These incidents, the people who did them, I recollect with a touch of humour to save my sanity, conversely, there would be nobody laughing if any escaped. Most will kill on an impulse and not even think about it or be conscious or remorseful of it. We perceived these events, occasions and the perpetrators as amusing when we had it under control but we knew they could be in an instant, unimaginably horrific if they had the chance and choice to do what they wished.

There was a fear palatable in the unit and so many incidents occurring when Charlie was 'home' in the wing that it was decided, following some threats of rioting from other 'homey' inmates, he would be placed temporarily into his seclusion cell to ease the atmosphere. This was fine with Charlie.

CHAPTER 17

This week I was on Midnights again, no problem because *Paris* had been on a hiatus from his "brown series" – thank God. Finishing the count, doling out the prescribed meds, I ventured to segregation where I knew Willie and Charlie were waiting in their seclusion cells for the accustomed talk, a kind of debriefing on their part that could illicit a lot more information than we received from the Directors and Warden. Get it *straight from the horse's mouth* we would say.

"So...Charlie?" I glared at him, "How did you do it?"

"Disappear you mean?" he asks with a smirk.

"Yeah! Do you know how much shit, how much work you caused? For everybody!"

"Yeah, sorry about that Boss. I didn't mean for it to get that serious...or go on that long."

A few awkward moments pass as I wait for a 'scoop' that would explain everything. Something that will absolve me in this farce and put me in a better light; many thought I was to blame partly for the confusion but investigation clearly showed I was just the 'messenger' in the midst of a communication breakdown. Records show all I did was report the fact that inmate Charles "Charlie" Fuhr was missing.

Willie retorts in self-defence, "Well don't ask me nothing Boss. I don't know nothing!"

"And I didn't do anything but stay in my room Sam." Charlie remarks with a smile.

"There were probably 15 people that looked into your room Charlie...and none saw you there!" my voice a little too loud as Charlie shushed me. "Don't shush me...and quit calling me Sam!"

"It is your nickname, isn't' it? Your friends call you Sam"

"We are not friends Charlie!" I saw a hurt in his eyes then as he turned his head away. Another minute or two drags on like an eternity as I wonder what to say next. I didn't want to be on 'bad terms' with him or anyone else. Things inside here were bad enough for both sides so we acknowledged (in silence) a Treaty of sorts and an unmentioned code of respect. Besides, my discussions with these two had offered invaluable material that had prevented assaults, hostages and probably saved a life or two. "Okay, I shouldn't have said that but be realistic Charlie, we are not friends. Not in the sense as friends on the outside. Okay? We can never be real friends…you know that Charlie." This seemed to ease his ego.

"Yeeeah, I know." he says softly, "but we can be friendly."

"Right, exactly."

"So then be friendly. Why are you shouting at me?" He asks with a scowl.

"Okay, yeah, you're right Charlie. Sorry. I shouldn't be biting your head off." A smile crosses his eyes for a second as I apologise. He takes his eyes away from the dark corner he was staring at.

"All I can say – Boss," he stops in mid-sentence to emphasize his cooperation, "is I saw it all. I saw everything going down when they were looking for me and I was there…well, in mind anyway."

"That's impossible. I looked for you myself."

"Well you guys didn't look hard enough. What can I say for you to believe me?

"Tell me who was there looking." I had him.

"What will you give me in return Boss?

"Nothing! And you know I won't and you know I can't, Charlie."

185

"You know…you can call me by any name and I can't do anything about it. Right?" he nods to me.

"Right, if I want to be nasty I guess I can call you whatever I want."

"Well, here's a little innocent favour I ask for if I tell you who was there. All I want is to call you Sam with you not getting all worked up about it. Okay? It's no big deal…we have a deal?"

I thought this over from all angles and couldn't see the harm and I was sincere about being sorry. But the real issue that bothered me was the fact he knew my nickname. So as an afterthought I added. "Okay Charlie, but I also want to know HOW you know my name? If you answer that and who was there I will let you call me Sam. How's that for a deal?" I was sure he could not answer.

"Okaaay, let's see." He proceeds to list off all who were there in his cell in the three days including the ERT, the Directors and Police. He does this without hesitation while my mind races to comprehend how he would know. The fact he does know all this confidential evidence and procedure starts to scare me. I take a step backward while he observes my shock. "Hey Boss, it's alright, no big deal…didn't mean to scare you."

"You can't know those things, you can't know everything that happened." I tell him hoping he can explain. I'm anxious in my disbelief but I restrain any posture or emotion that will tell him.

"No, seriously Sam, oops…sorry." he covers his mouth after calling my name, "Really though, I didn't mean to scare you. Here's the trick. Look, I had how many weeks to find out who was there. Even people who were there that you didn't know about, I can name because I got them from my cellmates, the nurses and the Doctors. Over the days I listen, ask questions, watch. Ha! I even use reverse-psychology on the Psychologists so that they divulge information and not even know it."

"Really?" I was incredulous, unsure if this was possible, if a person can gather that much info isolated in an 8x12 foot cell. No direct contact, no access to physical material and no secret spy tools to identify and assemble all this information?

"Of course – really! Do you think I'm some sort of magician or shaman who can shape-shift or disappear? Boss, I have been in here how many years and what do I do? I look and watch and listen…and pretty damn good at it by now."

I thought about it, it made sense as he put it in words and in context. It was also what I wanted to hear. This eased my incredulity, calmed that crawling fear that slid up my spine as I questioned what was real… and the aftermath of another reality.

"Okay, that's pretty good Charlie, very observant. You should have been an artist." I smiled.

"I was... a long time ago." he smiled back.

"With that said, how do you know my nickname Charlie?"

"You don't know, you don't remember?"

"Nooo, I don't remember. I got a good memory and you are not in it Charlie."

"Call me Charles…and do you recall a night sometime in 1963…64?"

"No." I interrupt; this was beginning to bother me. "Get on with it."

"Campbell used to love my playing the violin, the fiddle. Remember Campbell; he had lost his son under the ice? His son used to play too – he had a gift. And the Syds? I loved their stories, man."

These were long lost memories he was drawing up. How did he know them? That feeling of something creepy crawling up my spine started to come again. This was downright disturbing. "How can you know about them?" I shouted.

He placed his long index finger to his lips to quiet me, "Think. Think back. There was a dance. You and Kelly watched a couple screwing in the back seat."
That statement panicked me. This was beyond 'real' with no reason. Instantly my heart began pounding in my ears. *No one knows this!* I screamed inside myself. I felt like someone who had just been photographed masturbating. I was ashamed, mad, powerless and impotent all simultaneously.

He realizes I am about to walk away. He raises his hands pleading to let him finish, "Let me finish Boss, let me finish. I'll explain."

"Do it then!" I am holding the tremble in my voice. The fear subsides momentarily as he offers an explanation. He raises his boney finger again to his mouth, his smoke-yellowed nail touching the tip of his nose.

"Boss, I was there…I was the guest fiddle player with Smiling Johnny at that dance. Remember? Syd called me

188

the nephew of Johnny? I was on stage when a fight broke out and somehow I got pushed onto the floor where I got knocked down."

In an instant it all came back and I could see him there on stage playing the Ranger's Waltz with that violin moaning. Then another snippet came to me. As he went down close to me I recall someone calling out Charles. "Charles" I repeat in a whisper.
"Yeah, right. I was Charles...Charles on the floor." He laughed as he repeated me. "I had been watching you. You know why?

"Why?"

"Well you were the only white face in the whole crowd. I wanted to talk to you, get to know you...why you were there, what was your story. That was the reason why I walked out when you did, to see if I could talk to you, be friends. Then you two snuck over to some bushes calling each by name as you walked. I followed and that's when you guys looked into the car."

It was all there now. I could see it like it was yesterday. Faintly in the background the band was audible while we intruded on an intimate moment. I reflect on that moment realizing it wasn't that bad. We never bragged or made fun of that incident but kept it to ourselves as something cherished, a secret knowledge to be unveiled, as we became men. The emotions faded and a weight lifted off my shoulders.

"You got to be kidding! That was you...on the floor?" I smiled to myself referring to the scene of him falling.

Then it occurred to me, "Wait…what the Hell were you doing there? Your home town was in British Columbia?"

"One of many places Boss when I was on-the-run from Gramps and my parents. We also lived in California, Utah, Nevada and Montana."
"Montana! You lived in Montana? Where?"
"Shelby for one, then Great Falls." He has this big smile like a kid sharing a secret.
"SHELBY! Whoa, stop Charlie. This is getting too close for comfort." I feel that anxiety coming again, crawling. "I don't know if I believe you. There is nothing in the files that says you were anyplace but B.C. Are you playing me?"
"No, honest Boss. What's with Montana…and Shelby? Why does that bother you?"
"I lived in Shelby. That was my home before we moved back to Canada."

"Hoooly Shit! That is weird, huh? There is no way I would know that, just a whopping coincidence. Nobody here knows that about you."
"What do you mean by that?"
"I've asked a lot of questions about you since you came. I figured I remembered you so I asked around. I was curious plus what else am I going to do here for 23 hours?" He looked wounded that I continued to question his integrity. "Everyone thinks your only home was the Reserve."
"Yeah, okay, I get you. What years were you in Shelby?"
"I'm not sure, maybe '60'…. or '61'. We were there for only one year…I think. I was in Bitteroot School. How about you, huh? What school?"

"Bitteroot! Jesus Christ Charlie! That was my school too! What the fuck is going on here?" I ask out loud to myself.

"Well I don't recall you in any of my classes and I can't see your face back then but we would look different, really different I would think. Oooh man this is just fucked up!" he exclaimed with his mouth open, eyes twinkling.
I wasn't that amused, thinking this fantastic coincidence was compromising. "Listen, this is not funny and I don't like it. I want you to shut up about this Charlie."

"Hey, Mum's the word, Boss." he motions to zip his mouth. "Can I call you by your nickname now Boss? It was a deal, Scout's honour you know."
"Maybe...well... yeah, I guess so." My mind was not on this issue. I was kind of in shock, not scared but just overwhelmed. As an afterthought I added, "Don't call me Sam though if other guards are around. Doesn't seem right that an inmate knows and calls me by my nickname. Know what I mean?" he nods his head. "And this Montana thing, don't mention anything to anybody...got it?" He shook his head again. "And if I find out you're fucking with me Charlie I will take away every God Damn thing you treasure!" I turned to Willie, "You too Willie..."

Before I could finish he raises his hands in surrender, "I don't know nothing Boss...and never will." which sounded like a Yogi Bera misquote.

"Sam, I'm being honest with you. There's nothing happening. We just seem to be connected. So what? I think it's kinda neat – cool."

191

Beyond my control was a term I never liked but it did seem we were connected and now did share something together, a secret. I told both I had enough conversation to last a week and needed some quiet time to digest this. I still wasn't sure about it and I felt uncomfortable with this newfound knowledge. I took it home with me that morning and told Claire about it. She didn't find it alarming or compromising; in fact she thought it was sad, profoundly sad that a classmate from some 30 years ago would be in such terrible circumstances that he must be locked up in a criminally insane asylum. It takes a woman to make a man see things in a different frame. I felt so relieved, refreshed, unencumbered after talking to my wife - as I always did.

I resolved that it was nothing to fret about, a coincidence, a connection that I was sure had and will happen to many guards. I bore in mind the incident of Sol and his sad demise within these walls; a sad and rare coincidence that nobody knew. The more I thought about it though, the circumstances that led him to be here and for me to be here seemed more than serendipitous.

The old People say we are all connected; that everything in this world is connected in a circle. The circle is harmony, infinite; break it or remove something and it becomes finite with a beginning and an end. I wondered how this applied to life in general and acquaintances in our life. I know I don't believe in Destiny. There is no mystery to Destiny or Fate, well-used words to explain everything. Words, subtlety divine, meaning someone else is directing your future that you have no freedom in your future, no choice to change what may be but imprisoned to a predetermined end.

How about Freedom, what does it mean to be Free? Free of what? Free of rules, borders, responsibility, religion, morals, values? The lyrics by Kris Kristofferson, *"Freedom is just another word for nothing left to lose."* played - I thought of Death. The bound-man of the Shaking Tent flashed before me making me think, "Maybe that's what happened or supposed to happen…a man shakes this Life, becomes free, transcends the supernatural borders then comes back with answers."

I dreamed of Shelby again.

Chapter 18

It took a while longer than the two months for the scheduled deportation. It was postponed for another two months; everything in administration remained chaotic since Charlie's escape and would be for a while longer as the investigation reports and recommendations came in. By this time Charlie knew of the transfer, seeming to be okay with it, maybe content in a lazy laid-back way.

I was on an infrequent day-shift roster. My post for that week was in the Jeep on outside patrol where I got the word to come to Admin. A relief officer came to take over or assume my duties while I was away. I came into the administration area adjacent but separate from the security parameters that surrounded the inmate living dorms. The receptionist motioned me to the executive assistant to the Warden so I walked over and stated my name.

"Okay, come right in and have a seat." she was fifty-ish with a matriarchal bun on top her head, a pale pearl necklace or whatever it was that held her glasses. She moved with short steps to her executive office chair and sat, saying nothing else. I felt uncomfortable waiting, wilting under her gaze.

Finally the Warden's door opens and he asks me in, standing there with a stilted military posture looking to be taller than his five and a half foot frame he stood ramrod straight. He was slender, shallow in his chest with narrow shoulders. I see him as a timid postal worker. His facial features all point forward as if they were pulled and the shirt he is wearing seems to be choking him. He seats himself, his face pink with pressure from his too tight collar.

"I hear from the Keepers that you know Charlie Fuhr well and are keen on his psychological demeanour, his profile if you will."

"Yes, I have been with him on unit for quite a few years."

"So you think then, you are knowledgeable in his actions, his attitude, or any habit or bearing he manifests prior to his outbursts, or any planned misdeeds he may embark on?"

"I think so."

"Mr Fuhr, as you know, is a considerable risk, one who must be secure at all times, all times, no illusion to his violence, his impulsivity, the seriousness, the absolute resolve we must adhere to in his secure deportation." the Warden continues on in his staccato way repeating the importance of this escort when it occurs to me. He was determining if I was to be the Canadian contingent to officially transfer Charlie over to the U.S. authorities. I mulled over this as the Warden droned on and on. I wasn't too sure if I wanted to do this.

"Well what do you think?" he ends his little speech and I wonder if I missed anything.

"Aaah...I'm not sure Warden..."

"Call me Wilbur," he orders in a baritone belying his physical stature. I kept expecting a squeak.

"Okaaay ...Wilbur."

"Questions, you have questions, good, that is good, can't ask too many questions, can't assume normal procedure in this escort."

"Yes, exactly," I lied. "What is the process?"

"You will follow this to the letter, don't deviate, don't let your defence down, don't assume a natural progression in the process, be consciously aware, constantly."

I assure him that I would. He takes out a manifold of documents and Commissioner Directives I must follow, sign and hand over. The route and destination are in detail. A private RCMP security plane is to be dispatched for this escort along with passports and the firearms. The Marshal for the noted district will be forthcoming to FPC for debriefing on our procedure and a psych profile on Charlie. "He will be here within the week. I want you to meet him, get acquainted, have dinner, and meet your colleagues in Churchill unit. He is a veteran, been a Marshal for 10 years, in Police service for 8. His name is Peter Douglass," he signals two 'S's' with his fingers at the end of the name scrutinizing the docket before him, looking closer, "Peter Douglass Klin,"

I shout, "**Peter Douglass Klin!**"
"What?" The Warden jumps at my exclamation.
"Sorry Sir. Can you repeat that name please?"
"Klin, Mr. Peter Douglass Klin."
"You gotta be kidding. Holy Shit! I know this guy!" I laughed apologising, "Pardon my French, Warden." meaning my expletive. His eyes narrowed.
"We will not in any way refer to the French, or their language, in a derogative manner."
"Yes Sir, Warden…I mean Wilbur, Sir."
"This is convenient that you know him, nice, good for relations, great for communication. Use that, use it for your benefit and take these documents, study them. " He pushes the pile to me with a photo, an official I.D. photograph of Peter…my old friend "Pug".
I scanned the picture. Yes, it was Peter, my long-lost friend, Pug.

I walked out on cloud nine barely aware of my feet moving. I couldn't believe it. A whole lifetime has gone

196

by and we finally get to meet again. I wondered if he would know me, if he remembered me and if he even cared about meeting me after so many years. *He's got his own life* I reminded myself, *and probably family, other friends...*" It didn't matter. I still thought of him as a friend and would remain so even if he didn't reciprocate the feeling. At the very least we can rehash old memories, brush up on who is who and where they might be. I never forgot anybody there, but my life, my circumstances were different when I moved away from the place I called home and the friends there. They, on the other hand had their life there in Shelby; home never changed for them and they kept their circle of friends. It still didn't matter; *Que Sera Sera* - whatever will be will be.

Coming to the exit I met Murray. "Hey," he asks, "What the Hell you smiling about?"

"Me? I met the Warden and he told me I could call him Wilbur!"

He laughs, "That's not what I call him. Serious though, what's up?"

"I am going on a trip...to Montana, my old home."

"Really. What do you mean home?"

I explain briefly there in the lobby ending with details on the planned escort. He had a concerned scowl on his face, "Are you sure you really want to do this Bran? This is Charlie you're gonna escort, not some delinquent punk doing time for break-and-enter?"

"Yeah. I really did think it over – a lot."

"I think you should think about it more Bran. This guy is dangerous, very dangerous."

"I know. I looked at everything, even talked to Claire about it. There will be two of us accompanied by RCMP in a private plane and when we land a security bus will meet us."

"Okay, guess I'm not gonna change your mind, eh?

"Nope. I gotta do this Murray, it's like going home. I always wanted to go back but I was scared at what I would find...or not find, so I always had excuses not to go. It was better, more comfortable to stay in this world."

"In this world? For fuck's sake Bran, you're starting to sound like these guys." He waves his hand around in a circle. "You sound institutionalised, like you're in prison." He smiles at his remark knowing the irony.

"Maybe I am. Maybe we all make our own little jails. Besides, what's the difference Murray, between them and us except that we get to walk out at the end of our shift, but we still take home the shit?"

"Yeah, got that right," he looks at the floor "and we have to wait a fucking 30 years to be free. Yeah," he snickers sarcastically "Charlie will be paroled before we retire and he killed two people – at least!"

"Yeah, no shit." I mulled over my decision, "I don't know, it's something that's compelling me to go. I have procrastinated for so long, suddenly, all these things fall together. I got no more excuses Murray." We parted company, going back to our respective posts. I was excited, for the first time in years I looked forward to what was coming - and who was coming. A new roster was redone as a result of the escort and showed the following week I was on Midnights, Churchill as usual, with a note that at the end of my last shift I was instructed to meet Pug at the airport.

My days off flew by in a blink. Posted to Churchill SW again didn't bother me. For a while now I had been changing shifts to be on Midnights, I was getting tired of having too many people around. Lately I anticipated without reluctance my little talks with Charlie and Willie on the graveyard hours when everything was slow and quiet. To date all of us in that unit had been more relaxed and I definitely noticed Charlie being more open. I assumed he was eager for this break to which he confirmed on my first shift.

"Hey Sam," as he now called me, "Guess we're gonna be going on a trip, huh?"
"Looks that way Charlie, in about 10 days I think. Gonna be on your best behaviour?"
"Pfft," he pursed his lips in mockery, "No problem. Why would I fuck up a trip? Look at my record." I had and he was *clear of any incidents contrary to security* as they put it.
"Good. Looks like we're gonna be tripping together then." I was immediately aware of that inappropriate word. "Wrong word, it's going to be business, all business."
"Don't worry 'bout me Boss, don't do drugs anyway 'cept the shit they shove into me."
"So you never took drugs Charlie?"
"Nope, not even grass. Man, I was raised in a strict religious family, don't you know? Maybe it was a fucked up religious way but we were allowed nothing to corrupt or damage our bodies. Mom, Dad, Gramps, were always watching, always on the lookout and I didn't go out like the regular kids did. I wasn't allowed."
He went on and on that night, stopping only when I had to do my rounds. Willie stayed up too, silent but there, behind, as a friend sharing dark secrets only they could understand. Both had been persecuted, molested and abused in their youth. Now bound with that past and those memories, they sought solace within the physical walls of a Pen. It was more secure, even peaceful in keeping those mental images locked in within a physical prison - it was easier. The rage, always there, could also

199

be contained or controlled in these walls. This had become a home shared as brothers. They had each other and they had their 'space'.

"What about your Grandpa?" I asked at one point. I couldn't believe the tirade, the garbage that came out of Charlie's mouth. Apparently, Gramps was not your typical warm plump Grandfather we like to cuddle with in our fond recollections of childhood. From what Charlie told in vulgar description, I could picture as a boney wiry young-looking man who carried himself proud, gave an air of aristocracy and was generally smug and conceited. He didn't reveal his age in appearance or mentally, being quite sharp, witty with a sarcastic bite.

Charlie rambled on in descriptive dialogue and a picture of Dorian Gray began to form, only the face, the body was not his Grandfather but himself – Charlie. I thought *'He's describing himself'* as I looked at his face. I was going to bring this to his attention then stopped as it occurred to me this would not be wise or viewed as a compliment. He, the Grandfather had a prominent brow with dark eyes always scrutinizing those around him, especially Charlie. Always under his glare, Charlie became quite paranoid, with reason, since his Grandpa was very strict, not 'sparing the rod' in raising this young boy to an acceptable status for his planned future. His parents Rob and Rita were never there for guidance or support. His Mom, Rita, was well off, receiving a generous allowance from her Dad (Gramps) who in turn was filthy rich. Nobody ever knew where his money came from; he was wealthy before he entered Medical School, having doing so as Charlie claimed, more for the fame and prestige. The entire family and there were a number of European cousins, would come to be part of the 'Hollywood in-crowd' of the Thirties into the Sixties. His Mom was a

200

twisted puppet of old Gramps, his Dad (step dad), a stooge who from sheer boredom would beat Charlie without provocation. Charlie could take his Grandfather's abuse but from his Dad, who was not a Dad, it became personal since he wasn't part of the Family and didn't look it either.

He was as Charlie put it, "A waddle of a man, an oversized penguin with a red face, or think of a pig that can stand up. He was a piss-ant version of a human and to top it off he was a fucking lawyer...a fucking insurance lawyer. That's the only reason my Mom married him, because of orders from Gramps and for his money. Gramps, my real Dad, figured there should be a Father for me...looked better for public relations."

I asked, "You still insist that there was an incestuous relationship between your Mom and her Dad?" mindful of what he had told me a long time ago. I needed to hear this from him, although the facts, evidence and confession confirmed this. To confess and share such a secret meant I could trust him. This was not something you want other people to know, much less the inmate population and guards – or the Psychologists.
"I am not screwing you Sam. It's the truth." He looked away his eyes focusing on something not there. He startled me with his next revelation. "You know my mother never sang me a lullaby. Did you know that Sam?"
The words that had been burned into my subconscious, screamed in an echo, '*You know my Mom never sang me a lullaby*'. The same words he said when he came to me in a vision in the Officer's Mess.

201

"What?" I asked in shock. How could those same words be repeated verbatim from a ghost I had dismissed as a dream?

"True. In all my life she never sang me a lullaby…or a song, or read me a book." He gazed at me with a question, "Ever hear of that Sam?"

I was recoiling from the words, not in fear but in the sense of *Déjà vu*. I felt empathy, not trepidation, that wasn't there when he first said those words. *Am I dreaming this again?* No. This was real.

"She was never a Mother, never meant to be. She learned from her Dad and eagerly used it on me – her son. There was no hesitation, no regrets, no guilt in what she did to me. So, I waited for the right time and for the right thing to do." Charlie searched for the words. "I think I loved her…but maybe, because I wanted to. A child needs that, you desire that closeness so you do anything to please."

I was aware of this from his history file but it hurt just to hear him tell it. Out of curiosity, moreover, to stop him in his torture I asked what was in Montana. "Charlie? Why do they want you back in Montana, what's the link?"

"Oh, you don't know?" he grinned leaving his memories behind. "We killed a couple people there. Well not so much me, it was my Gramps who did everything but he made me watch. Part of a retribution thing as I remembered, vengeance for something these two did or were going to do. I was only about 9 or 10 at that time."

"You're kidding?"

"No."

"Why didn't you say this before? Why didn't you tell the U.S. authorities?"

"They never asked and I wasn't going to tell anybody. Don't forget Sam, nobody ever believed what I said – never! They said I was delusional, crazy, a lunatic…" He raised his shoulders opening his hands in surrender. "The only time FPC even thought of listening to my story was when the U.S. comes into the picture, who by the way, didn't believe me either. The sole reason I was questioned by the U.S. back then was because my folks were U.S citizens and did so for that reason, not because they suspected a connection. They never discovered we were all related, our names were different for one thing. My last name after the marriage was changed so the authorities, the cops, didn't bother to look any further. The two killings were also years apart you know. They never did tie the two together for a long time."

"Why would they tie the two together?"

"The skinning! Mine…and those in Montana were similar, the same method."

My eyes were open wide. "Two skinning? You skinned another couple in the states, in Montana?"

"Nooo…my Grandfather did, not me. Where do you think I learned it from – the skinning?"

"And he made you watch?"

"Yeah. He spouted off something about justice and loyalty and how I should know what this all meant, how I was expected to deal with it in my later years when… I was going to be the Master," he added as an afterthought. "So he took me that one night, made me wait in the car while he did his business. Afterwards with the two in the big trunk of his Cadillac we drove outside Shelby to the Marias River."

He stopped. "I need a cigarette Boss."

"What?"

"I need a cigarette."

"Jesus Christ, now?" I didn't want this break but also fearful he would stop if I refused his request. "Okay." I hurried off to find his pack.

"And bring one for Willie too!" he shouted in the hallway.

I was back in seconds with the two cigarettes. I gave each a smoke through the tray hatch used for their meals.

"Where's the light?" Charlie asks.

"What?" I ask again impatiently.

"The light, the light. We need something to light up our cigs."

"For fuck's sake!" I hurry off, back again in seconds. I light their cigarettes and keep the hatches open. Charlie takes a long long drag on his, appreciating it with a sigh as he blew out the smoke, manoeuvring his lips to weave little circles of smoke, each following the other. He paused to admire this. "Charlie!" I yelled.

"What? Oh yeah...yeeeah. He pulled them out, a young couple. There was no blood on them." his forehead creased thinking about this. "Then he placed them on the ground side by side, went to the trunk, brought out some knives. He began skinning them, peeling their skin away, showing me the proper way while he worked, mentioning the Indians and trappers' ways. He ran the knife along the sides from armpit to hip to groin. The arms were cut lengthwise from the shoulder to the wrist. The neck area was cut circular so the face was separate. The hands and feet were left 'cause they were too hard to do, *'didn't have time'* Gramps said. He knew what he was doing."

He stopped. "I wonder why there was no blood? When I did it there was blood all over the place." He shook his head, "Anyway, he taught me there, hands-on experience you might say. After all he was a Doctor. He started with one corner of the skin and pulled on it so it separated from the meat. Pulling harder, he would at the same time, put the knife into the edge where the meat and skin joined and keep cutting. The skin comes off pretty easy you know." Charlie told this like he was reading from an instruction manual. "It's the hands, feet that are hard, skin there is tough and of course more ins-and-outs to the fingers, toes. The face is not bad but you gotta go slow. So when he was finished, he strung up the skins, like you would a pelt. He put them on some branches of an old Cottonwood tree and dumped the untraceable bodies into the River."

"So how did they connect this murder to yours if nothing was found?"

"I'm not sure, guess someone took a closer look and saw the similarity, the *modus operandi* – maybe the names, the family connection."

"Not because of evidence, physical evidence like identity of the faces?"

"Oh no, they found the skins. An old Métis trapper found them dried and still in the trees but they were hard, maybe impossible at that time to identify them. They knew two people were killed and skinned but who were they – and who did it?"

"How about the faces?"

"Try to see what's left and what it looks like after a summer in the sun. Ever see dried meat…jerky?"

A frightening thought occurred to me then, "Charlie? Charlie, how old were you then?"

"Don't know…maybe 9 or 10…not sure. I stayed, lived with my Grandpa off-and-on when I was young. Why?"

"Were you going to school?"

He looked at me, disbelief coming over his face as he realized the context of the question,. "Yeah, like I said before, Bitteroot…in Shelby at that time. I remember going back to school the next day."

"Holy shit. You mean a killer coulda been sitting next to me…in the morning…in Grade 4?" I saw him different at that moment. "Fuck. Maybe you even had blood on you still."

"Hey, hey! I didn't do the skinning and I didn't kill anyone! You think I wanted to be there. I had to be there or be dead. I got no illusions what Grampa would do. Sam, you don't know the man. I swear the guy was the Devil."

"How about your Grandmother, you musta had a Grandmother?"

"Nope. He never married. I heard from Mom he chose his sister to impregnate then she disappeared. My Mom never had a Mother. All she knew was this degenerate who was called her Dad. She also said she was the only one to survive. Her Mom, also her Aunt, had numerous miscarriages before she, my Mother, was born. Did you know my Gramps was into Selective Genetics and Eugenics too?" Charlie added. He shuffled his one foot. "That could be one reason she sexually abused me. She thought or maybe was taught, that this was scientifically normal like inbreeding dogs to get what you want?"

Charlie wrestles with the idea then becomes conscious he is minimizing the act. "I don't know, I really don't give a fuck; she had to die…and her pink piggy, for doing what they did to me. I knew it was wrong!"

"Wow. That is some serious shit." I began to wonder what I would have done. I didn't think I could survive something like that. I most probably would kill myself

206

rather than to go on with that abuse and memories. *But what if I didn't know anything else?* I thought, *what if all the rules, values, beliefs were ingrained from birth?* I doubted if I could be trained, taught or corrupted enough to do it, I reassured my self.

"But you also knew that to kill them was wrong."
"Hey Boss!" Willie says behind me, "I woulda done the same fucking thing, fucking bastards! And don't tell me I wouldn't."
"No Willie, I know you would."
"We're kinda the same, me and Charlie. We both got screwed by the people who were supposed to care for us, supposed to love us. What happens when you don't plant love? You don't get Love." He put it concisely, Willie suffered in his English but he was no fool. "We did wrong but we did right. Now we share the same home, the only home we could go to."

"So Charlie, when did you decide to kill your parents?" I interrupted. The dialogue was going so good I couldn't let this go by. This may never happen again I assured myself so I pressed on.
"Don't know really. It was always there, especially after I had watched Gramps do it and it seemed so easy. He wasn't aware at the time but he gave me a tool to get outta that prison and into another. Understand? If I'm in the Penitentiary, Gramps couldn't get a hold of me; I was not accessible to him, the others and his plans. So in my revenge, I was making damn sure I got caught and put away for a long time after the old bastard died. I planned to return home to my parents and put an end to all this shit!"
"His plans, what plans?"

207

"What do you think? Gramps had always been grooming me to take over his little empire...or kingdom as he called it. There had to be a leader, a Master to continue his Bull cult and that leader would be called the Minotaur. That is why my Mom was consummated with a bull...I am the Minotaur."

"Do you believe that Charlie?"

"Of course I do. I had seen the same thing done when we moved back to Los Angeles. There are others out there but I was the chosen one, chosen by the Master. Maybe you're asking if I believe a bull sired me? No, I don't. But having your own Grandfather, as your Dad is not much less horrible. Is it?"

I nodded in agreement, not looking at him. I was beginning to see *the unforeseen circumstances* as my wife mentioned that could arise and put a man in jail for life. Some things are beyond your control, life deals you a shitty hand and all you can do is make a deal with the Devil.

"You said, *Others out there*. Where?"

"All over the place; New York, New Orleans, L.A., Seattle and even in the smaller cities, towns where there was an interest. And money was a big part too; money usually means power and protection. Each society made and accepted had its own Leader."

"So this is widespread, nationally?"

"Oh yes, internationally too but L.A. is what we called the headquarters. Headquarters, get it?" he laughs "Like head of the Minotaur?" Charlie stops, seeing I am not sharing the humour. "He was on the go, always recruiting, travelling, putting on shows." He sees my eyebrows rise at the word 'shows'. "Yeah, the old man could do some weird stuff. He could go through walls

208

and levitate, know every secret you had, and some said he could change. That's why these people with money wanted to be part of his world because money can't buy that – the supernatural."

"I don't believe this, walking through walls, shit."

"I was there Sam, I saw it. It is not a trick - I saw it. I used to go on his travels and help with the shows. There were never any gizmos or equipment used to fool the crowd." he paused briefly ending with a revelation, "I inherited it too, Sam. Honest."

"Hey Boss," Willie again, "what about us and our 'Shaking Tent'? What about our shape-shifters…our bad medicine…or the Devil?"

I recalled an event a long time ago in my youth. Yes, I had seen something a long time ago. I couldn't explain it then. I could see the shadowy similarity here but those beliefs died when we got older…and smarter. Or did they? *Deep roots and deep waters'*, I recalled the thought.

"Sam, some people are born with powers and some are given powers. There is no such thing as impossible nowadays, you know that. People are starting to find out there was a lot more to those old mystics – and prophecies. How do you think I escaped, Sam?" That jolted me.

I spin towards to him, "Oh come on Charlie! You don't expect me to believe that bullshit?" I start to laugh, "Good God you guys are getting stupid – loonier, a couple stir-bugs in the fruitcake!"

"You know my Mom never sang me a lullaby? You know that Sam?" This time the words scream instilling a dread in me. Charlie looked at me with charcoal eyes, "How do I know that is what you heard, and that you saw me dead

209

and standing in the Officer's Mess room?" He looked hard at me. "How do I know that Sam?"

I fought for an answer and the willpower to stay there. Everything was telling me to get the Hell out of there. I was rattled, losing all composure and confidence I had in controlling this conversation. I fought to ignore it and continue the questions; I needed answers even if they were lies. Whether it was false or factual, I had to have the full story from Charlie as he saw it - because that would give insight to the true story. But, *how did he know this, how could he?* I put the fear behind me. *There is no such thing as supernatural* I said to myself. The image of that Tepee shaking and the **bound-man** in its belly kept repeating. My walls were starting to crumble, walls I put up a long time ago against that which I could not explain. Things like knowing what was going to happen, hearing voices that gave you answers, dreams coming to life. The old People used to say these were gifts and we should use them or we would lose them. My new culture with education and religion said to renounce from practising such witchcraft or to believe in such, *for they are tools of the Devil.*

"Sam...Sam." Charlie brings me back. "I am not the Devil – or a Devil. I am a man who escaped a Hell by going to prison. I made my bed, now I got to sleep in it but I am not my Grandfather. You got to understand I didn't ask to be what I am."

"I understand." I fight for control, "I can understand your actions but I don't' condone them Charlie." I really did see how he would arrive at his solution if any of this were true. What he told me however, I believed, or hoped it to be a contrived convoluted yarn to justify his crime. I refused to believe in his paranormal claims even while my memory did cast doubts on my own faith. I wanted this to end.

"Charlie, how, when and why did you kill your parents?"
"Stupid question. I told you how and why. I skinned them. When? I was 13. I'm sure you read the file." I detected an edge to his voice. "I skinned them just like my Gramps did except I took longer. I also didn't bother to hide anything. I hung them up for all to see as well as that fucking dog. Ever realize dog is God backwards? Whoever came up with that idea to name an animal – dog? Remember you named your dog 'Sol' after an old friend who use to work for your Dad?"
"I never told anybody that, how can you know?" I blurted out without thinking.
"Got you again, huh? Quit trying to ignore what I'm telling you Sam. It's all true. Every God damned thing I told you is true. Once you believe me you will believe in your self. Willie doesn't have any problems with what I say because it's true."

"That's right Boss. The old ways are still there, in you, but you gotta find them. Charlie always said you had a gift but you put it away."

"If I tell you one more secret will you believe me? All right? Just listen, then you can make up your own mind. Okay?"
The last bit about my dog really shook me. I had to know now if he really was honest about what he claimed. Slowly I gave him one nod.
"I see you with 'Pug', your old friend. You were saying good-bye." I stood back, no one here knows of my friend and what I nicknamed him. "This is when you were moving back to Sandy lake, your reserve. And what

211

did you guys do, what did you promise to each other?" he asks me. Then he tells me, "You two cut your thumbs and vowed to be 'blood-brothers' for life" He was wrong. Charlie interrupts my thought, "Except, and Pug doesn't know this either, you didn't cut yourself. Right Sam?"

He was right. He didn't have to say anything else. It was done and with that secret said, I believed him and the whole story he had told me. In one instant, everything is now different. There are things you can't explain - some events are unexplainable. It came to me then in a rush why this is so hard to believe; *it means another reality, our world is more than what it shows to be.* You can't convey this as a fact to the authorities though. You know it's true but you are caught in the paradox.

"One question Charlie," I forced this question even as I trembled. It was all-important, I asked scared of the answer, "Why stay here if you can just disappear…and why can't your Grandpa come and take you away through the walls?" I still refused to believe.
"Gramps died. I was on the run from him and others when I heard he had died. That was about the same period I was in Canada moving around. That's what I waited for; for him to die before doing my thing. And me not disappearing, why should I? I feel secure and comfortable here…in my home. There are others out there, powerful people, very rich people that want me back and will do almost anything to get to me."
My senses returned with that statement. "So when we do, if we do, escort you on your deportation you wouldn't try an escape?" I concentrated on the reality now, practical logical measures to ensure my safety. What he said rocked my world, the world I believed in,

212

not the other from childhood tales. I hung onto what I believed was real but his confessions questioned all that I knew.

"Absolutely not! I am looking forward to the trip; a change of scenery, maybe some old memories. Really Sam, Scout's Honour! You gotta believe me, I don't want to escape. What do I escape to?" His eyes had grown in shock fearing I might back out now that I was aware of his 'gifts'. He realized where I was going with the questions. "Hey…hey Sam. Forget all I said there. It's just a buncha BS; I was trying to impress you so you'd give me some respect. It's all explainable."
Now I was pissed off. "You don't do something like that for respect. And fucking with my beliefs for a little game you're playing? That is bad – and sad. You just lost any trust I had in you; I don't believe any thing you say now."
"I'm sorry Boss, really, I am. It just got outta hand because I knew all these small secrets you had. I lived in Shelby too; secrets are not so secret in a small town when there is nothing to talk about. Kids talk….and inmates talk. Sol had told Willie he knew you."
I had been duped and felt stupid.

"What about your disappearance, your escape from your cell?" I asked point-blank. Charlie began a smile, "Don't fuck with me Charlie! If you don't tell me we are not going, end of discussion!"
"Okay, all right. Remember my room and the layout? Did you notice the acrylic paints there on the table?"
"Yeeaah."
"I painted myself, body painted myself. You're an artist, you would know this," I did know this and it slapped me hard in the face.

'Why didn't I ever think about this, it was right there in front of my face — staring at me? Body-Painting! SHIT!' God I felt horrible at that moment. He kept on not aware of my shock. "On the table behind my desk lamp, which is the darkest corner, I had painted my whole body to look like the corner with all its bricks. I painted myself into the corner that was away from the window. I knew they would look first on the bed, then under, then to the window where their eyes would be dilated, blinded momentarily….and then they would panic. My lamp was also on and shining with the shade up and pointing to the door. You ever try and look at someone who is shining a flashlight on you? Funny no one ever thought to turn off that lamp. So I just stayed there, got up once in awhile, and watched all the excitement…till I got tired and hungry."

It made sense. It was the only thing that made sense. And it was a welcome relief; I needed that. What hurt, or dented my ego though was that fact that I am an Artist and should have seen it. *'SHIT!'* I told myself. I could see it now as his room came to mind and what he said is exactly what we did, what we all did. The fact nobody had seen anything made me feel a bit better. *'But I should have.'* I reminded my self humbly.

"Okay. But I am going to see the Warden this morning at 8 and tell him. If he says the trip is a 'no-go' that's it then, we are not going."

"Okay, fair enough Boss. I am sorry – really sorry Sam." he ended.

I was about to walk away when Willie says, "Boss, he was telling the truth."

"Willie! Shut up." Charlie tells him. He presses his face to the Plexiglas window, "Give me those paints. Come back in 1 hour and I will show you." I went to the hobby

214

room got the paints minus the brushes and got him the acrylics and closed the hatch. "Be back in an hour?" he asked and I nodded an okay.

I radioed the Keeper to come over. I realized I needed an official witness, someone with authority to record this. I relayed what Charlie had confessed and he was reluctant to accept the whole story, so we waited. After an hour passed we went to his cell. We turned on the hallway lights then approached his window. "Okay Charlie, what you gonna show us?"

"Watch this." he said as he moved to the back wall. He turned his forearms so the insides were to us and all of a sudden he had no arms from the elbow down. Amazing! He had created an illusion. By recreating the exact colour and lines of the masonry walls he had rendered that part of himself – invisible. "Whatcha think Boss?" he was obviously happy with himself.

"Wow!" we both said in harmony. It was a professional piece of work, especially getting the exact colour and shade to blend in.

"Now, if your not looking for this...you're not gonna see it. Right Boss?"

We both agreed. Now that we knew what he was doing we could see faintly the outlines of his arms but if you had the time you could paint the edges and shadows away too. I was convinced, so was the Keeper who immediately went to fax an urgent "heads-up" to all prisons across Canada as security procedures dictated. Charlie was told not to erase his work of Art. I detected smugness in him as he agreed whole-heartedly.

We met the Warden who I assumed would scuttle the trip after these revelations. I probably would be verbally reprimanded too for not 'seeing' this. To my astonishment after a briefing from my Keeper, the Warden shakes my hand muttering, stammering accolades not only vocally but also in official memorandums. I received, was awarded a *letter of commendation & merit!* Unbelievable. An hour ago I was wondering if I should just resign considering the seriousness of my oversight. But the fact ERT and everyone else had missed this too and I had managed in getting Charlie to divulge the secret through *case-management disclosure* as the Warden had written in his directive, I came out on top of the mess. Upon releasing his commendation and subsequent Directive to National HQ, all our staff, personnel were hurried to Segregation cells where the Warden looked at, then scrutinized the arms of Charlie, amazed at what a little paint could do. Nobody recalled the former incident when ole 'Whodunit' made his ill-fated attempt at escape. All staff present that day were ordered to come and see firsthand the masterpiece. I was designated the 'expert' who presented the case before them in a Sherlock Holmes kind of way with Charlie in his cell showing off, basking in his fame. "Ladies, Gentlemen, I show you – the Amazing Charlie!" It didn't quite sound that way but in his ears it did and in my mine too, but maybe not as loud. We both wallowed in our celebrity; everything was forgotten and forgiven. The transfer process continued with no hesitation. At the end of that week all documents, licensees, permits and passports were delivered. We were set to go.

Pug would be there on my last shift - Tomorrow. I was to meet him, bring him for an extended tour and introduce Pug to our beloved Warden whose image had softened in my eyes, become more saintly since his elevation of me. It was hypocritical and I thought I

216

should set aside such juvenile antics for a while… but we are all human, enjoy this while I can.

I was a bit intimidated by the circumstance; I will be meeting my best friend….who I had lost decades ago.

Wonder what he looks like, if he married, does he have any kids, why he never wrote to me. Geez…I dunno, might not be all hugs and smiles.

Chapter 19

I saw him come off the escalator, I recognised his posture and walk immediately. He was slender, not skinny, carried himself with poise and military deportment. He had a full head of dark hair, almost black, with a slight wave on the sides that swept over his ears. No grey yet. He had a face well defined, features that were carved with definite lines; eyes sunk, wide apart and enhanced by long dark eyebrows arched over them. His nose was straight, narrow, a subtle bump at the end and his mouth was tucked in at the corners. Looked much better than his ID photo. *Handsome*, I thought, *not cute like he used to be; kinda reminds me of Rick Nelson*. The tune *of Lonesome Town* sounded in the distance. That's quite corny, a bit too saccharine; I then realized it wasn't me but someone else playing on their Walkman. I waited for him to eyeball me, see if he recognized me. He came closer. **He didn't.** I had grown to a size XL the last 3 years and now at this instant I became self-conscious, discerning of the time passed. There had been no photo of me attached to the documents he had received. All of a sudden it came to me - I don't look like anything he probably remembers. Now.... I'm shorter than him, with a Van Dyke moustache and overweight. God! I could kick myself. *How did I ever get this way?* I bemoaned. Well, too late. As he was about to walk past me I reached to him, grabbing his arm.

"Peter?" I asked.
He turned with a start, puzzled at who I was, then it occurred to him, "Braaann? Is that you?"
"Yep...the one and only." I couldn't think of anything smart to say, total blank.
"Wow, look at you, you're so – different."

218

"Yep…the one and only."

"Wow, so different." Pug repeats, frustrating me.

"Yep… the one…" I was going to repeat that intelligent phrase again but caught myself. "Yeah Pug, what the Hell did you expect! It's been over 28 years!" I did a quick mental count that wasn't quite right. We looked each other over, another awkward pause then laughed as we hugged. "Yep, Wow is the word. You're looking pretty damn good. Wish I was looking like that." I waved my hand to present him.

"Well, you're looking pretty damn good yourself Bran." He lied.

This was Pug, never saying a bad thing about anybody, clean-cut and always courteous to a fault. It did feel good for someone to pay a compliment to me so I ignored the inaccurateness of it. Anyway I was healthy, still had my hair and not decrepit, so yeah, I was okay. We went to the coffee shop while waiting for his luggage, sat down and immediately began rehashing old memories mainly about him, his life. He was married, had the typical 2 kids, a boy and girl, went to college after Vietnam, then served as a police officer before becoming a US Marshal. There was nothing drastic in his life other than Nam, which he wouldn't elaborate on.

"So how 'bout you Bran, huh?" I noticed the 'huh' just like Charlie. They say 'huh' in the U.S.; we say 'eh' here in Canada. I told him in as many few words as I could about my life and home here. Most of the history I related was about my kids and what they did and were going to do. I didn't want to bore him, besides I needed to hear more about him and the home I had left behind. He expounded a bit more on his wife and family, that his brother had died in Nam, his Father passed away, his sister 'Molly' (I had a crush on her) married and moved away and Dianne, his Mother, had sent greetings to me. Pug had informed her of our impending serendipitous meeting. It surprised me that she would remember me. Apparently she was in great health, had remarried and still living in Shelby. I reciprocated by instructing Pug to relay my greetings to her then asked about Shelby itself.

"Oh Bran, nothing's changed. The people have grown, moved on, had families but Shelby is still exactly the same. It's like stepping into a time capsule and returning back to the 50's and 60's. The old Capital Café is still there, the Oasis bar, Alibi Lounge, Lot 13, Roxy, O'Haire Hotel..."

I cut him off, "O'Haire? Where are the brothers? I remember the brothers, great football players and we used to hang around with their younger brother too? What was his name? Remember when you got knocked out – at the game?"

"Yeah, yeah. Brothers all moved away, think his name was Dillon. I kinda remember the game...some of it, and after in the hospital..."

I cut him off thinking of the cheerleaders, "How about our girls? We both laughed.

"Well, Heather had 7 kids..."

"Seven! Seven kids?"

"Yeah, she's still there but Mary and Linda married and moved away, don't know where. We all parted company in high school, besides they were a little older than us so I never was in their crowd." He filled me in on all he knew about our friends, classmates, teachers and other residents we happen to know. By the end of our recap we had sat there for two and a half hours, his luggage still going round and round the giant baggage carousel.

"Geez Bran," he looks up at the clock "Don't we have to go?"

"Oh yeah! Don't panic though I'm off duty. This is the first of my days off. We are supposed to meet the Warden, a couple of my friends then the rest of the day is ours." In spite of my reluctance to move since I wanted more on the history I lost, we got up slowly walking to his luggage. A thought occurred to me, "Pug, do you ever remember a Charles Fuhr – Charlie? He might have been with us in a class at Bitteroot."

"No, doesn't ring a bell. Bitteroot is now shut down, finally, after some 50 years."

"Demolished?"

"Nope, think it's used for books or archives. I'm not sure. Why do you ask?"

"Well the guy we are escorting, deporting was, according to him, enrolled in Bitteroot School at the same time we were there. I don't remember him in any of our classes."

"You got to be kidding." he stops. Mouth open, eyes wide Pug pauses a second to get his breath. "He's a killer….and he went to school with us?"

"No, I don't think he was in any class with us but that was my expression too when I first heard it. He was the one who told me… but he could just be playing games, he likes to do that, screw around with your mind. Be real careful if you're alone with him Pug." I looked sideways at him making sure he heard.

"Oh don't worry. I'll be with you all the time Bran. Wow! I didn't realize this escort had any connections to Shelby at all – or to us! I thought this was a plain pick-up and drop-off to our Pen and that was it."

"Why exactly do they want Charlie in Shelby?" I ask recalling his story.

"It's not Shelby, it's the FBI who have questions because they think his Grandfather was in this…in the Shelby

221

area." Pug corrects himself realizing he's in Canada. "We are to admit him into the new Penitentiary close by where they will hold him till the FBI are satisfied he has told them everything. Probably a day, two at the most." He pauses for insight, "So maybe he was in Shelby?"

"New Pen? Wow, things are changing."

"That's the only thing that has changed, no kidding."

"Well the FBI are gonna have a good time. Man, the shit-is-gonna-hit-the-fan I tell ya."

"What do you mean? They just want to know when and why his Grandfather was here – there."

"You don't know Pug? You don't know his history with his Grandfather?" This alarmed me, he had also said *killer* when referring to Charlie, not serial or multiple. I wondered what he knew, what information he had on Charlie

"No. I was informed to pick up a Canadian killer who the FBI wanted for questioning. Routine, except he was a murderer."

"Charlie is a multiple killer, killed his parents then skinned them… in British Columbia." "He's a sadistic Psychopath who maybe involved in other ritualistic killings." His expression exposed his shock and the minimal info he actually had. "What the fuck did they tell you Pug?"

"None of that! What is going on here?" He looks to the floor wondering, "Geez, this is supposed to be a routine trip. I'll have to phone right now. Excuse me Bran. This is disturbing." He says to himself walking briskly to a private corner, speed-dialed his authorities, the shock still showing in his wide eyes. From a distance I could see the animated conversation; a sagging of the shoulders then activity again, his arm rising over his head then in ending Pug puts his fingers to his forehead in a resigned

222

affirmative nod. He walks back a slump in his shoulders. "I have no choice, I can't withdraw my acceptance of this escort. I could but they would have to send someone else and I'd be deemed inactive. I didn't read everything in the folder assuming this was just another pick-up and drop-off and my immediate superior had assumed the same. No diligence here, and missed communication."

"Hey Pug, brighten up, it's not that bad." now I was lying. *You have to read everything, everything!* I yelled in my thoughts. "There will be a team of RCMP to take us over the border, they will be there until we hand off Charlie to your authorities. They have to be."
"Really? Well it's not that terrible then is it?"
"No. We will look after you Pug, just make sure your people are there. Maybe phone them back right now." He hurried off and within 5 minutes he was back, this time a smile on his face and looking relaxed.

We met the Warden and I informed him of the 'missed communication,' who in turn assured Pug that we were the tops in security and procedure, - that he 'was in very good hands.' It wasn't that Pug couldn't handle it but that he got blind-sided so the Warden promised to look after our part of the order, he wouldn't have to do anything until Charlie was handed over. This eased his anxiety and doubts so we thought to end this tour by visiting Charlie. Get acquainted with his questionable package.
We entered SW and into the security station, the banging doors startling poor Pug every time they opened by remote. Control was monitoring where we went so our every approach to a door was met with a bang; there were five doors from entering the building to the seclusion hallway inside SW. A person not accustomed

can be weak-kneed by the time they get to where they're going. We loved to do this to new staff, banging, opening the doors before their approach. I expected this was what was going on in control and told Pug.

"Bastards!" he said. It was the first time I heard him swear – ever! I was surprised but then he was a man now, a father, not a 10-year-old kid. The image just wouldn't relax its hold on my perception. A reflection of myself smiling while looking at the obituaries crossed my mind and for a long period, many years, I had wondered why I did this. Was I demented and relished the bad luck of others? Then it dawned on me – everyone in the obituaries was smiling; I was smiling back. Reactions and perceptions are all relative to the situation and the time they are in. Mine was still in yesterday Shelby with Pug, and I was treating him unconsciously as if he were still that young. I had to get rid of it and treat him like the adult he was. While these reflections drifted in-and-out, I was aware of someone playing violin. Inmates, as part of their therapy through the Arts programs, were allowed to 'sign out' instruments to play or learn to play. We also had instructors coming in every two weeks for individual and band instruction. My ears perked up, I caught the tune of 'Ranger's Waltz'. Someone was playing my beloved waltz that I used to demand from anybody that played the fiddle. It was coming from Charlie's cell. I loved that tune; it brought back so many memories, good memories. I could see my Mom and Dad dancing whirling to the tempo as my Mom's favourite scarlet dress flared out when my Dad stepped around her to a turn. My smile broadened as the music got louder with each of our steps. Arriving at Charlie's door, I stopped and soaked in the last moans of that waltz. He had played this very tune at the Dance.

"Did you like it Boss."

"Mmmm, yeah. That was nice. You never forgot how to play?"

"I play now and then, not like when I was touring with 'Smiling Johnny' but enough to keep up with the new waltzes." We both giggled at this inside joke. Pug looked puzzled and maybe a bit surprised at our friendly relations. He looked apprehensive, alarmed at Charlie's next question. "So how are you doing Pug?" Pug turned with a stare asking for answers with his eyes. "Whoa! Don't spazz out on me. I knew you were coming and I knew who you were. Bran told me a few weeks back."

"Funny, I don't remember telling you that." I searched my memory.

"Well maybe it was Murray or the Nurse but I knew about it. I also had to sign papers concerning this deportation too you know."

"Hmmm, anyway Pug, this is Charlie also known as Charles Fuhr whom we will be escorting to your country. And that's in four days Charlie, in case nobody has informed you."

"Yep, know it already. Thanks."

"So you are Dr. Fuhr's grandson?" Pug asks.

"Yep...the one and only." An awkward pause ensues as Pug and I look at each other. "But grand is maybe not quite the right term, right Boss?" he turns to me.

"Yeah... right." I turn to Pug. "The story is convoluted but yes Charlie was very close to the Grandfather. He in fact lived with him while they were supposedly in Shelby and area." Pug keeps his calm but I feel his eyes on me.

"So everything is alright with the trip Boss?"

"Yeah, there were a few 'hitches' but all seems to be in order now. Everything is okay with you? There is not going to be any games or incidents during this trip?"

"Oh no Boss, Scouts' honour. I am not gonna screw up any chance at a temporary vacation from here. I'd be crazy to do that. And Peter don't worry, nothing to worry about."

"I would prefer you keep calling me that, my proper name, as opposed to my nick-name."

"Will do Boss...Peter it is...will do." Charlie salutes with a crisp salute. I see that Pug approves. His straight frame from years in the service relaxes a bit.

"That's it then, I'm off for a few days, so see you then Charlie."

We walk a ways before Pug says anything. "He's a multiple killer? He looks so young to be our age and his disposition...doesn't match with a sadistic killer."

"Don't be fooled by his words. He's a charmer, maybe the best I've seen." I gave him a tour of the Center, a more in-depth look at the different units on whom they housed and the security measures, tools, equipment in place for treatment and protection of all staff and inmates. Pug was impressed, affirming his decision to continue in this deportation.

"My wife Claire has made dinner for us. So if it's no bother, we will go and pig-out then later, if you're not too tired we can have a few beers?"

"No bother, no bother at all." his eyes lit up.

We did pig-out, so much so we didn't have much room for the beer. Claire had made a beef cross-rib roast with all the trappings of gravy, mashed potatoes, steamed vegetables with a butter mayonnaise cream sauce. They took an instant liking to each other, especially following Pug's excessively lavish accolades on her cooking – his kudos somewhat similar to the rich gravy...and too much of it.

We carried on into the wee hours and it seemed we had never been apart. We talked openly, laughed at lame jokes, and recounted numerous occasions, accidents of our youth. Before he called a cab, the topic arose (in some weird way) on why we never remained in contact. I told him I had but he and 'our girls' slowly quit replying; so I quit writing too in that special summer, the magical summer of '68'. Unbeknownst to me as we drank and made merry in the Saskatchewan Pines most of my old classmates along with Pug were drafted and undergoing training for their compulsory tour in Vietnam.

Pug replied, hesitating, "I don't know, I wasn't aware of anybody at that time. The odd memory would creep back and you would want to talk to that person but then it seemed so much trouble and you didn't want to rekindle old flames or friends because you might not be back. I did think of you Bran but back then it was the wrong time. So three years later I'm back and alive and going to College…and I meet my wife to be. How about you guys, when did you meet?"

What the future held through their view of '68' was so different than ours. "Well there was no Vietnam for us, thank God so yeah I don't envy what you had to look forward to. From what I heard it was a future on hold till you get back alive. Here, we didn't stop, the drinks kept flowing, and we didn't have such a thing as Vietnam hanging over our heads. But yeah, even then amongst our parties in the 'Pines' I forgot too. That was pretty well where we met; our first date was in the Pines.

This kindled a recollection and he raised his finger, "I do remember one incident and it was during one of our

227

parties. It was out by the Marias River where some pines grew." Pug had a strained look as he remembered. "We were partying, sitting under a Cottonwood and I had to go for a leak, go relieve myself. So I was alone behind some pines and as I was looking about me I saw someone or something move…about 30 feet away. It was dark of course, I asked *who goes there?* and a person appears, turns around and looks at me." He hesitates for the longest time.

"And? What happened?"

"It was you Bran. You stood there, still young, looking at me. No words, nothing, you just stared at me…."

"Oh my God!" Claire cries out, cutting off his words. She grabs my arm staring at me with a puzzled look as I stared back wondering what she was saying. "Don't you remember? On that date, our first date, you said something to me?" I was ignorant. "I remember because that was our first date. You came back from the bushes, you saw something."

"Oh my God!" I echoed her astonishment. "Yes! Holy shit, that's right!" I turned to Pug, "I went back into the pines for a piss…a leak. I'm standing there, doing the same thing…looking around…and someone is standing there, 30 feet away, staring at me." My neck hair started to rise recalling the event. "I take a step closer, then start backing off. It was you Pug! You were standing there looking at me. No words either, just staring."

"Holy crap! That is God-damn weird!" Pug, like me was at the edge of his seat. He recoils throwing himself back onto the couch. "Jesus…"

"I know the time too. It's so clear in my mind now." Claire adds in a slow soft voice, "It was a Saturday night, Sunday morning, July 21st and it was 2 am."

228

"What!" We're startled at Pug's shout. He stands up, a mad stare in his eyes like we were doing something bad to him. "You're not serious, you're kidding?"

"Nooo…" Claire says nervously. Regaining her composure she states, "No. I recall exactly the date and it was 2:01 because I remember Sam asking me the time right then. And I wrote it all in my journal the following morning."

I now remembered that night along with the distinct time as the memory flashed before me, that shadow of him and that exact time.

"That is the precise time I saw him too." Pug pointed to me. "I know because the next day, that afternoon, we were to travel and report to boot camp. Sunday July 21st…and it was 2 in the morning. When I got back to the car that is what it read on the clock…in cold neon blue, on the dashboard, it said 2:01." He sat back down in slow motion reaching for the armrest, "Hoooly Crap…" he dragged the words, his eyes focussed on something not there.

"What is happening here guys?" Claire breaks the silence. "I don't like this – it's just too weird." We both say nothing but stare at the coffee table between us. "I don't know, should you guys go on this escort?" Claire asks.

.

"Of course we go! We have to…can't back out now." I retaliate maybe in too harsh a tone.

"Right. We have to go. But you know, what happened… this coincidence? It happened what…some twenty-plus years ago?"

"Right…riiiight," I turn to Claire "Twenty years ago Claire, it was twenty-plus years ago." Pug's breakdown of the years passed made the coincidence trivial. "That's all there is to it, just a weird happening. Maybe for an instant we were together as one, our vibes jibing. Right Pug?"

"Right, and I do believe in stuff like that. For people to share common events separated by distance happens; it happens all the time. Don't worry Claire. I'll look after Bran and I'm sure he'll look after me."

"Yeah…right. And we're not alone. There will be four RCMP with us." Claire knew of Charlie but not the whole story and I wasn't about to disclose anymore at this juncture.

"Hmmm," She replied, "maybe it's a warning."

"Warning? Naaah…no way. It happened long ago, way too long ago."

We left it at that. Following a friendly argument we convinced Pug to cancel his taxi and sleep over. His contention that he was putting us out didn't wash so he stayed with us for the duration. We must have reminisced about our whole life together in those three days. I took him to my reserve home, which he found amazing and enchanting. I couldn't see the fascination he had with my life, culture and tales. My family, my life were quite boring, even shameful, I concluded as the dilapidated houses we had to pass by came into mind. He didn't see it that way though. He was cognizant of the persecution, pressure brought on by the Governments here and in the U.S. and how the Natives were subjugated to a life that wasn't theirs.

"They took away their Tepees," he said, meaning a way of Life.

It was refreshing to hear someone else say that. Having to always explain 'matters' on why our People lived the way we do was maddening. On desolate reserves, back alleys of cities, pow-wows and headdress in our hair, riding horses - we didn't all live as the media and movies portrayed us but that is what they saw. That is what was shown to the public. Christ, I was scared of horses... and never danced in a pow-wow! I took him to meet my Mom and Dad pointing out our house was further in, away from the highway. He was exuberant to meet them again after so many years and the fact my Dad had been Chief added to his delight. My Mom and Dad greeted him asking many questions of his family and on Shelby itself. We stayed for a dinner my Mother had prepared consisting of slow-roast Elk, garden potatoes and snap peas with a fresh slab of baked bannock. I wasn't too sure of this recipe, assuming stereotypically in my ignorance he was more into beef steak, mashed potatoes and sliced white bread but Pug was ecstatic.

"No wonder you're...plump" he looked at me. We all laughed then he added, "but you carry it well Bran. I would be 350 pounds if I was fed these fantastic dishes your Mom and Claire cook." My Mother loved him. We talked awhile at the table as Pug asked countless questions on politics, treaties to which my Dad was more than eager to answer.

My Father was devout in his pessimistic analysis on Government policy and it made sense now unlike in my youth when I didn't want any part of this new life back here. I listened to them talk. It came to me then, in my anger I had rebelled; I had stubbornly shut my ears, shut my eyes fantasizing instead of returning to a lost time and place I called home. Now sitting here with Pug's infatuation with our ways and how we came to be at the present was fascinating. We were in a 'warp', still traditional but striving to grasp our future in a contemporary society. I felt good after Pug shared his

231

opinions on these issues that harmonized with my Father's and I came to understand why we had moved back. Hearing them talk made it so easy to understand as opposed to my Dad saying the same things to me; I never wanted to listen to the reason. To fight for immaterial things, ideas without substance, rights every culture should have to survive was beyond my reason those many years ago when Dad tried to explain. In my youth I was self-centered and the world revolved around me, there was no empathy yet unless it served my purpose. The clock ticked on, before we knew it the sun was setting. My Mother hugged Pete, as she called him, making him promise to come back. My Father shook his hand firmly; he was never the 'huggy' kind. They walked us to the car, small-talked about the hot weather, tepees and air conditioning. 'Tepee' struck a chord and the Shaking-Tent Ceremony came to me.

"Hey Dad, remember that guy, the Bound-Man inside the Shaking Tent?"

"Yeah, when you were a little kid?"

"Yeah, about 5 years old. What did he say to you, what did he whisper?"

"That something lost would return. He meant you."

"But there was something else...at the end of it that you didn't tell me."

"Ah, yes." Dad gazed upward then to me, "Beware the bad spirit... the Devil. But that could mean a lot of other things, kind of a general warning. He could have meant watch out for vices like alcohol, drugs or certain people. In our language, 'Muts-a-mun-to' the Devil, doesn't have to mean one person. Evil doesn't always show itself so you should know what to look for and listen to."

"Really?" Pug asks.

"Yes. The danger is not listening with your heart; our mind tends to disguise things so we see what we want. A lot of times we can't see what is there before us. We need a guide to show us." Dad gazed upward again; something seemed to catch his eye. "I'll tell you a short story." It was like being 10 years old once again; we rested against the fenders of the car, anticipating.

"An old Man was talking to his Grandson, trying to teach him to be patient so he could learn - see what he couldn't see. The boy was at that age where he believed in only that which was visible to him. They stood on a hill silent for a long time. *'Do you see that Eagle?'* the Moshum asks his grandson. *'No'* the boy says. His Moshum points to the sky where the Eagle was but still the boy could not see. *'Look harder'*, he was instructed but the boy still could not see no matter how hard he stared at the sky. *'Listen then'*, he was told and he listened turning each ear to the sky. The boy became restless, impatient and didn't want to listen anymore. So the Moshum tells him, *'be silent, sit there and let it come to you.'* For many minutes they sit in the quiet then the boy hears something, a faint cry a long ways away. He waits, listens for the next sound. It comes again and he looks to its source, another cry comes and in the boundless sky a speck appears. He sees it...then hears it and shouts; *'Moshum I see it, I see the Eagle!'* He points to the sky as the Eagle calls and circles above them, becoming larger. With that, the boy began to listen and see from that day onward."

My Dad stopped here and everybody was silent for a long time. Then like it was meant to be, we hear a cry way high above us and we strain our eyes to see in the vast blue. My Mother points to a spot. Another cry came and there it was, an Eagle so high it was barely visible. We watched as the sun set, casting its orange rays across

233

the horizon, the Eagle glided down and with a soft scream soared skyward where it became a point then disappeared, swallowed by the Autumn blue. It was all so sudden, surreal in this silence, not a sound other than a soft wind in the pines.

"Wow…" Pug whispered in awe. I was so happy he experienced this special moment with us. Mom put both her hands on his, a tear in her eye; my Dad put his hand on his shoulder smiling. Pug looked down not wanting us to see the tears welling in his, but we all saw.

It took someone else for me to see, to see how special my parents were.

Travelling back to Saskatoon we never said a word for about an hour. Pug finally opened up with, "Wow your parents are something else Bran, I mean - real special." I agreed in typical fashion but I did have an epiphany, a full appreciation of my family and life on this momentous occasion. Unexpectedly he adds, "And your life, I wish I could change mine for yours."

This shocked me because all these years I had envied his.

A lazy thought came to me and I realized tomorrow we would be leaving, *'Leaving On A Jet Plane'*. The tune came to me immediately so I tried to sing it and Pug harmonized – or tried to. This initiated Pug to find an Old Classics station on the car radio, which he did in short order and Kristofferson belted out *Me And Bobby McGee* in his raspy voice. We howled along Karaoke style singing, adding our words…

With those windshield wipers keeping time,
And Baby slapping hands,
We did sing up every song that driver knew.

Freedom is some other word for nothing left to lose,
Nothing is worth nothing when it's free...

We did sing everything up we knew as Kristofferson put it and it felt incredible. We were behaving as two kids did a lifetime ago on some concrete curb in a dusty little town. Now in our adult years it looked silly but we didn't give a shit. It was great!

Chapter 20

In the morning we left early to get documentation, the firearms and ourselves ready. I had insisted Claire not get up for us, that there was a breakfast at the Center waiting for us before our departure, but she did anyway. She planted a sweet little peck on my lips, walked to the door and said good-bye to both of us. Pug bent down, kissed her hand, *an English Dandy* I thought as he swept his left hand in a gentleman's gesture.

All went well as other officers brought Charlie to the airport in a security van complete with a double-cage. He stepped off the van with some difficulty, the body belt and shackles limiting the range of his mobility. The last step he couldn't manage himself because it was too high so he jumped with all the chains around him moving slow in their weight, making clanging sounds while he landed in graceful motion. He looked so young for a moment. We moved him into the RCMP jet where the four officers there took charge as they placed him into an archaic chair that looked eerily similar to the Executioner's Electric Chair of the early century. He was strapped to the wooden armrests, the legs to the chair legs and a transparent porous hood was placed over his face.

"Holy shit Boss, they gonna fry me, do the job right here?" Charlie asked in fake bravado but I could tell he wasn't comfortable.

"Is the hood necessary?" I asked the RCMP who referred to some article stating the required procedures. "He has never tried to bite or spit at anybody." I added but it was useless, they had their orders.

"Like, where in the fuck am I gonna go...or do?" He shook his head in defiance as they put it over. A lattice cage door was then pulled down from the ceiling and fastened to the floor then locked. "You think maybe I'm gonna commandeer the plane and fly myself to Hawaii?" None of the RCMP said anything as they stuck to their routine.

"Easy Charlie. You thought you were going to be in first class, maybe with a stewardess…with big 'knockers' who invites you to the Mile-High Club?" I could see he broke a smile under the translucent hood. "Don't worry. In less than two short hours we will be in Montana, Charlie."

"No problem Boss." he invited me closer with a shake of his head, the only body part not tied down. I went over, bent my head to the cage. He whispers through the mesh, "I'm okay Sam. I won't screw this up. Just that…. I'm scared. I never flew before."

"Welcome to my boat. I never did like flying either." I had never seen Charlie scared or fearful of anything.

We took off and it was uneventful until we crossed the border where the pilot notified us, then added that we will be hitting some turbulence. He didn't mention to what degree but we found out fast. We felt the drop first, our stomach travelling up to meet our throats then the jet shook. We bounced around, little play figures rattling on a floor as the engines roared in protest. It wasn't that long but the anxiety gnawed at us while we sat stoically anticipating the next drop. I glanced at Pug across the aisle, he was fine, smiling as if it was a joke but Charlie was gasping. His hood was milky or fogged up, his breathing laboured; I couldn't tell what was obstructing his breathing so I jumped to the cage. He was choking. He had thrown up his breakfast and it was all across the hood in front. I rushed to the cabin telling the crew to open the cage but they were adamant on not doing so. Pug comes beside me and hollers his support notifying

237

them of his jurisdiction now that they were in the United States.

"Get that cage open and that hood off or he's going to die from suffocation. We're in my country now. It's my call and I will accept the risk." Pug hollered over the engines.

The Sergeant in charge looked to the pilot then back to Pug. "Okay but anything goes wrong it's your neck – you gave me this order in your jurisdiction. Understand?"

"Yes, understood! Now get that God-Damn cage open!" *Way to go Pug* I mutely cheered. I could see the authority now; I was impressed.

I grabbed the keys and disregarding protocol, we hurried to open the cage and I yanked the hood off Charlie. He took in deep breaths coughing up some remnants and spitting them out. "You look a little green Charlie." I wiped his face with a towel the Sergeant had tossed me.

"Thank you Pete, thank you Boss, I heard you give the order. God…coulda been dead in another minute or two. God! Thank you again, both of you. I'll never forget this!" He glared to the cabin. "As for you guys, the Fucked-up Four… I hope they ship all four of you to Tuk-ta-yak-tuk for 20 years!"

"Okay, that's it Charlie, it's over." He quietened down quickly now that he had expressed his disdain for their actions. A subtle smirk covered his face as I remarked on his knowledge, "I see you know your geography." Being stationed way up North, isolated, was not a good move for the RCMP; posts in Ottawa or Montreal were the favoured.

It was only minutes later that we began our descent, landing at the Municipal or County airport outside Shelby. The small tower and authorities were notified and a single van approached as we taxied closer to the buildings.

"Where's the prison bus…or the armoured transport van?" Pug asks, talking to himself. "What the Hell is going on here?" The RCMP opened the entrance door anticipating someone to be there with the portable stairway. "Stop, hold it right there guys!" he shouts pulling out his service cell phone. They hesitate, holding the hatch when Pug yells, "Close that fucking door! Something's wrong here!"

That was the first and last time I heard Pug swear to that extent – or degree. I asked him what was going on, but I had already deducted the security meeting us was not sufficient. This was not what was expected, it wasn't proper procedure for such a high-risk transfer, not to mention that this was an international deportation. I had a gut feeling something was amiss and Charlie echoing my sentiment says, "Hey Boss, I don't like this, I got a bad feeling."
"I know, I know. Peter is phoning his proper authorities right now. Charlie would you ever set up a 'break' like this - escape on an escort?" I knew he didn't have the resources or inclination to do so but I needed his word on this.
"No way Boss, absolutely no way. I don't want to escape…escape to what, Boss?"

A few minutes passed till Pug came to us. He repeated what was relayed to him and it wasn't good news. Apparently the Pen, although very close, didn't have the manpower to supply an armed escort because they were having a 'lock-down'. Until the problem was contained, they could not afford anybody so the only option was to use the county Police van they sent and transfer the inmate to County Jail. Our other alternative was to just

239

wait inside the security plane until State Corrections had the men to send...and the secure transportation to transport. We could be waiting for days if the uprising continued. To this the RCMP exclaimed they were not going to be waiting around for answers. They were scheduled for numerous transfers across the country, their country. They had no interest or authority here, which was true, and they did have an official schedule to follow. The only choice for us if we wished to stay inside the jet was to fly back to Saskatoon. We talked about all the options, Pug made a few more phone calls but time was wasting.

Finally the RCMP gave us the ultimatum, "Okay, time's up guys, we have to book our next flight plan to Headquarters and we are doing so – now."

The Sergeant attempted to push away the stairway, Pug grabbed his arm, "Wait, wait...let us go out and do a search of the area." The Sergeant agreed to wait for this. While they guarded Charlie in his secured chair and cage, we went outside doing a quick but effective search of the immediate area surrounding the plane. We ran to the adjoining hangar and old-fashioned airport depot where we did a superficial scan for any suspicious activity or vehicles, then did a search of the van for any guns, keys, or shanks that could be hidden. At least the van had a security cage. We motioned the RCMP to bring Charlie to the van as we waited, armed and standing opposed to each other so we could survey 360 degrees. It didn't take long for them to release his bounds, doing so in paired unison. In moments we were locking Charlie into the van cage. Wasting no time we bid good-bye to the RCMP who released all permits, licenses and passports to us and we sped away with urgency. We had mutually agreed on locking Charlie into the county jail on

240

condition that they, the County Sheriff provided security for the time needed. Pug arranged the necessary manpower through the Sheriff to cover twenty-four hours surveillance with 2 guards always there; one with him, the other watching the entrance. Approaching the outskirts of Shelby, I was struck by the familiarity of everything. The sky, the dry hills surrounding us, sage and tumbleweed all hit me - the smell of my youth. Nothing to many who were probably bored by the 'commonness' of living here but I was ecstatic as we entered... my Shangri-La.

We soon pulled up to the County Jail; I was amazed, aghast! This was the same town jail my Mom and Dad had taken me for stealing a silver dollar out of my mom's purse. I never forgot the incident that left an everlasting lesson in me about lying, stealing and doing what was right. At the time, the building had struck me as huge, intimidating with its whitewashed brick and mortar towering over me as a 6 year old. But now this quaint tiny hacienda was to hold one of the most feared killers I had known? The jail hadn't changed a bit along with the neighbouring residential area and Main Street that passed blissfully by, ignorant of the peaceful chapel-like building's true purpose. I wondered if it had bars on its cells – I wondered if it had cells!

"Wow!" This is nice Boss." Charlie remarks looking at the short steeple adorning the white arched wall of the entrance. By the olive oak door in nice western Texas font done in brass it read, *County Jail*. "Right fucking on! This is like a private jail for the privileged. I feel privileged! Did you arrange this Boss?" I shook my head for a 'no'. "Well it's got to be you then Boss," he turns to Pug with a Cheshire smile. "This is the cat's meow. A big

241

thank you Boss. I haven't been in something so charming since my time on the run."

"On the run?" Pug asks, everybody looks sharply to him. "Can you elaborate on this?"

Without hesitation Charlie rambles, "Yeah, in between the time I left Gramps and the time I killed my parents in British Columbia. Oh I loved that time – I was free!" While beaming his shiny pearls in another smile the Deputies took a firmer grasp of their rifles. "Oh yeah, best memories. I travelled all over the place playing in any band that needed a guitar, fiddle or sax. I was good, man - damn good. Got it from my Gramps, he used to say but..." he frowned at this, "I never ever saw him play anything...come to think about it." Charlie drones on like a bad record that nobody really wanted to hear. Breaking his thought he adds, "Anyway that's when I heard Gramps had died so it was a perfect time to finish the job and kill my parents too. Then I would be free, really free, except I didn't take into consideration the rest of those sick bastards." The deputies are staring hard at Charlie.

"What is this Bran?" Pug looks to me. "What the Hell is he ranting on about?"

"It's true, read the history. I thought you knew all of his history? Why do you think we were concerned about only one Marshal coming? We thought he could be a flight risk."

"Hey Boss, remember my words? I am NOT gonna try and escape, no way!"

"It's all right Charlie. I'm just reassuring these guys you won't try." I turn from the deputies back to him, "Right, Charlie?"

"Absolutely. I have nothing to escape for, or to. Look at this," he lifts his head waving a hand at the same time, "I couldn't be happier. I got this cabin to vacation in and brick walls and guards to protect me from those lunatics...and my Grampa."

"Your Grandpa is dead Charlie."

"Right."

"Besides, if your Grandpa could slide through walls how are we going to protect you?" I ask mockingly realizing Charlie is doing a job on the young guys.

"Hey Boss, Sam, I explained that bit on disappearing but Gramps could do it. I swear. The thing is though; it didn't always work for him and he could only go through one wall at a time, so that's why a prison keeps me safe... lots of walls. I saw it Sam, honest. And there are other powers, ungodly powers nobody should have and he wanted me to have them...take them over. The best place for me is a maze of walls, a labyrinth.

"What the fuck is this?" the two young county deputies both echo the question simultaneously. "Nobody told us about this shit, man." They look to each other for support, their wide eyes giving away their fright. The one standing closest to me surprisingly looked like ole' whiney 'bug-eyes' we nicknamed in Bitteroot School because of his protruding eyes and irritating voice. I speculated on the possibility this guy could be his son.

I interrupted my imagery, "Jesus Christ you guys, you're not spooked are you. You don't believe this shit do you? He's trying to scare you."

They quickly catch themselves, "No, no, just wondering 'bout the escape risk." I could tell however, Charlie had implanted a seed of fear in them. "Okay, we better lock this guy up right now."

Briskly they grabbed his arms taking him to a vacant cell that, to my relief, had bars. True to Charlie's imagination the jail inside did have that Martha Stewart décor to it

243

with pastel walls, freshly painted green bars, suspended adobe lights and on each side of the cell – a 2 foot vase full of yellow daffodils and mauve tulips. Inside the cell on the toilet was a doily with a box of Kleenex on top and overhead a sign reading, *Jesus Loves You*. Pug, Charlie and I stared at one another then together we all began to laugh. This was hilarious, incredible after coming from a grey colorless cold institution of clanking doors and hollow screams. Obviously the jail was not used that often, more of an office for the Sheriff and his Deputies. We shared our inside joke with the deputies, now jail guards, while Charlie exclaimed his pleasure and wish to stay there permanently. This eased the tension that had built up; afterwards we locked up Charlie, isolating the vases to a few more feet away so they were out of reach and removed the *Jesus* plaque.

We briefed the deputy guards on procedure, risk, management and departed after giving our service mobile phone numbers for any information, advice or emergency. We checked in our rifles, mace, handcuffs and keys; we kept our personal side firearms. The RCMP were scheduled to stop on the following third day on their trans-Canada escorts. Pug arranged all necessities, service and legal matters with his seniors leaving no loose ends between them and the local Sheriff. He was well organized and a good manager.

Chapter 21

Stepping outside, I breathed in that air I had never forgotten about, country air with a wet pavement tang and wet tire aroma. I marvelled at the strong pleasant odour, questioning if the pavement here was made or applied differently than in our cities. It was peculiar in its fragrance, remarkably unique, or maybe it was my heightened senses that magnified the scent. Nevertheless it was a bouquet of memories I drew in with a deep breath, looking around me in wonderment. My focus went from the jail, Main Street, across to the tracks, to the hoodoo hills and down again to Main Street as I glimpsed and recognized each icon of my lost home. I walked slowly to the corner, my senses replenishing everything the long years had dulled. A slight rain had fallen, it now was drying up on the streets; the mirrored pools of water reflected the blue sky. I summon up the many times after a rain, I had zipped through such pools on this very street.

"Bran, let's go for a beer or something. We got to stop somewhere and get a rental car too so I can show you around. Mine is in Great Falls where I flew from, I don't live here anymore you know." Since his workplace was in Great Falls or originated from there, I was not sure nonetheless that he had made it his home. He did keep ties with old friends here as well as his mother but his wife and kids were in Great Falls, a mere 60 miles away.

So we walked down Main Street from the jail, which was at the east end of Main and followed my memories due west. It was uncanny, eerie; everything was the same. I got giddy as I glanced side-to-side passing by fond worn-out recollections now distinct, my hands caressing the

245

masonry walls while we strolled along them. My hands unconsciously kept reaching up to touch the walls, the lamp posts, the parking meters, reminders that we were really here – home in Shelby. I had a feeling like we had stepped off the plane into a time capsule or maybe I had been dreaming a long dream and now I was awake feeling for the tangible of a real world, the smell of the pavement, the concrete that bound all in my world. There was the Dry Cleaner down across the tracks, Penny's Clothing, a hardware store, the Five-and-Dime and further down with its neon arch – the Roxy where my dreams began. The Modern Café, the Capitol Café all there still playing our classic tunes on their Wurlitzer and the counter mini jukeboxes on each table. It was all here, still. I told Pug to go on, I would meet him at the Alibi afterwards. I strolled down one side then the other, entering whatever building flashed me an image of its soul so I could inspect, verify with my saved images of yesterday. I knew the past never lives up to your expectations, but here in this dusty little paradise, the past was alive. People keep their past in the present by not changing so why change if the past was good to you? I stood there, viewing all through my fifties 3-D Master Viewfinder and it all looked so good, so clean, untainted by the corruption of progress or commercialism. I was thankful that something... something in my world never changed.

I met Pug at the Alibi later, discussing the values of a small town as opposed to a city, specifically this town, our town. He quickly shot down my inflated perspective on civil values with revelations of dirty secrets and corruption. I listened, coming to a realization that every town, every person has secrets in their closets no matter their glamour or aesthetics. I also realized that most others would look at Shelby as old, dated, but to me it was an old friend who never grew old. A contradiction in comparison but with its age on pause, to me it had kept honest to itself not pretending to be what it couldn't be. I guess you could say that about every small town that never grew... like Peter Pan. The thought and image brought a smile.

"My Mother stays in an apartment now, a small townhouse. I was wondering if you wanted to stay with us? Mom sent an invite. One problem, there is only one extra bedroom and one bed, we would have to sleep together."
"Oh God no!" The thought revolted me. I couldn't imagine either of us having a good sleep, each having habits and idiosyncrasies of our own. *What if he unconsciously hugs his wife through the night,* I imagined. Adding to this uncomfortable notion, I visualized my habit of rubbing my feet with Claire's. I hurriedly ended the debate, "I'll rent a room, no problem."
"You sure?"
"Yeah, absolutely. Pug, we're getting along so good, why destroy it?" We both laughed.
"Okay but you have to come for dinner- tonight?"
"Sure." and we did have a marvellous supper as we call it in Canada. She asked a lot of questions, the same everyone asks and I answered accordingly. We leafed through some old photos, the 2 hours dragging impatiently as we ran out of things to reminisce over so I politely excused myself with a lie. I was never that close to Pug's mother, preferring to look at her through young idolizing eyes from afar out of respect and awe. She was that stereotypical Mother of the Fifties in her white house of white curtains with dorms, green shutters and a career minded husband. As a child I had not been aware

247

of, or valued our family differences until now when Pug had acknowledged how unique and interesting we were. That is when the insight dawned upon me as I came to appreciate how hard my Mom had worked while still being a Mother and wife at home. Now, too many years later, I fully understood what she endured to keep us together as a family. In a scant six days, not even a week, my attitude and the gratitude, admiration for my life had changed.... thanks to Pug.

My real reason for leaving was this chance to walk through my past in the streets, starting here. Pug offered to drive me but I insisted on walking, he understood, letting me go on my own. Walking, with each step interrupted by a pause I gazed upon my memories, my eyes stopping at every house and tree. They were different but still alike; the old Oak was there, the houses were of different colours, the streets unchanged and there was that curb at the end where we sat to say good-bye. From there our lives changed, branching out like that old Oak tree growing older. Along the way to Main Street, my destination, I went past two of the places I had called home; one a small white house now blue and the apartment where I squealed on my aunties. I stood gazing, not really focusing on anything physical but on a scene playing in my mind so many years ago. Pug had been there... then left me on my own.

I crossed the railroad tracks, stopped, and looked back. I recalled an event one warm Sunday afternoon coming upon a mob of people all raving about some person on the train. They pointed to some guy inside; his shoulder resting on the window, the other hand waving boringly, a slight smirk on his lips. I learned later it was Elvis Presley. I knew who it was on the movie screen but not

248

in real life. I was mad at myself for not paying more attention; I could have gone up closer, maybe gotten an autograph.

Passing the tracks, I walked uphill where I stopped at a hobby store. I stared at the large window, seeing my young self standing, nose to glass, staring through the same window 30 years ago. The many model cars, planes, ships and Knights of Armour still adorned the platform set up for display. One instance came to me when I had bought paint for my 1954 Monarch Ford model that I had assembled at home, ready for finishing with a paint job. In such a rush to get home and start painting, I tripped close to the tracks falling flat on my face – and stomach. The paints, mostly red, had broken as I crushed them and the paint smeared all over my chest area like blood. I got home, crying all the way and my Mom sees me. In her anxiety and fear she grabs me, hugs me and starts crying herself until she finds out it was paint. I got a scolding for the ruined shirt but there were still some tears in her eyes when she did. Nobody appreciates a parent's fear for a hurt child until you have kids of your own.

A half-block up was Main Street illuminated by the same Neon lights of the Fifties; the Capitol Café, its sea-green Martini glass on black, and around the corner to my left was the Roxy Theatre, its fat bulbs blazing and dancing in Flamingo red. From its façade a canopy craned over the sidewalk in a blinding Marquee, billing a double feature; *The Blob* and *The Thing*. Enclosed in parallel red lines was the note; *Tuesday special for seniors begins at 9pm*. I glanced at my watch; it was 8:50pm, just in time! I wasn't Senior yet but what the hell, you're only young once.

I ventured in, watchful of everything around remembering the glass-covered posters, the ticket teller and the counter with all its goodies sprinkled in fluorescent colours. The popcorn popper was adorned in a golden yellow light popping out white kernels in a magical melody and the word 'Popcorn' in red circus font pasted the sides of the bin. I am sure I had the biggest grin on my face; this was like yesterday as I bought my regulars. I cradled my body into the soft seat (now maybe a bit too narrow) as I looked upwards admiring the splendour of the Roman architecture. I had a feeling this decor was here before; I just never saw it – too busy watching for the girls. The movies played exactly as I remembered although not as scary, recalling the numerous times Pug and I jumped, our popcorn flying. At one time I turned to see if that old lady snorting her tears was there behind me. There were probably only 20 people in the theatre as I glanced around; everyone alone except two couples, quiet figures not moving; all bordered in a neon blue becoming memories again, those old ghosts that had haunted my mind.

I thought, later on in my motel room, I should have asked Pug along, *damn it!* Ah well, I'll see him again. Tomorrow is another day. Would have been nice though to remember together, remind each other and giggle over that wicked old lady snorting in her hair rollers.

'One more day here – tomorrow,' I repeated silently as I looked to the blank wall of the Motel. The next day we would fly back to Saskatoon. Pug will have to remain on the plane and come back to Great Falls immediately, to his home and family. I wondered when we would meet again.

I turn over; the red neon sign is casting a hot glow on my ceiling, the TV on mute stabs the dark in flashes. The heat is coming, they said in captioning. My eyes grew heavy, the engines and wheels outside die a distant echo, sounding lonely. A soft velvet curtain falls; black in weight, light as a speckle of dust dances the rays.

Chapter 22

Tomorrow was here...and it was hot. The morning sun rose over the dry hills, a wind stroked a wispy cloud of dust off the hoodoos. I stuck my head out the open window and felt the heat on my face. I saw the tree beside my second story window; its leaves limp, looking lazy on this dog day morning. I had slept in but so what, nothing to do but enjoy my last day here and Pug wouldn't be coming around till the afternoon so I made my two cups of coffee on the Motel mini coffee maker — after I read the instructions. God what happened to those good old drip machines?

I sat lazily thumbing the selector through the TV channels, not too much available so I gave it a rest, it had been on all night. I turned on the radio and what do you know, they were playing the rock & roll classics. That perked me up a bit. I had a separation anxiety brewing since the movie last night knowing one more sleep and I would be going back home. What was the big deal though? It wasn't like Shelby was across the ocean. Hell, jump in the car and I could be here in six hours especially now after breaking my decades of procrastination. The fact cheered me so I hopped into the enamel tubs they had here, those with clawed feet, probably vintage, the real thing since this Hotel turned Motel had been around before we came to Shelby in the early fifties. I felt more comfortable, relaxed in these old-fashioned tubs; we had had one in our house on Cascade Avenue. Wasn't long and I was out of the tub drying off and pouring some fresh java into a mug. On the cream coloured sides it read **O'Haire Motel** in Sienna colours. '*Hmm*', I hummed appreciating the mug and found another one, a clean one, which I stashed into my duffle bag. '*Great memento.*' I recognized and made a note to take the other mug back for Claire. Another ten minutes I had finished all of the coffee and my lone cigarette, bringing to mind I had to go someplace and get me a pack and a couple cartons of those American smokes to take back. Everyone on the Rez was always so crazy for them, the most favoured being Camels and Winston. And there was the beer. I had forgotten about the beer, *got to get some beer to take back to my friends*, I noted for my list of must-do. I phoned the Town and County Jail where the two guards on duty said everything was in order. Pug had already been there in person to check up making me feel a little guilty but '*Hey*' I *was off-duty* I reminded myself since handing Charlie over to the local authorities. Apparently Pug was off to the Pen to see if the lock-up was still in effect so I left a message for him to phone me or just find me someplace on Main. I mentioned I did have my mobile too.

"Man, you mobile phones are so cool, wonder what they will think of next?"
I said aloud to my mobile phone like it was a person. Although heavy, big as a brick they were now becoming a necessity on escorts. I wasn't too fussy about the purse thingy that held it which kind of cheapened our tough-man look.
 I walked down to the main level, initially with my mobile phone slung over my shoulder but optioned for the waist belt instead. Surveying my surroundings I realized I was a block away from the old poolroom and Bowling Alley so I ventured forth to see what was inside. As I entered, there was one person inside who must have been the caretaker since this was still morning and he pretty well ignored me. *It used to be full all the time, wondered why there could be so many in the afternoons when school was on,* I

253

thought recalling the crowds and times. Taking in the surrounding I could see nothing had changed; the pool tables were there where I last saw them decades ago and the bowling lanes were still there too. There was the same counter with the same stools, Coca Cola signs on the wall and written in coloured chalk on a black board was *'Cherry Coke Malt'* the favourite drink of every kid I knew. Separated to the right by a beam were the rows of beer cans; there was Hamm's, Budweiser, Coors and an assortment of others I never heard of. Wow! So many choices, and in cans too.

In Canada, specifically in what was considered the Wild West until very recently, never had beer available in cans and beer in Poolrooms with kids around? No way! It made me mad thinking of the glaring differences and the why of it – the temperate politicians we elected. God, it wasn't till the late Sixties when men and women could drink together in the same barroom. Before then there were two sides, divided; one side for the Men and the other for the Women so if a man and his wife went for a friendly beer they had to sit separately – maybe wave to the other while they sat alone. God! Who made those laws…and why did we let them?

After an hour walking the back streets I decided to venture again down Main, this time on the opposite side, the south side. It was cooler on this side of Main being in the shade and easier to see as the sun beat down. At noon I entered the Capitol Café and for just a second I expected to see my Mom there behind the counter dressed in white, a classy coloured insignia of the Café on her lapel. After school, 3:45 every day, I would come by here and Mom would have a hamburger waiting for me, a deluxe burger! If Mom had to stay past 6pm and

254

my Dad was out of town working on the railroad tracks, then that burger would also be my dinner, or supper as I now called it. I learned to cook early; fried eggs, boiled eggs, scrambled eggs and Kellogg's Toasted Flakes. I should have been a Chef.

Manoeuvring my butt onto the swivelling stool I ordered that famous Deluxe Burger of my youth. In front of me was the black marble counter that continued the length of the café and back again shaped in a big U. The swivel chairs of silver with bands of black on the sides lined the length and around, and at every third chair was a mini jukebox on the counter. I flipped the chrome pages finally coming to an old favourite, *I Fought The Law*, and played it with a quarter, one quarter inserted for one song. We used to get 3 plays for 25 cents, damn inflation. Waiting, wondering if it worked, I gazed through the humongous picture window and saw Pug peeking in. He waved, with a big smile. He came in, took a quick inspection then saddled up beside me.

"Still the same, huh." He spins around on his stool.

"Yeah, thank God. The town is pretty well the same too, don't you think?"

"Oh yeah. Shelby stays the same...year after year after year."

"That's what I love about it, more towns should be like this."

"Betcha I know what you ordered?" Pug pokes me with his elbow, "a Deluxe Burger, right?"

"Yeah, how did you know?"

"Some days I would stop by and say 'hi' to your Mom. If she weren't too busy she would make me the same thing, a Deluxe Burger. She said it was your favourite." A lump came to my throat not unexpectedly since waves of nostalgia had been washing over me since I arrived.

The song I played came on, "Oh God, I love this song!"
He looked far away tapping the marble with the tips of
his fingers. "Hey, remember the day you left...we were
sitting down...on the curb?"

"Yeah. Never forgot it." I was amazed he remembered
those times. I had come to assume it was only me that
had these memories. Another lump came to my throat.
My burger arrived; I took a bite quickly to swallow, keep
it down. If I had to talk at that moment I'm sure I would
have started blubbering all over my Deluxe...like that
woman in rollers. Pug starts to hum a bit then the lyrics
come in broken parts. "Oh God, don't sing." I mumbled
and I meant it because that lump was coming up again. I
took another big bite hoping the quantity would stop the
feeling. No luck as Pug, unaware of the tears welling up
in me, started to sing clearly as the words came to him.
Slapping in time on the marble top he turned to me
singing.

*Every time I phone my sugar-plum, and try ta getta date, My Dad
says...* he points to me for intro in a deep voice like we
used to but nothing comes out of me but a squeak. I
fought not to cry, my mouth full of hamburger, lettuce
sticking out at the corner of my mouth while trying to
smile at the same time. He had the wrong lyrics, just like
he used to do when we were pre-teeny boppers. He
points to me again oblivious, blinded of the tears
building in my eyes, repeats in a deep bass, *"No dice a son,
you gotta woka late..."*

That's when I broke down and started blubbering; I
could not hold it any longer. My mouth open, the lettuce
falling out, I attempted the lyrics with a smile still on my
face hoping he could not see my breakdown. As my

vocals strained some words crawled out that were more tenor than baritone, *"gotta woka late... eek"*, my squeaks betrayed me. Reminiscent of that cranky lady in the Roxy, I was now trying to snort back the sobs and breathe in, but the burger is there and I start to inhale. I begin to choke! Pug, shocked at my reaction stands up, staring, then comes behind me. I quickly push Pug away in his attempt at the Heimlich Manoeuvre when the burger finally slides down and he pats me on the back.

"You okay Bran?" in a soft voice Pug asks.
"Yeah, yeah..."
"Guess we should skip that song, huh?" A short chuckle came from the both of us. There was silence for a few minutes.
 "Sorry Pug. I don't know what the Hell came over me. I never thought you remembered any of those times."
"I remember them all Bran." he placed his hand on my shoulder, "and I felt like how you're feeling now."
I mustered myself up standing, my shoulders now straight, "Really? God, what a wasted time...we should have met a long time ago, gotten together." I reminded myself, mindful of the circumstances, "Yeah, but we both had a life by then."
"Would have been nice to meet though, huh? Maybe every summer break when we were kids. I wanted to, but I assumed you didn't, the letters quit coming, you were probably thinking the same thing?"
"Yeah, I did. I thought, why even try because he won't."
"Then we become adults, I go to Nam, and you're finding your sweetheart. After Nam I didn't want to see anybody – not even my Mother."
"Yeah, I can see that. The missed time, when we should have gotten together was when we were still kids." I recalled how our families were vastly different. "But, in

reality it wasn't going to happen. There is no way either of our families would have let us visit each other on our own – by ourselves? No way."

"Yeah, exactly. I agree. Conditions were just not there for us." Pug frowns then lights up, "But we're here, we are here now...and there's nothing stopping us from meeting again!

"Right! You're damn right Pug!" We looked eye-to-eye then hugged one another.

"We need a beer – a few beers! Right?"

"Right!" We walked out, the waitress wondering what just happened. By tonight there will be a local story of some strange guy crying over his burger. I speculated about the small-town rumours that could start... *maybe the burger didn't have bacon*, they'll ask each other.

"I'm alright now you know. It was just a stupid reaction to everything around. I haven't cried...since I left." The fact occurred to me; maybe that was part of it. This journey had been building up a long time - right from the time I left. While I was reflecting on those times long ago, an odd sight appeared before us right there on Main Street eclipsing my memory. A white limousine crawled past us, surreal white glowing in the glaring sunlight. The shaded dark windows mirrored our faces as we stood there watching it move slowly past us, south down to the tracks. "Did you see that Pug? When has a limousine been in Shelby?"

"Oh God, don't know, maybe at Grad time but they come from Great Falls...no service or depot here. I wonder if they're picking up someone at the Rail Station?"

"People still use the train for travelling, long distance travelling?"

"Oh yeah! A lot around the West and Mid-West prefer Rail to Air, especially the older folks…and tourists wanting to see the foothills and mountains. We're only 30 minutes away from Glacier National Park, remember?"

"Yep, forgot about that. We went to the mountains once or twice when we were here." I wanted to do more sightseeing, catch up on other memories. "Say, how about we wait for that beer till tonight after supper – dinner?"

"Sure. You're fine then?"

"Oh yeah, really. I feel stupid now - like that grumpy woman in curlers, or rollers at the Roxy. Remember?" I turned to him with the question. We both break out laughing at the memory then get the giggles thinking of my "burger moment" in the restaurant. We must have laughed there on that corner for 10 minutes, running the scene over-and-over and trading barbs, not to each other, but on ourselves. "God I must have embarrassed you Pug with that lettuce hanging out of my mouth?"

"Yeah, well how about when I panicked when you started to choke? My eyes were bugging out like ole 'Bug-eyes'! I tried to grab you for a Heimlich manoeuvre! Ha haaaaaa…" Pug had a long laugh that dragged on, and then died like the Doppler effect of a train. Mine was more of a giggle to a scream so once we started laughing it escalated as our laughs became worse and we laughed at each other. We finally got a hold of ourselves after our stomach muscles became too tired to take anymore.

"Okay, okay…let's walk around, I wanna walk around, visit some places." I had to hold in my stomach with both hands.

"Sure. Where did you want to start?" he had propped himself on the wall with one arm.

"Anyplace, anyplace, you probably still know some of these people?"

We walked the whole Main Street, door-to-door and he introduced me to those he knew. Most were younger, a generation after us but a few our age and older were still minding the stores. Two of which I recalled from my 'newspaper' days when I went to their businesses to sell, one being the **Oasis** bar or tavern. He actually remembered me when I did introduce myself, which felt nice. So we trekked, finally finishing where we began, the Capitol Café. It was close to 5pm by that time so we decided to eat out, maybe the Modern Café or the Chinese restaurant, which I could never remember. I didn't want to go back to the Capitol, not after my little episode inside.

"Let's do Chinese." I offered not able to recall the name of the restaurant. We dined in splendour but left room for the beer later. Through dinner we talked making plans for the night and the Oasis was what we mutually agreed on for our final get together. Pug thought some of our old friends might be able to attend if they were still around so he was going to make a few calls trying to track down whom he could. I was happy with just the two of us but yes, seeing others from our classes would be gravy and great for an update on what happened to everybody else. I was running out of time cramming as much as I could into these three days but I was in high spirits. To think we almost didn't make it here, glad we persevered.

"Well, that was great Pug. It's on me; I have an expense account for everything on this escort. What should we do now?"

"Let me go to my Mother's place and I will ask her about any of our old classmates. She might know their numbers since she still lives here… and who is still here."

"Fine, I need to go back to the room anyway, have a nap, have a piss."

"A piss? I haven't heard anyone use that term for a long time."

"Probably since I left, eh? My wife just hates it when I tell the kids to go for their piss. She says it sounds disgusting, but my Dad used it and so do I. Old habits die hard Pug. I guess I should change, getting older so I should know better."

"Don't change, don't change for anybody's sake." He raised his arm, finger pointing to the sky. What did Popeye say, '*I yam what I yam*', or was it Thor?"

I laughed at his attempt at impersonating Popeye. In our boyhood I was his captured audience when he auditioned his new impersonations. There was Elvis, Sylvester the Cat, Porky Pig and so many others of that time. We all attempted the impersonations and we all sucked.

With that, we ended our dinner. We were across from the Oasis on exiting the diner and about a block from the County Jail. I bent down to light my cigarette away from the slight breeze then thought of Charlie and his cigarettes. He had brought some with his package but they were together in one sealed canvas bag and forwarded to the Pen here.

"I just remembered Charlie doesn't have any cigarettes. I got to get him some. He's probably having a fit by now."

I went back into the Diner; got some Camels and we both hurried to the jail. Coming around the corner off

261

Main we noticed the same Limousine we encountered earlier pull away slowly, slinking down the hill into the trees. We looked at each other then ran across the avenue. We burst into the jail scaring the hell out of everybody. "Who was it that just pulled away?" we both hollered. Nobody said anything. "In the limousine, white limousine, who was it?" Pug asks.

"Limousine? Here?"

"YES!" we both yelled together.

"Nobody was here. There hasn't been anyone here. You're the first ones to come in. By the way, who in the hell are you guys?" they both drew their short 38's aiming at us.

"Wait, wait, I'm sorry guys." Pug says calming the tension. "Careful, just let me reach in and get my badge, I'm a Marshal." He moves his hands in slow motion, one to his inside suit pocket, the other holding out his lapel. The two guards aimed nervously, trembling while both moved apart. He pulls out his ID and softly throws it to the feet of the head deputy. "Bran, throw yours too." I did, also in slow motion. It wasn't a good feeling with two loaded pistols pointing at you and their shaky fingers on the trigger. They checked the credentials closely lowering the guns as they became at ease.

"Where is the prisoner, is he here, have you checked?" Pug asked but was more a statement, an order.

They were just going to check when Charlie bellows out, "What the Fuck is going on out there?" in his loud voice startling the whole bunch of us. I was glad he hadn't hollered before when the deputies were aiming at us, we might be lying on the floor with some bullet holes.

It's me Charlie…Sam." Pug looks at me quizzical as I say my nickname.

262

"Did you bring me some weeds Boss? I'm fucking dying here!"

"Yes, yes, that's why we came…got some Camels for you."

"Hold it!" the Deputies say, "We have to check what's inside." They take the pack for inspection then hand it back. *Good,* I thought, *this is good security.* I look to Pug to give him my appreciative look and nod on their procedure.

"Here Charlie," I threw him one pack, "sorry, we forgot that your cigs are in your personals."

"Oh thank you Boss. One thing I can't do without and that's a good ole weed. What was all the ruckus about back there?" he asked while pulling a cigarette out with trembling fingers. "I need a light Sam."

I held the lighter for him, his fingers too shaky to synchronize it to the end of the cigarette. "You okay Charlie?" The only time I saw him like this was when he was about to tear into someone. "You look nervous…or agitated, what is it?"

"Nothing Boss, nothing. I was just in withdrawal. Really."

"Nobody tried to get a hold of you? You didn't hear anything or …see someone?" The limousine came to mind. I was uneasy after seeing it crawl away as if it was watching. *'Maybe it's some tourist thinking this is some small museum'* I reassured myself.

"No, relax Boss. Go on. Go have some fun. You're making me uptight. Is the Bitteroot School still standing?" I ignored his question but the others all looked at each other.

"Okay then…that enough cigs till tomorrow night? I will inform the deputies you can have a cigarette every hour if it's alright with them."

I walked out satisfied that all was in order. The Deputies overhearing the chit-chat wanted answers, "What does he know about Bitteroot School?" They crowded into me whispering. I debriefed them on his history, the possibility his Grandfather had been here and that Charlie claimed there was a murder, a skinning done here along the Marias River. Following this, I instantly regretted telling them as a subsequent shock formed on their faces. But then again, I surmised, they had the right to know so that security remained tight; *keep up their Guard* as it were, so that nobody made foolish, maybe fatal mistakes.

"Holy shit!" was all they said. They all looked towards the cell hidden from sight behind the wall, staring blankly.

"I can get another Deputy to guard, a third person if you want. Would you like one more to help, maybe someone to stay outside by the door?" Pug was great at this, telling them in a question. They agreed so Pug made a few more calls and within 10 minutes he had all the paperwork and logistics completed with approved authority. I realized he, and the Marshal Justice Department had quite the power when needed. We would have wasted two weeks to pursue and complete the necessary documentation to do what he did in 10 minutes.

About another 15 minutes later the Sheriff, along with a new Deputy guard arrived, who we also debriefed. Pug left a set of keys with the Sheriff and took the other set; no one else was to have the keys. Any emergency, requiring the opening of Charlie's cell was to be relayed to Pug. This may have been contrary to State corrections but this was a town jail and the Keeper of the keys was within walking-distance of the jail. Another set was given to the Sheriff in case we became indisposed. Everything seemed to be in order, so we left, but I still had an uneasy feeling about that limousine.

CHAPTER 23

"I wasn't aware of the supposed skinning at Marias River."

"Yep. That is what Charlie claimed. He said it was his training, his first lesson in killing. In fact what he learned from his grandfather there along the river, under that Cottonwood, gave him the skills and inspiration for the murder of his own parents. There was never any confirmation on his Grandpa's killing though – the Marias skinning could be Charlie's invention."

"Did you know there was an old urban legend that a couple were killed – somewhere along the Marias? I recall the story being passed around at party campfires in the late sixties, some of them along the Marias."

"No kidding? Maybe there is some truth to what Charlie says and you know... every story has a beginning, where there is smoke there is fire." We both thought about this, walking in solitude. Arriving at where we departed in haste, we made plans to meet at 9 pm at the Oasis; it was already close to 8. Time was wasting, another 'sleep' as we used to say and we were gone – or I was anyway. With the uprising not settled and investigation pending, it would be awhile before Charlie joined us back at the FPC. Willie would be lonely as I envisioned the empty cell beside him.

I laid down as soon as I got into my room, set the alarm and immediately drifted off. An eerie blackness fell about me; so black I could feel it, a dismal soot spilling through my fingers as I held them in front. I was apart from myself watching me from a short distance but I still felt what my other self was feeling. The emotional fear felt though, was his alone as I saw him tremble and I was unmoved. Suddenly without reason the both of us were before a campfire and we were waiting in fear for something. Our heads darted to and fro looking for that overwhelming presence we felt coming. Out of the darkness came an unnatural cry with a wind. The wind rustled the blackness as a curtain then a gap appeared in the filament, transforming to a door that changed to a flap. I recognized it as the flap of a tepee and bent my head upward to see dim faint outlines of a tepee towering above us. The flap opened wider as it shook. Without any sound, a huge black mass came out hovering, changing. I began to see a semblance of some face when it disappeared all together. Now there was a sound, a heavy hum that reverberated around us, shaking our bodies, behind, came a hot moist current of air that flowed around my neck tightening its fingers. Instinctively in horror, my other self and I turned. There behind and over us was a huge black bull, its massive head swaying side-to-side with its horns. We saw beyond its head and there were only two legs – and they were of a man. In abject fear, we scrambled to run but it held us down with its cloven hands and one clawed thumb. On our backs, we stared into eyes blood red as it raised its head, opening the mouth wide to feed. It didn't. Instead, it tried to speak. I listened intently as the terror held me, the hum broke to something distinguishable and I began to hear words. I knew they were important but a noise kept interrupting as the words became lost, meaningless. "Beep beep beep…" the shrill screamed in my ears, suddenly I was back, back in my room. I lifted my head, gazing around for the source. It was the timer. My radio alarm was blaring - it was nine o'clock.

"Jesus - nine o'clock! Pug will be waiting." I brushed my teeth quickly, splashed my face and slicked my hair with water. In the mirror, I thought I saw something behind me, I spun around but nothing was there. I dismissed it as a passing shadow from outside; it was still light with the twilight descending. I wondered on the words hushed by my alarm.

I jogged the brief distance to the Oasis, a flash came to mind of the other time I had run down this street with Pug and 'our girls' hot on our trail. I recalled their reaction, which was what scared us. I came into the entrance straining my eyes in the sudden darkness to see. I heard from the corner, "Over here Bran." so I followed the voice. "Hey, got someone here you haven't seen in a while." he waved his hand to present 4 people. He introduced them as Rick, Allan, Mark and the last one was a lady – Heather. I couldn't believe it! She looked good; gorgeous was more descriptive especially after what – seven kids? She had her blonde hair, naturally curly, 5 foot 7 inches with a knockout figure. She had arched eyebrows over lazy blue eyes, a classic Scandinavian nose, high cheekbones, and a wider mouth tucked in at the corners with dimples on each side. It occurred to me then, God she looked like Claire.

"Doesn't she look like Claire?" Pug asks reading my mind.
"Wow, yes. I was just thinking about you… you know…and the other girls," I said to Heather.
"Mary Jane, Bonnie and Lynda?" she asks softly.
"Yeah, yeah and you guys, girls, were chasing Pug and I down the street here?"
"You mean when you pests were bouncing around with water balloons as tits - making fun of us?" she mimics our poses back then, lifting her one arm, hand bent daintily, the other holding her hip. "You little buggers sure took off when we got up!" Everyone laughs at this

as I find a chair to pull up. "So tell me Bran, what have you been doing for the last, what – 20, 25 years?" I gave her and the rest a condensed history leaving out much of the Reserve life. I was still uneasy about disclosing that part of my youth because it was uncomfortable; I wasn't sure how to handle it. The guys all filled me in on what they had been doing, their families, the future and what was planned. I found that interesting, that most everybody planned early on what they foresaw. On the reserves most didn't dwell on the future, it was too worrisome. So we all sat in the surprisingly small Oasis, drank, reminiscing about our high school days and on other friends now spread across the globe. We compared jokingly on mannerisms, habits, and cultural idiosyncrasies of our countries with exaggerated anecdotes and laughed at ourselves. A few more beer and we were talking, debating on the present and future legal, ethical and moral issues facing our kids and grandkids. Funny how we get serious over beer and too many beers make us geniuses in our eyes, as we get stupider. We never reached that level thank God. All present were a tad too conservative and grounded.

Pug pulled out an album from under his jacket that had been folded on the bench. "I thought I should bring this. My mother mentioned it when Bran had left yesterday. It's an old album of my childhood years but a lot of you guys are in it. My Mom was obsessed with her Kodak back then." He opens it, we all bend forward, a collective "aaahh" as we recognize Pug in his smock jacket, fifties hair, blue jeans with upturned cuffs and white socks. He offers each of the four albums to us and we raced through the pages to find ourselves. We were all there enshrined forever in memory. In black and white - birthday parties, school trips, events, the fair was there through all the seasons. I came to Pug's class photos and we all looked, each pointing to themselves except for Heather who would have been probably two classes ahead of us but there were a few with her and Pug's sister who was about the same age although they were not best friends. Pug's other family members filled most of the albums and although interesting to the guys because we were in them, Heather soon found it boring as she sat back. It was getting close to 11pm as I saw Heather check her watch. The slideshow was winding down.

I scanned each row of the class photos, mentioning names I came across. In the middle row second from the left was someone we didn't know.

"Who is this Pug?" we asked and he couldn't put a name to him, a young boy with tossed up crumpled dirty blonde hair and a shoe with the sole separated, maybe an itinerant worker's son, we thought. His shirt appeared wrinkled, un-ironed and he seemed to be the only one in the class who was not smiling for the camera. Pug tore off two corners that held the photo to the page turning, it over to read the names of each. "Charles...' he drags the name looking up at me with amazement, shock. "My God! Charles - Charlie!"

"What? What..." the others ask noticing Pug's eyes.

"Holy shit, he was here – in our class!" I bend over to get a closer look.

"Who? What? What's going on guys?" Heather sits upright demanding an answer.

"This guy," Pug points to the photo, "is the guy we brought down. He's in the county jail right now."

"Really? What did he do?" Mark looks up from the album.

Pug and I hesitate, not quite sure if we should tell them. It wasn't contrary to protocol, but this was a small town, by Tomorrow it would be common news, consequently, maybe a sideshow. I envisioned a bunch of cars passing by the jail, banners flying with balloons all over the place. I shook my head '*no*' in reply to my thought. This wasn't the 1800's and most here in this dusty little town didn't care. There was a Maximum Security Pen down the road so this shouldn't matter all that much.

"You wanna tell them Pug?"

"I don't know. There is nothing saying they can't be informed, but things could get – too exciting?" He suspends the sentence thinking of possible consequences. Our friends are staring to each, to us and back again. I knew we had lit the fuse; they wouldn't let us get away without some explanation especially now with them knowing their Grade 5 classmate was a felon, a multiple killer.

"Hey listen you two," Allan pipes up, "I'll just go up there and ask the Sheriff what the Hell is going on."

"Yeah. Yeah." the others chimed in.

"Okay, okay, but don't go blabbing this all over town." Pug looks at everyone in the eye. "Alright?" they all nod in agreement. "You can pass this on when we move the guy to the Max....but not till then!" He relates the story, as he knew it, downplaying in condensed form, not including the gory details of the skinning or the Cult. Pug also emphasizes the fact that the killing was in British Columbia, Canada, not in Shelby. Regardless, they find the fact startling; that someone they sat next to in class 25 years ago had killed his parents. I identified with them in their retrospect, but this feeling of sideshow wonder had left me a long time ago. To Pug too, to a lesser degree, it was no big deal. "There is more, but we can't divulge because it will be part of an FBI investigation. In

271

two weeks time I will personally tell you the whole story…if I'm here."

Ooohh Geez Pug…shouldn't have said that, I thought. From what info I had with its subsequent involvement of many powerful 'others', this could take awhile. Mentioning the FBI also added fuel to the fire. This had brightened our reunion in a macabre way, adding to a scene to be concluded later. *Great excuse to get together again,* I smiled. The conversation now turned to us, what we did for a living, what our duties entailed. So I typically brought in stories they would soak up, those tried-and-true tales I learned from practice that would hold them. Stories Hollywood wouldn't think of, stranger than fiction, some too gory, even for Hollywood. I soon stopped, tired of the repeats everyone wanted to hear replayed, and those particular gory items or actions they would want again and again. I was indignant with myself that I had retold these factual events and now I was stuck but it had done what I had intended – to take away prying questions about Charlie.

To my relief, Pug assumed the storyteller when someone asked about where I grew up so he retold last week's trip to my home reserve and meeting my parents. I figured from past experiences people didn't want to hear about this, that this conversation soon would tire but he went on being very graceful, generous about how he saw our distinct ways of life. To my relief they listened and asked questions; no ignorant remarks or Grade One queries such as, *you guys still live in Tepees?* Soon the whole topic had migrated to Native Cultures, the History and beliefs. I was surprised; I was basking in the interest they showed. For once, I spoke freely on my true sentiments not having to explain away stereotypical myth like why

272

we don't pay taxes. The dialogue was open, fresh, providing me a 'rush' to continue speaking about my culture. They asked without prejudice or presumptions so I explained with no hesitation. They wanted to know. Maybe part of this was the fact they never knew anything about me when we were in school but back then no one cared – we were all the same. It's when you get older that you change.

The topic we had escaped from slowly returned as someone speculated on where he, Charles, had come from and the 'poor' state he seemed to be in at the time of the class photo. Nothing was further from the truth, making me aware of how perception was so influenced by image, especially when we have grown older. None of us thought this back then, we probably didn't even notice him. "Oh he wasn't poor." I spoke up, "This guy's Grandfather rubbed elbows with the very rich. He was part of the in-crowd of Hollywood, colleagues with the famous, a member of an elite artist's group…" I cut myself off. *What the hell was I doing?* I had been taken aback on the misconception of Charlie because I knew his situation, and his wealth if he ever received it. I had inadvertently opened the topic again, to my chagrin.

"What crowd, who? How rich was he? He was an Artist?" All the questions came at once. I had to retract or just shut up which was proving harder to do while being in the spotlight.

"Hey Bran," Rick turns to me, a frown on his brow, "why bring him here if he killed in B.C.? It doesn't make sense. What about his Grandfather?"

"Well yeah, his Grandpa passed through here, maybe lived here briefly, so the FBI are just tying up loose ends. Maybe it's something to do with fraud or tax evasion, I really don't know. FBI won't divulge in an ongoing investigation." I lied to curtail the questions. The FBI had called for all our information after opening their files to us. The documentation we received from Los Angeles church dioceses were forwarded to them also which resulted in the order for deportation. I suspected Charlie would be here for a while. "I'll probably be returning to Canada with this guy, Charles, tomorrow when my escort arrives." Pug lifts his eyebrows knowing full well the FBI hadn't questioned him yet. "That's it, we can't tell you anymore....honestly."

"Man, one of you guys should write these stories down you know. It's interesting." Rick stabs his finger into the air towards us.
"I did start writing but all are about Native lore, legends... and history."
"Yeah Bran, you and your Mom and Dad know a lot of stories." Pug adds.
"But they're all Native."

Heather pipes up," So? People are keen on that. They love stories like that – myth, legends." Heather continues, sliding to the edge of the seat, "Why don't you tell us one... before you leave. You're leaving tomorrow so leave a present, leave a memory till next time." Everybody agrees urging me to tell a story.

"Okay, okay." My mind files through the many short stories for one that would fit the occasion, something I could leave with them to mull through after I was gone; maybe they would retell to their kids and grandkids to be. "Okaaay...here's one I did write but it never left my desk. Because so much time has elapsed since we last met and who knows what is in our future, I think this

274

story fits the occasion. It's based on an actual event of mine, between my Father and I and how he explained my question."

I think back, "In this memory I was maybe 5 or 6 at that time. I was sitting, staring at a beaver pelt stretched over a circle of willow branches." Here I decided to use the words I had written, it sounded better, more literary

"The fur shimmered orange by the dancing flames and as a waft of smoke escaped reaching for the ceiling I watched while it encircled the stovepipe caressing it delicately with grey fingers, seeking direction like a blind woman. It smelled warm, comforting; soon I saw only the thoughts in my head. I was in another world when suddenly my Dad poked me with his foot."
Time for sleep he says.
"I reply with a question."
Dad? What is time? People always say it but don't explain, like time was good...or bad...or what a time.
"He recalls a memory and says, *I will tell you a story from my youth.* In a deep voice he began." I imitate the voice and assume my Dad's character.

Many, many summers ago an old wise man came to us in his travels. His truth, knowledge and wisdom had come before him. I was a young man with similar questions in mind so I sought him out. I was not allowed to see him till all the Elders smoked the Pipe with him. They ushered me in, seating me in front of his great fire. In spite of the heat I quivered, my voice trembling, I said, Great Elder, I have but one question. I waited. Speak then, young man. Any confidence was now gone like shadows of a cloud as his thunder shook my spirit.

275

I stammered, what is time? A long pause was broken by laughter as I crawled into myself. It was long for the reply as sap seeps from the trees. I waited. Slowly, he raised his hand demanding some quiet. A hush came over the tepee while this bear of a man looked about. With my heart in my ears I could not even hear the silence.

I expected a growl; instead he directed soft words of warning to the others. Do not mock his question. He stared at each sitting in the circle, demanding respect. Has time clouded your reason that you laugh at Him who is without age? From birth he will control you and everything in your life; like the night, we never really know him. He is there but not welcome. He now had his grizzled hand up pointing to each. Sometime you will see him in your children or grandchildren, other times you see him as you gaze upon your self in still waters. He passes from face to face so you never forget but is so common we lose him all the time. Even in the green of spring, the white of winter and fiery reds of the fall you see him. He is with you all the time and has been since we have had the mind to see him. Now he posed a question to them. Can any of you explain him and why he is here? None did as they thought silently.

He then turned to me. In comforting words he gazed into my eyes making me feel alone as he apologized. I am sorry my son. I do not have the answer you seek nor does anyone. An ant, the trees or the mighty eagles do not wonder upon this because they live only to live. If all the people were to die, time would remain but no creature would know him. Forever… eternity is a measure of time used by us, a name. We need to place names to that which confounds us…so we think we know it, but in fact we do not know. Time has many names and like friends lost in youth, we don't recognize him as we meet. As you get older, wiser you will get to know him again till finally you will not let him leave lest you die. Dying? Don't be afraid. Death is just another world where time knows no home and dreams live. Time is the earthly reminder of our humanity here on this earth - Spirit knows neither time nor border.

276

I leave these words with you. "In memories you will walk with him to where you want and you will try to keep him but it is He who keeps you."

I stopped. Seeing they were expecting more I added for their benefit, *"The End."* They remained silent; I considered the story a failure, maybe not so much in content but as to how I told it. They continued in solitude staring at me. I was getting uneasy, uncomfortable in the wait, contemplating how to get out of this awkwardness.

"That is a great story Bran!" Mark exclaimed.

The others followed, "I felt like I was a kid again."

"Me too" "You have any more Bran?" "You have to write those stories – definitely!"

I was overwhelmed with relief. I was never at ease storytelling, preferring to write the stories because there is an Art to telling them so that the audience feels enchanted. I did a thank you with a brief bow,

"Thanks, and yes, I did consider writing more, maybe get published a few years down the road. But, yeah, I'm glad you liked it 'cause now that gives me confidence to continue."

We spoke at length about stories, myth, and novels as we sat there soaking up each other's presence. It had been so long with no contact whatsoever amongst us; with Heather it had been only a dream I had that we would ever speak together. She reminded me so much of my wife. I recalled then that I was to call and remind Claire I would be flying home tomorrow without Charlie. This would put her mind at ease. I excused myself, went over to the bartender asking for a phone for long-distance and he offered his. I informed him twice it was long-distance and both times he said 'yes, it's okay'. I reflected on how old he must be. As I recollect he was old when I used to come in and sell newspapers making me wonder his age now – 70, 80? But then again anyone older than you by 10 years was ancient back then. Claire answered so we talked for a short time as I let her know my arrival time and asked how the kids were and if anybody important called. I wasn't expecting someone important to phone, it was small talk but she took it the wrong way.

"Why? You expecting someone important to call?"
"No."
"So why did you say that?"
"I just said it for small talk."
"You don't say something like that if you're not expecting an important phone call....or someone important. What If I called you and asked if someone important had called?"
"I'm in Shelby, Montana. Who would call here for you?"
"What…I'm not important?"
"Yes, yes you are Claire."
"What?"
"Yes… you are important to me."
"So why didn't you say that in the first place instead of insulting me?"

I stalled for her next words, waiting. They didn't come so I apologised, said I loved her then she laughed. She had arranged the conversation so I would be on the defensive. She loved doing this, twisting my words then pretending disdain. In response I told her I was sitting with Heather, which didn't work to my expectation. I wanted to evoke a bit of jealousy, instead she replied, "Whatever, see you at 3." In spite of the rebuttal, I grinned at our short chat.

CHAPTER 24

I sauntered back to the table, sat down mentioning my wife when I noticed Pug wasn't there. They updated the activity since I was on the phone. The County Jail had phoned requesting Pug attend an issue regarding overtime and the Deputies. Someone never showed up for the Midnight shift and the present staff was not staying unless overtime was authorized – or something to that effect. They weren't sure but he said he would be back in 30 minutes. My impulse was to go right away but it wasn't my business, mine was finished when we handed over the papers and passport. I figured I would stop by in the morning, maybe give Charlie another pack of cigs, let him know I would be back whenever they finished with him.

In between conversation and questions, my mind kept returning to Charlie and his life history, his delusions and the explanation he gave when I threatened to put a halt to his escort. At the time, his answers had satisfied me, probably because I wanted some reasonable account for what he claimed. Specific incidents did not correlate with his rationalization and explanation. Nobody, I had come to realize, let alone Sol who had died before I got this particular dog, knew I had named my dog Sol. That was why I had given the dog that name – in memory of Sol. Charlie's quote and description of my vision inside the mess on *his Mother never singing him a lullaby*? Nobody knew this but me, I didn't tell anyone, not even my wife. How would he know that? That was a dream, a vision. And the secret of not completing the Blood Brother Ceremony with Pug, did he really get this from the other classmates. They don't even remember him, much less would have talked and shared a secret with him? I decided to ask my old friends about this.

"You guys, Heather... did you know of a secret ceremony Pug and I did before I left?"
"No." they all responded.
"What kind of ceremony Bran?"
"Nothing?" I persisted and all repeated they had no idea what I was talking about. "It was something Charles claimed that he learned while he was here in Shelby. So Pug never told any of you about our blood ceremony?"
"No, what the hell is this? This is way too interesting. Bran, are you pulling our leg – legs?" Allan jokes but all note the seriousness in my voice.
"No, just wondering, I'll tell you later when Pug gets back." I kept watching the clock; it was close to 1 am. It was over 30 minutes now. The abbreviated dream I had while on my post-dinner nap returned to me. The Bull reared its head but not in hate or aggression, I had imagined, but in agony while it attempted to speak. The words began to form, make sense as they erupted in a guttered rumble, *'Don't come, don't come!'*. That is what the Minotaur was trying to say, *don't come, don't come*, the words played softly on my lips. I guess I said them loud enough and Mark replied, "That was what I heard."
"What?" I yelled.
"I overheard someone saying that on Pete's big mobile. Sounded like it was in the background – in the distance, you know?"

I took off as fast as my legs could go, I felt something was wrong; I hoped, I wished that it was nothing but that dream I had, the bull's head rising, filled me with dread. Approaching the jail a short block later, I saw that white limo perched on the hill, not far from the jail. I wandered

281

cautiously around so a set of trees covered me. It was quiet with the odd car or truck speeding by on the interstate, here there was nothing, no noise or commotion, just a peaceful calm under a blanket of stars. I snuck to the limo on my knees, tried the doors but they were all locked. I looked into the front windshield and saw there was no one inside. I approached the oak door putting my ear to it, there was no unusual noise coming forth but a faint conversation. No yelling, no screaming, so I reasoned there was no cause for alarm, but I would enter with extreme caution so I took the safety off on my .38 Special and placed it back into the holster with the strap undone. I walked in casually, noticing on my first glance that the Deputies were sitting typically with their hands clasped together behind their heads then saw to my right Pug sitting on the floor, his hands behind. Seeing this my focus turned to the Deputies again, this time I could see the glistening reflection of metal on their wrists, and they were handcuffed with hands raised in submission not clasped behind their heads. Now I could see that Pug was handcuffed too and all were looking at four men standing who seemed to be having a discussion.

I shouted, "Hands up. Freeze!" while reaching for my gun. One of the four reached to his side and drew a pistol, looked like a 95mm. As he brought it up to aim, I threw myself to the floor, rolling, and drew my 38 shooting into the crowd of four. Within a milli-second I fired twice but only one shot found its mark and that was the person who drew the pistol. From his action I saw he had been hit in the forearm, in the other arm not holding the gun. He fell to his one knee cradling the arm on it, the others all turned to me raising their hands in surrender. I watched them in astonishment, *'This is it, they're surrendering?'* I marvelled at the revelation. No damage done, no one hurt except the one stranger. I observed that they were young men dressed in high fashion suits, black with shining soft leather shoes to match, white shirts and maroon neckties. They all looked the same.

"On the floor!" I screamed. Instead, they slowly moved apart spreading across the floor with their hands still above their heads and as they continued the hands gradually came down. *What are they doing?* Their unexpected action alarmed me.

"I will shoot! I'll blow your fucking heads off!" I warned. "I've got four more bullets!"

They stopped, the one on the left raising his hands again, "Don't be foolish. We're here for our Leader. Let him go and no one gets hurt."

"What Leader? Nobody leaves here and that includes you guys. You are all under arrest. Understand? Get to the fucking floor!"

"We don't want anybody hurt, just tell us where he is and we will go."

"What the fuck are you talking about?"

"The Master, where is he? Where did you put him?"

I stare at this bellboy yuppie not having the foggiest notion of what he was talking about. "I don't give a shit about no Master – get on the ground – now!" I raised the 38 to center target on his chest pulling the hammer back, ready for a fast fire.

"We're not scared to die Sir. We will die but there is no reason you or your friends here should die. Listen, tell us where he is, give us the other keys and we are gone. Nobody dies, nobody gets hurt."

283

Suddenly a voice close to me says, "They have the keys already Bran but no one was in the cell." It was Pug informing me calmly.

"What?"

"Charlie is gone! There is nobody in the cell!"

"How can that be?" I glared at the Deputies but they knew nothing, shaking their heads.

The one Deputy points to the remaining three men, "When they came, took us hostage, and took us behind to the cell, he was gone! Then they made us call the Marshal."

Pug interjects, "Bran, I checked too, nothing there. I even gave them the keys for the cells but now they think we have some other special cell – and keys."

"Tell us where and we're gone." one of the young men adds.

"There are no other cells you morons, this is it…or the Pen."

"We know he is not in the Pen, we have people inside who know."

"Who the Hell are you guys?" I become aware they had moved further apart so I stepped backwards.

"That is not important, what is important is that we rescue our Leader, bring him home."

"No fucking way, nobody is leaving…and that includes you."

"We have been searching since the Old One passed on. We will not leave without our Leader. We will die if needed." He stepped forward. Instinctively I fire, seeing the bullet hit the center of his neck as his head reels back from the concussion. In a flash the others reach for their sides bringing out pistols firing instantaneously. Nothing finds its target. In a moment I fire once more, flashes of

284

more gunfire, another falls down then I feel a burning in my side and shoulder. My arm falls limply, my 38 slides across the floor. The gunfire ceases as fast as it began and a lone stranger, one who was shot earlier in the arm, is above me now. I see two men in suits on the floor, as I lay down unable to keep my body erect. The supposed leader who had been doing all the talking and was shot in the throat rolls over fighting for his breath, blood spurts out of a small hole below his Adam's apple and with each exhale he wheezes.

Pug screams, "You bastards, you fucking bastards!"

"Give us the keys, tell us where he is…or you die too."

"Shoot me then…shoot!" Pug screams. The young man steps forward placing the gun to Pug's temple. Abruptly there is a silence, a presence that is palatable. The Deputies are staring behind the young man, a paleness washing over their faces. A shape steps forward from the wall, somebody is there. The leader of the four lying there stirs then crawls to the figure's feet, grabs the leg then dies in a groan.

"What did you do?" Charlie grimaces switching glances to the remaining young man and me. "What the fuck did you do? Do you know who I am? Look at me!" The lone stranger gazes in wonderment followed with an awe-inspiring fear replacing it. He gives a short bow stepping away still holding the gun at his side. "This is my friend…my friend."

He kneels beside me holding my head in his hands. I can't believe this, what is happening? The words I hear don't make sense, the scene before me doesn't register. Indescribable pain stabs me with every breath and my focus blurs.

"Master, we must go!" the lone man implores.

285

"I am not your Master!" Charlie bellows, the roar throwing the guy back on his heels. "Get out of here! I am not your fucking Master!"

"We can not leave without you Master. Please…come with me."

"Get the fuck outta here or I'll kill you myself." Charlie glares at him as he puts my head down softly and prepares to stand.

The man backs to the wall, "If we don't succeed Sir, many others will come. They will come and come till you are back home- they will not stop. Others, many others will die or kill to release you." Charlie seemed to listen to this. I caught a glimpse of an insight in his eyes, a resignation. He stepped over me reaching for Pug's arms ordering the young man to release him. He refuses.

"Release him… or I don't go with you."

The lone stranger realizes the only option to him had been offered. He says some words to Charlie unintelligible to me while I surveyed what was around me, searching for my 38. I saw it behind Charlie's feet. The stranger scrambles to unlock the cuffs on Pug so he can leave successfully. Charlie spins to watch him take off the cuffs kicking the 38 to me in the process. I grabbed it with my good arm, placed it under my jacket and rolled over to my face, chest to the floor. The pain was gone. The young man approached Charlie reaching out warily to grab his arm.

"We must go now before others come. Hurry."

In an instant I heard a gun cock, then another shot. I saw the lone man fall back and glancing over to Pug, I saw him collapse head to the floor, hard, from his kneeling position and his right hand clutching his personal firearm. He had shot the young man but he also had been shot in the process. They didn't know or didn't bother to search Pug for a gun since he was handcuffed with his arms behind. To my amazing eyes, the lone man rose from the floor, stood and rushed over to Pug in anger; his pistol drawn he aimed it and prepared to fire. Charlie charged the young man and the pistol flew across the room after it had been fired. Both now momentarily over Pug, I drew my 38 from under my jacket and without aiming, fired it; I felt two shots rang out before I dropped the gun. The lone young man spun in agony, fell to his knees and crawled to the entrance...and to my dismay I saw Charlie slowly crumple to the floor. I gazed through half conscious eyes and could see Pug lying in a pool of blood; the last man had shot Pug again. Beside him was Charlie, both motionless. I crawl to them through the blood already thickening on the floor, sticking to me, as I manoeuvred between the two. I reached for Pug feeling his neck, hoping for a pulse.

"Noooo!" I screamed out. There was nothing, no pulse. I repeated it on both sides, on his wrists; I lifted his eyelids wishing for a flicker. Nothing but a vacant stare; the pupils dilated, looking obsidian. I cradled his head to my chest and rocked. I cried and cried no longer feeling the physical pain of my wounds. Strobes of memories flashed as I closed my eyes, the tears flooding down my face onto Pug's. I saw us in the distance, smiling, laughing, and riding our bikes. I called to him and he turned around, smiling. He stopped and standing still he began to wave good-bye.
"Nooo!" I screamed again, demanding, "Don't you go!"
I hung onto him squeezing tighter. I felt for his hand, holding it to my face remembering just an hour ago we were laughing. I let his hand go and it fell with a deathly thump onto the floor. I picked it up again whispering,

"Pug, sorry…sorry man. I didn't mean to hurt you." I rubbed his hand caressing it.

The small wound he endured to be my Blood Brother was there on his fingertip and I touched it with my finger. I let his head descend to a resting position on my lap. I pushed away some hair that had fallen over his brow. I recalled his little habit of flicking it away with a swipe of the hand. I thought of his family, wondering if his son would ever do that…or see his Dad do that. Through closed eyes, a vision came to me as I saw him and his son walking away, Pug holding his boy's small hand in his, he stopped and turned to his son. He bent forward to his boy and smiled, smiled that loving father smile. He stood up erect and waved good-bye, his son reached for him. The vision hurt and anger overwhelmed me as I contemplated the aftermath and I cried out again, "Aaaahh!" I clenched my teeth then I cursed everything, everyone around - myself, Charlie, the world. I screamed in despair then cried in defeat.

The Deputies were still bound to the desk by leg shackles; one shouted to release him, the other was dead. I threw him the cuff keys and he quickly unlocked his cuffs. I told him to contact the Pen as he ran past me. I was beginning to lose consciousness, fighting it temporarily with a will power to stay alert. I hear a moan. I look at Pug, shake him, shake him hard, "Pug…Pug!"

"Ummm." a distinct moan.

I hold Pug's face in both hands. "Wake up Pug…stay awake!"

"Unnnh. Sam… Sam, you still here?"

"What?" the voice didn't match.

"Boss…Sam, is that you?"

I realized it was Charlie, not Pug and left out a sigh of dejection. "Yes…I'm still here…but Pug is gone." I laid his head down onto the floor as I laid my self down. I felt it was time to die, my body was giving out. Face down I could see Charlie beside me his head slowly angling in my direction.

"Sam, I want you to do something…something for me."

"What's that Charlie?" The words were becoming an effort, my eyes closing.

"Shoot me."

I opened my eyes, stared at him.

"Look at me Sam – can't move. I try and there's nothing, can't feel anything past my neck. I can't live like this Sam."

"At least you'll be alive. I think I'm gone. Pug's gone." I whisper

"He is?" He looks over to Pug then stares to the ceiling, "Oooh man, sorry boss, sorry. I knew he was your best friend." He stops for about two minutes. "Sam, I need you to do this, for me."

"I can't Charlie, I can't shoot you in cold blood. They'll take care of you."

"Sam, please." I felt the urgent pain in his voice. "Imagine them feeding me, wiping my ass. I can't live that way….and they will come again…probably more will die. They're sick, Boss. The only home I've known is FPC; going back like this will be a Hell. Think about it. What if you were me?"

I did think and reflected on his life, *what a life lived and what was in his future* I concluded. I am probably going to die anyway so why not free him. Let him go to the only peace he could find. I began to cry again.

"Hey Sam, don't do that. It's no big deal…you'll be freeing me."

I looked over to him. Tears were coming down the corners of his eyes. I knew I had to do it. I pulled a little closer to him putting my hand on his chest as he stared to the ceiling. I reached to his eyes wiping away the tears.

"Charlie...thanks for trying to save Pug. I got something to say first."
"Don't worry about it Sam, don't stress over it. I knew you shot me. It was an accident."
"How did you know I was going to say that?" my energy seemed to rebound.
"I have this gift, you do too... but you deny it. Your Dad and Mother know it, the Bound-Man knew it. Time to go back home Sam."
He turned stiffly and smiled, "Let's get on with it, it's time to go." With a knowing and reassuring look he adds, "I'm not afraid of dying, Death is just another world." He smiles, briefly and painfully, at his words knowing I would remember the story.

I lay back down staring at nothing but seeing so much. His words rang in my ears. I knew Charlie was not evil but a prisoner of his life, a life manufactured for evil. He had prevailed in spite of all that happened and all he ever wanted was to be free of it.

"Okay, okay Charlie, I'll do it. But you got to forgive me...now, before I do it."
"I forgive you Sam. You are not doing anything bad. You're setting me free." He turned his face to the ceiling again as more tears fell. "I always wanted to be your friend Sam and if you do this you will be a friend."
"I am your friend Charlie, wish we had gotten to know each other when we were young." tears began to well in my eyes as I reached for my 38.

"I can't look at you Charlie." I brought the gun to his head, cocked it then I faced away from him. I shut my eyes tight fearful of what I would see.

"It's alright old friend. This is the best you do for me."
I closed my eyes, tears came and I cried more.
"Don't do that Sam, you're hurting me."

I felt my finger tighten the trigger and faraway I heard a gunshot. My eyes remained closed; I floated away, my body had no substance as a peaceful blackness engulfed me.

CHAPTER 25

My eyes were met with an airy whiteness surrounding me, I felt a slight breeze lift me and I imagined a lacy white curtain swaying from an ocean draught. A tranquil comfort washed over me but as I opened my eyes wider, it was replaced by a harsh paleness devoid of colour. A person was close to me also in dull white moving briskly around and I realized this breeze was the drifting air I felt. The figure came closer, my eyesight focused and an elderly lady appeared out of the whiteness.

"You're awake? How do you feel?"

"Aaah, I don't know. Where am I?" I searched around for something familiar. The pain hit me as I tried to sit up. Soon I began to distinguish things, slowly recognizing the white décor as the interior of a hospital. A glimmer of some nightmare pounded my vision as I kept witnessing a horrible scene replying in a broken reel. The images and action were disjointed yet they came to make sense and the full impact struck when I suddenly comprehended the whole picture…and I screamed. I purged my pain in another bout of crying recalling the last moments of my consciousness, muttering, "Pug, Pug…"

"What's a pug?" she asked. I swayed my head back-and-forth not wanting to answer. "You repeated that word in your dreams – and nightmares."

I ignored her with a defiant look.

"You should tell me Sam – really."

"How did you know my nickname?" I shot back.

"It's right here… on your info sheet. Somebody wrote it in here." she raised the clipboard to write something else.

"It's Bran. Bran is my name and Pug is a name…not a thing."

"That's unusual for a name. Pug? I never heard of it before. Does it mean something?"

She was starting to piss me off, this chirpy older lady with a forever smile. Quickly I was beginning to detest the saintly demeanour she exuded in her talk. "It's a fucking nickname, okay?"

"Ooooh… I understand your pain Mr. Bran but we mustn't get snarky, must we? I'm just here trying to do my duties Mr. Bran. So who is this Plug…Pug?" She smiles as she gets my name wrong and calls Pug – Plug!.

I screamed in my head, *God! Help me God cause I think I'm going to kill her!* I couldn't take it any longer, "Bran! Bran is my first name, my last name is…" I stopped yelling as a name flashed, then I resumed, "Flakes! – Bran Flakes!"

"Oh my, we mustn't yell. I have perfectly good hearing you know. Bran Flakes? I never heard of that name either. My, my, my…such strange names, Bran Flakes and Plug."

I began to cry again, and laugh, not from pain or sadness but from excruciating frustration, "Ooooh God!" I whined, "It's Pug, not Plug…from a combination of Peter and Douglass!"

She perked erect, stopping with her rear end sticking out, "Peter? Peter?"

"Yes! Yes!" I mimicked her in a high voice.

"You listen here young man," she stared over glasses, "I have had quite enough of you. You sit there and bawl like a baby while others are in real pain. I'm leaving now, go tend to someone who appreciates my care!" she briskly turned and waddled away, her ample rear end swaying side-to side with each step.

Fine I thought but caught myself as I considered my Mother. *She was just caring for me, making small talk* I thought and hurriedly added as she went through the doors, "Sorry!"

A short time later, maybe 15 minutes, she came back in strutting like a conquering General, smiling. "Well, I hope we are in better form now. We will get you all comfy for your first meal…you have been without a real meal for some time." She puffed my pillows and took a quick peek at my wounds. I had been shot in the side through my lower rib cage and my clavicle was shattered. "They will put a metal rod in there for you," She says matter-of-factly pointing to it, "You'll be fine. Now what was that person called, Pug or Peter?"
"Peter." I held myself, groaning and getting ready for the next round.
"And what's his last name?"
"Klin." I repeated the whole name to stop further questions, "Peter Douglass Klin."

"Well, isn't that interesting?" She bent to me gazing over her eyeglasses. I didn't want to be interested; I just wanted to be left alone so I turned away. She poked me seeing no response, "Look at me young man." It was an order so I turned to her in defeat. "We have a Peter Douglass Klin here."
I stared hard at her. I couldn't comprehend her statement; what was she saying? I kept staring as the words rolled through my mind. In what felt like an eternity, I managed a timid "What?"
"You heard me, we have a Peter Douglass Klin here."

This couldn't be right. I had seen Pug die - he was dead. I had held him in my arms, checked for his pulse. "That can't be, it's impossible, he's dead." I whispered my disbelief, tempering my sudden expectations, I told her,

"No, no…it must be someone with the same name…or maybe a relative, an uncle or Grandpa he was named after." My words trailed off and my hope relinquished to despair as I became conscious of that fact.

"Well young man, I checked that. It could have been a Peter Douglass Klin, Senior I said to myself so I checked his records. Nope, no sir-eeee." She paused for a moment. "What is his occupation?"

"Marshal. He's a United States Marshal." I whispered, choking in anxiety as if it were the last question for a million dollars.

"Well young man that is what it says on his examination clipboard." she was smiling ear-to-ear looking like the most beautiful woman in the world. "You eat these veggies and I will get someone to come and help me get you in a wheelchair. I think you're strong enough for a visit."

I couldn't believe it, I was terrified to believe it yet I had to know. 'No, no… now. I gotta see him now; see if it's really him. Please Lady?" I raised my hands in prayer. I added as if it made a difference, "I'll eat anything…everything you send me…after I see him. I have to know."

"Wellll… okay. But you know there is a possibility it isn't him. Do you understand? Are you ready for that?"

"Yes, absolutely M'am. He died beside me — in my arms."

She radioed for security. A burly gruff man came to help, protesting all the while that this wasn't his job. She reiterated in a no-nonsense tone that she was the ICU head nurse, which I hadn't realized, and she could order whatever she wanted. I was starting to love this woman.

295

We exited my room and immediately turned right into another room that was next to mine. We cautiously, quietly entered the private room stopping on my hand signal while I scrutinized the bed and the person on it sitting semi-erect with his head back onto the pillows. My heart fell. *This wasn't Pug, who was it?* My muscles became lifeless, drained by the dejection leaving me slumped in the wheelchair; she understood my reaction.

"Wait, let's go closer."

"No, no. It's not him. Let's go back."

"We came this far young man and we're going to look closely and see if this is your friend. If it isn't, you will say 'hello' and we will then go back." Her voice hardened while she attempted to stay positive and patient with me. We creaked a bit closer and the noise awakened whoever it was in the bed. We looked at each other, a scant yet infinite second passed. I saw the eyes under his swollen brow, the one cheek purple in a puffy mass. It was him – Pug! I knew those blue eyes anywhere! He saw my reaction and smiled with those gleaming teeth worthy of a commercial. Not able to lift his arms he motioned with his fingers to come closer.

"Hey, know what I was dreaming? We were biking, you and I, going to the fair. Remember the fair?" His voice seemed to be in the distance. My mind was still trying to grasp this; my dream world and reality fighting for ownership.

"Oh yeah, like it was yesterday Pug. How you feeling? Man, I was sure you were dead." The shock was unshakeable, still there, as I heard myself speak in a monotone.

"I thought so too, even after I came to, and I thought you were dead...I thought everyone was dead!" His voice was strong. "I came too briefly and saw you laying face down and Charlie was beside you…and he wasn't moving. How about the others?" The tone lowered in his question.

"Aaaah, bad. The one Deputy was killed, one of the strangers was dead…and yeah, Charlie was killed too. I killed him." I bowed my head remembering Charlie's prediction and said it out loud; "I killed him in cold blood."

"No you didn't Bran, it was self-defence, you didn't have a choice."

"No, you don't understand Pug. He was trying to save you; he jumped in between and grabbed the stranger's pistol. Then…I took my gun and shot at the same time, at the stranger…three times. But I guess, I must have shot Charlie too. The young man, the last one, spun around and crawled wounded to the door, Charlie fell to the floor." The scene played clearly.

"Still… Bran, you had to do it!"

I bent to him, "It was after, after I had your head in my arms and thought you were dead. Charlie was still alive but paralysed, couldn't move anything." I bent closer, whispering, "He asked me to kill him…and I did; there on the floor, point blank to his head." There was a long silence. "He begged me to, said he couldn't go back like that, forgave me, then I shot him…in cold blood." Charlie's words hung like a noose.

"Bran, it sounds like you did it out of compassion…out of mercy. Don't forget Bran, he's a killer and you said, you told me, he wouldn't hesitate to kill us."

The sentence didn't register as I heard Charlie's last words, "He called me friend before I shot him. We had been together for a lifetime. You know that Pug – a

297

lifetime. I think I had a friend and never knew him…he gave his life to save you Pug."

In the days to follow, both of us were visited and investigated by a slough of agencies; the FBI, Corrections from both countries, State Troopers, local Police and the U.S. Justice Board that we were aware of. There were also reporters but soon they were ostracized quickly because of the ongoing enquiry with subsequent charges to follow that would include many people. An undercover operation into Cults within the New York and Hollywood areas could be jeopardized, so great care and jurisprudence was taken to 'hush' the media but there were always leaks. The Black Dahlia connection to Charlie's Grandfather was a favourite item on the Internet but the L.A Police had no evidence to support his involvement other than what he told Charlie and what Charlie claimed. The FBI, on the other hand, took the story Charlie had related to me in detail, more seriously. They had discovered associations and associates of Dr. Lewis Claymont Fuhr in other cities such as New Orleans, Miami, Seattle and in New York where he reputedly was the Leader of a Satanic Cult; the same Cult supposedly behind the Son of Sam killings. If this was all true, what a legacy to leave for your grandson – and son. How could you escape such a dark cloud of Evil?

There were too many unanswered questions to what transpired in our case. Who shot who? They persisted in questioning how Charlie was killed; we didn't know. All we knew, as Pug and I agreed, that one young man (the one left behind who was shot in the throat), Charlie and a Deputy were killed.

So *where were they?* They had asked. *Where were the other two young men we shot and Charlie? They were missing!*

Missing!? Who in the hell took their bodies, they were dead, and where did they go, such as the surviving Deputy who was still missing? They also suspected the uprising inside the Pen was planned, a note scribbled inside a cigarette pack corresponded with a date and phone number that tied into the limo registration which in turn was traced to Los Angeles. The young strangers of the limo were all wearing Kevlar vests, they surmised after discovering a vest on the dead stranger left behind. Our friends Ricky and Allan, curious to our prolonged absence came to the jail and saw one of them jump into the car and speed away, so obviously not all were killed. The CSI (Crime Scene Investigation unit) revealed that there were only small sporadic pools of blood, mainly ours. There was evidence a quick 'mop-up' had occurred. The lead stranger I had shot in the throat had bled considerably, so someone must have cleaned up. Why? Why take the time to do this? This shocked me, I knew I was in a wide pool of blood and much of this was Charlie's. And since I had shot him through the head, where were his brains? There should have been a blanket of pink grey matter on the other side of his head spreading across the floor!

Too much confusion, too many questions, I shut down unable to comprehend the full picture but after all was said and done, I suspected that they did cart off Charlie's body along with the others. That is what they came for. I could envision these people mummifying his body for worship…or maybe enclose it in some formaldehyde-laden coffin for all to see. A scene flashed of clandestine

299

figures crowded around him, around his green aquarium. I recoiled at the image.

After six days of interrogation, they left us alone. They took up the new leads they had uncovered, dispatching officers for surveillance and infiltration to expected areas of activity. For now we were finished, so my presence was no longer necessary, they would be contacting me at my institution. I bade farewell to my old friends promising to return soon... 'for a beer'. Pug was walking, now mobile, but he had more tests to undergo, more therapy - physical and psychological. He had been shot in the chest and hip area and suffered a broken cheekbone from an assault by one of the young men but he was doing fine.

"You going to be okay ole buddy?" I asked while packing my service bag.
"Oh yes. I am due a long vacation, my wife always wanted to go to Tuscany in Italy so that is our plan. I am insured, compensated for life Bran, I don't have to go back to work if I don't want to...but I probably will return, we'll see."
"Yeah, that's weird you know. I'm okay too for as long as I want...no overtime though." We both snickered.
"It's damn crazy, eh? We both meet after so many years, suffer a shooting, thinking each other is dead, then come out smiling like we won the lottery."
"We did win the lottery, Bran. We're both standing, alive and have a future and a home to go to. You know, I am going to bring my wife along the next time I go up north to visit you. She has to meet your parents."
"That would be great Pug!" We embraced with a shake and hug. I left the room for the lobby downstairs.

Kel, Shake and John from the Rez came down to drive me back. My injuries although healed were too tender to the air pressure of air travel especially the abdominal walls where a bullet had pierced. Corrections had offered an ambulance which I denied because there was no way I was going to lie down for the whole trip. Instead I managed to convince them to let me rent a big SUV where I would lay down if the need be, I only had to find a driver to drive and pick up my rental in Saskatoon so Claire suggested my friends. Claire had arrived the day after I regained consciousness staying for two days but had to return for the kids. She had been in touch all this time but I refused her travelling all that distance again when I would be home soon via chauffeurs and a Lincoln Escalade.

I was going home, that sounded strange, almost alien since I had never considered the Reserve my home. I had promised my parents I would stay with them while I recuperated, Claire had to return to her job and the kids had school. But the return turned out to be more aesthetic than physical and I could feel it, there was a kindred feeling with my land, my culture, the Spirit I had forsaken for so long. It had taken someone I had lost to find it for me. My heart and recollection of a treasured past is there in Shelby and I will never forget my dusty 'Shangri-la' but it was a home of memories. My family, my culture was where I lived.

Epilogue

In the period following the shoot-out while we convalesced in the hospital, I heard Willie had killed himself subsequent to hearing of the disastrous breakout and successful abduction of Charlie – Charlie's body. The staff had allowed him to undergo a ceremonial fasting in his grieving, unaware of the hardship and danger of his request. He had asked for tobacco, smudged himself then presented his prayers to the four directions for Charlie in memoriam. For four unrelenting days he ceremoniously danced without water or food akin to the sacred Sundance then, on the traditional fourth and final day he released his spirit, his body to the Creator and died there in his cell on a cold hard cement floor. All food and water that staff had presented or made available was flushed down the drain without their knowledge.

Both of them gone! I could envision, feel the word **emptiness** that portrayed the Isolation Wing and Seclusion cells but now the word was more sublime, so definite in it's meaning – maybe void was a better word. I knew I would not walk those hallways again.

On the ride back to Saskatoon with Shake, John and Kel, we talked, most of the conversation dwelling on what had happened. I asked in futile attempt on how their families were doing, etc.; kept trying to change the subject, but the topic kept popping up so I resigned myself to telling the whole story.

When I arrived at the ending Shaky asks me, "Where did this Charlie all of a sudden come from - in the jail? Wasn't he gone, didn't he disappear?"

"And why would he reappear…for what?" John added.

I had no answers. I did not want to entertain Charlie's claims of the extraordinary, the supernatural because that conflicted and contradicted with my real world. But here was a fundamental, reasonable question so… 'Yes', why would he reappear, why return when all his life he had been consumed with avoiding these people? How did he reappear when he wasn't to be found before? Where did Charlie come from all of a sudden? And myself, I think of Pug, how did he survive? The atmosphere chilled, became solemn as we all sat silent contemplating this. A few miles passed, the tires whining and the radio blared over the wind rushing through our open windows. The station was an 'oldie' station playing Kris Kristofferson's *The Pilgrim* and the lyrics shouted from the speakers.

"Hey Sam?" Kelley asks over the song, "How many shots in a .38, or .38 special?"

"Six." I wonder why he should ask this. He should know. "Why?" I ask in disgust.

"You shot two times coming, rolling into the jail, right?"

"Right! Shot the guy in the arm and missed with the other shot."

The Pilgrim played on, Kris singing, "*from the cradle to the Hearse*"….

"Then you fire off another round when one of the guys comes forward. You hit him in the throat, and then another stranger is shot. Right"

303

"Right. So what?" I holler above the song and wind howling through the open window.

"Then, when the inmate Charlie tries to save your friend, you fire another 2 shots. Am I right?" Kelley looks to me.

"Yes! Right! What the Hell you getting at Kel?" I didn't want to relive that memory and this third degree interrogation was pissing me off.

"That is 6 shots, Sam – six! So where did the seventh bullet come from to shoot Charlie through the head? You shot seven times – **seven times!**"

Kelley was right! How could that happen? I knew I had fired six times; I had felt the recoil and heard the shots. I had shot six times before killing him with the seventh shot... with the same gun! I could see the picture and hear the shots. Where did the seventh bullet come from?

I hear Charlie laugh.

I close my eyes to shut out the paradox. I wonder on his last words and the destiny he chose. In the background, the **Pilgrim** ends his song.